BRESSIO

BRESSIO

Richard Sapir

Random House New York

Copyright © 1975 by Richard Sapir

All rights reserved under International and Pan-American Copyright Conventions.
Published in the United States by Random House, Inc., New York, and simultaneously in Canada by Random House of Canada Limited, Toronto.

Library of Congress Cataloging in Publication Data
Sapir, Richard.
Bressio.
I. Title.
PZ4.S242Br   [PS3569.A59]   813'.5'4   75-10341
ISBN 0-394-49741-4

Manufactured in the United States of America
First Edition

FOR
Martha and Joseph, parents and sweethearts

BRESSIO

I

Alphonse Joseph Bressio woke up thinking about the bills he had gone to bed to stop thinking about. Besides his personal affairs, which he felt he could always straighten out somehow, there was office rent, office-furniture payments, quarterly payment on the large loan which last year was supposed to consolidate his indebtedness, Clarissa Duffy's salary and her summer-school tuition, which she had explained was part of an understood fringe benefit.

Bressio had said he would finance her college education—nights —as long as she was his secretary but hoped she would someday learn that nowhere in the law was there such a thing as an "understood fringe benefit."

"It's a moral understanding, Al. It's above the law," Clarissa replied and Bressio had acknowledged that while many things might be outside the law—"not above, Clarissa"—a labor contract was not one of them.

Because of his pressing financial problems that muggy morning, Bressio did not weigh himself or begin a diet, which naturally would be doomed to fail. He ate a chocolate cupcake in two bites and licked his fingers as he waited for the two coffees and Danish to go at Moochie's Luncheonette on Canal Street, a few blocks from 1250 Broadway, his office. He did not have to say, "Two Danish pastries." In New York City two coffees and Danish meant two coffees and two Danish pastries.

"What do you like?" said Moochie after Bressio had placed his order. Bressio knew Moochie was not trying to rush him. Moochie liked Bressio to hang around. He said it made him feel safer. Not everyone knew that Moochie's was a connected, and therefore protected, place, especially the young kids. To disrupt or rob Moochie's meant assaulting an entire organization which could break bones and spleens and visit all sorts of awesome grief upon those who threatened it. Unfortunately, to many young men in dungaree jackets, Moochie's looked like a luncheonette with a lot of breakable glass and pocketable goodies, and a thin bald owner who whined when he talked. All his connections were useless against youngsters who pocketed cupcakes and threw coleslaw.

When Moochie talked about feeling safer, he always nodded to the .38 police special shoulder-holstered across Bressio's chest. But Bressio knew it was not the gun. It was the appearance. At five feet nine and a half and two hundred and forty pounds, Bressio's dark craglike face and burning black eyes deep under fierce bushy brows took the fighting desire out of almost everyone who saw him. He looked as though he could throw a man through a wall, and want to.

"What do you like, Al?" Moochie asked again.

"I like the Cubs very much," said Bressio.

"It's six and a half five and a half you pick 'em," said Moochie.

"That's even money," said Bressio. "The Cubs always fold in the stretch. The Mets always come on strong. How come it's even money? This is New York City. You should be dying for Cubs money."

Moochie shrugged, that very Jewish shrug which signifies one is dealing with the unfathomable laws of the universe, which one can no more explain than one could change.

"You pickem isn't a bet. It's a lock, Moochie," said Bressio. "Three yards."

"With you, Al, I'm not worried about money. That's my last worry."

"I know the tab's over thirty-eight hundred dollars. I'll take care of it. I haven't forgotten."

"Hey, Al. Al. Don't be upset. I toldya the money don't bother me already. You're good for it. I've carried you for three times that much. No worry. With you a little phone call could make you rich. Any time you want. With the talent I have heard that you have, you would never have to mess around with taking the bar again."

When Moochie referred to "talent" he purposely looked away from Bressio's shoulder holster.

"I'm not messing. I'm not taking the bar," said Bressio, supervising with his eyes the countergirl who was filling his coffee to go. "No cream," he shouted.

"Clarissa was in here last night, said you was taking the bar."

Bressio made a little wave of his hand, signifying that Moochie should know better than to believe such a thing.

"She seemed certain, Al."

"I'm forty-two years old, Moochie."

"You should be rich, Al. As a friend, I'm telling you. You should be rich."

"You're rich, Moochie. You could buy half those investment people who send over here from Wall Street."

"I'm talking about rich," said Moochie, whose face squinted in an ecstatic, voyeuristic appreciation of a certain wealth somewhere between a great inherited fortune and an entertainer's brief, glittery success. "Rich, Al. Rich."

"Make that three Danish," said Bressio.

By Broadway the coffee leaked, so Bressio ate the most-soaked Danish. But when he reached his seventeenth-floor office he stopped worrying about wet, dissolving bags or how to continue maneuvering the morning newspapers free of the drip.

The door to the hallway was open and the office was dark but for a line of weak yellow morning sunlight coming under his inner office door. He could make out the file cabinets behind Clarissa's chrome-and-teak desk. The top three drawers on the left file cabinet were open. Someone had gotten to the medicals.

Bressio smoothly removed his .38 police special from his shoulder holster, shielding the action from the crowded morning hallway spilling workers from arriving elevators.

He moved into the office with a decisive quiet for a man of his bulk. He checked the outer bathroom. Nothing. He checked his inner office. Nothing. He snapped open the door of the inner-office bathroom. Still nothing. He looked at the gray metal safe, untouched behind his desk.

"Ahhh," he said in a disgust that was more acceptance than grief. He returned the gun to the holster. If it had been a professional job, they would have gone for the rinky-dink safe behind the desk and picked up a couple of hundred he left for that purpose. If it had been a professional job, they wouldn't have bothered with the files left unlocked and accessible in the outer office, and even if they had, he could probably put out the word to buy them back. If it had been a professional job. You could reason with professionals.

"Ahhh," said Bressio again and kicked the stupid safe. He hung up his jacket, locked the gun in the center drawer and put the coffee, Danish and papers on his desk.

By ten-fifteen he had skimmed the *Times* and the *News,* finished his coffee and the one he had ordered for Clarissa, and was working on her Danish. She still hadn't arrived. Bressio took a stack of manilla folders from the top right drawer and glanced through them. Work to be done. Clarissa, as usual, had organized it perfectly. The top file was labeled HOLZMAN, and Clarissa's note read: "Ripper's running again."

William "Ripper" Holzman was a client at his father's request. Bressio would never have taken him otherwise. The old man was a Brooklyn lawyer who had sent his son to Swarthmore and Harvard Law, then set him up in what the father proudly called "fancy-shmancy Park Avenue offices." Old man Holzman had asked Bressio to keep an eye on his son until he got "some *sechel,*" a Yiddish word meaning wisdom. "Brains he's got in abundance, but *sechel,* that will take a little time. Let me know how he's coming along, okay?"

It had been five years and Bressio had painfully avoided letting old man Holzman know how his son was coming along because he respected the older Holzman as a lawyer and as a person. Ripper, as the son was known, had showed little interest in making a good reputation for himself, helping his clients or even making money. He had one simple little ambition—to infinitely change the basic legal contract of American society. He was a "Constitution nut," according to Clarissa.

Bressio glanced at the case and shook his head. It angered him when lawyers attempted to transform a simple phone call into a philosophical battle. This was more common among young lawyers. Those who survived usually changed in three years. Bressio dialed the phone.

"Put Ripper on. This is Bressio." He waited, fingering Clarissa's typed notes.

"Hey, Ripper, this is Bressio. I got your simple-negligence case here. Do these people really want to play around with admissible evidence? I mean, it's a small plastics factory they got, not the Ford Foundation."

"We could take that tack I outlined, though, couldn't we? I mean, I would have a chance to get it off the ground, wouldn't I?"

"Yeah, you would have a chance. But do your clients want to march all the way to the Supreme Court? That's where it's going if their money holds out and you can maneuver that point intact through appeals."

"I got a chance, huh?"

"That wasn't the case, Ripper. It's a busted leg. A busted leg for this guy I figure is seven hundred, maybe five hundred bottom, to tops twelve hundred, and if you go to fifteen, you're screwing your client. Now, as to whether a doctor who had been employed by the Department of Public Health when—"

"That's the question," said Holzman.

"No," said Bressio. "The question is whether the plastics people —it seems like an odd spelling of Feldman here—would want—"

"Al, I gave Clarissa strict instructions that I wanted your opinion on whether we have a constitutional case. I'm not particularly interested in the grubby bargaining of someone's hairline fracture."

"For one, Ripper, you don't give Clarissa instructions, especially strict ones. Secondly, the grubby bargaining over a hairline fracture is what you were hired for. Thirdly, you will phone the plaintiff's attorney and make the deal. There's an area in here in which he's weak. It's something as grubby as the question over the entrance to this loading ramp. Now, you would probably lose on this thing if you fought it, but it is questionable enough to save your client some money when you deal with the plaintiff's lawyer. Tell them you'll give four to five and settle for anything less than twelve hundred."

"If my father—"

"If your father weren't paying your office rent out of his Brooklyn practice, you'd never use me. I know."

"He didn't send me to Harvard to produce another Jewish Brooklyn lawyer, Al."

"Son, you couldn't carry your father's briefcase and you never will."

"If I were Murray Blay Dawson, you wouldn't speak to me like that," said Ripper, referring to a famous lawyer he had been trying to meet through Bressio.

"I wouldn't have to; goodbye, Ripper, and don't let me hear of you in court with that case."

Bressio checked his watch again. The next folder was labeled McGuffin. Way back in his career Francis X. McGuffin had been with the DA's office. He had the reputation of trying to compromise with an avalanche. He was more afraid of appearing in court than most button men, Bressio knew.

Naturally, the McGuffin case required court action. He had sent it to Bressio to see if there was some way he could avoid this. Bressio dialed the phone again.

"Frank, this is Al . . . Yeah. I got it this morning. Look, we're going to prepare a simple brief for you. You've got the closest thing to an airtight case there is. Don't piddle with this guy . . . No, Frank. You don't have to take less . . . Yeah, I know they're recalcitrant. That's why you're going to court . . . Bronx Superior Court, Frank. You take the West Side Highway . . . Frank, listen to me, Frank. There's some nice money in this . . . Don't worry . . . If they fight, they're fools. You can really clean up for yourself and your client. Frank, money, Frank. Money. Money. Money. Okay? Don't worry. And, Frank . . . money. Goodbye."

Bressio outlined the thrust of the case, which was all Clarissa would need for a brief. He checked his watch again. Almost eleven o'clock and Clarissa still had not arrived. The next folder was marked Ward Whipple, of Whipple, Barnes and Trent. It was a long letter from Whipple's secretary posing a good and sticky question. Bressio would have to think about that one when he had time, probably a week hence.

The heavy click of wooden-soled shoes came down the hallway and Bressio leaned back in his chair. The outer office lights went on and the outer office door shut. Clarissa came into his office, a night school notebook held over her chest, like a square miniature shield. She was a fine-featured young woman with a grace of freckles over a delicate nose, and brown sensitive eyes that could at times show a world of sympathy, and a mouth that could smile a hermit into congeniality. When there was a smile. This morning her brown hair was stringy and her face looked like an old washed-out tennis court.

"I see the files are open, Al. Did you leave them open? You shouldn't leave them open like that. Someone might get to them, you know."

Bressio sipped at the remnants of coffee.

"Did you get coffee and Danish?" she asked.

"I finished them waiting for you."

"You shouldn't have. You know what that does to your diet. You look as though you've lost some weight."

"I gained."

"Oh," said Clarissa and glanced sideways in what Bressio knew was the formulation of a difficult sentence. "Al, I want to talk to you. I've got to talk to you. We've got to communicate. I think we've got to express ourselves honestly and communicate. I think that's where our difficulties come from. We don't communicate."

Bressio picked up the *Daily News* and reread a column, but saw only the words. Their meaning at that moment was irrelevant.

"Al, are you going to talk to me?"

"Yes. Go to the outer office and retrieve the medicals. It was the medical files you took, wasn't it?"

"You don't need compensation cases any more, Al. Dammit, listen to me. You don't need a list of doctors who'll swear a woman's nerves are ruined for life because she slipped on a banana peel. You don't need the shyster ambulance chasers. You don't need to be a goddamn private detective for Murray Dawson. You could be a great—"

"Did Dawson phone me recently?" Bressio asked, a sharp note of suspicion in his voice.

"For the last two days. He says it's urgent, damn you, stupid sonuvabitch," sobbed Clarissa and she dropped her notebook and covered her eyes and cried.

Bressio got his revolver from the center drawer, snapped it into the holster and headed for the door.

"For Dawson you'd use a gun," Clarissa shrieked after him. "Why don't you use it for the right people and make some real money, if you're going to use it at all. You dumb guinea cock-sucker."

She heard the hallway door open and shut.

"Dumb guinea," she said and cried for the rest of the morning.

II

_____

When Bressio entered the elegantly furnished reception room of Dawson, Hemler and Burns on Park Avenue, clients suddenly became very interested in magazines, briefcases or laps. Bressio was used to this reaction, but it never failed to make him a little sad.

"Dawson says it's urgent," he said quietly to a lush young receptionist with a soft artificial smile.

"Certainly, Mr. Bressio," she said in a clipped British accent while ringing the private line to Dawson's private secretary. There was no direct line from the reception room to Dawson's private office, nor was there need for one. Few of the people waiting would ordinarily ever see Murray Blay Dawson, much less discuss their case with him, yet all of them would feel he was involved in their legal matters and pay that much more for it.

This illusion was calculatedly fostered, Bressio knew, by the younger lawyers of the firm, who often told clients, "Mr. Dawson and I believe," or, "Mr. Dawson fears you might run into some trouble if . . . " or, "We think we see an opportunity that Mr. Dawson has been waiting for." In the floor-wide spread of Dawson Hemler and Burns, Dawson's office was secluded to the right because, as he had told Bressio, he did not like to run into the young lawyers who handled the caseloads. He could never remember their names, and that embarrassed him.

Bressio did not sit down among the clients, for there was always someone, usually an elderly woman, who would assure him that Murray Blay Dawson would get him off. And in support of this prediction they would invariably open up one of the magazines and point to an article. The office bought them in five-hundred-block lots so they were always new.

Bressio stood by the receptionist until he felt stares. He glanced at the room and saw a "Dawson cover," as the secretaries called them, go up in front of a portly gentleman's face. It was a two-year-old *Newsweek* and appeared when Dawson won acquittal for an Army colonel charged with ordering a civilian massacre in Vietnam. Dawson had virtually put the United States Army on trial and was working on including the State Department when the court-martial found the colonel innocent. A lieutenant who had followed the colonel's orders got twenty years to life.

Dawson was one of the few criminal lawyers in the country to have the strong and abiding respect of almost every government agency. He earned this by hurting them deeply whenever he could.

A U.S. Attorney General known for his rectitude, prudishness, and New England sense of fair play had once called Dawson a "cocksucking sonuvabitch" to the surprise of his staff, all of whom had assumed he did not know those words. Privately the Attorney General referred to Dawson as Dwarshkopf, the name investigations disclosed had been used by Dawson's grandfather before getting it changed by an immigration official at Ellis Island.

Other attorneys claimed Dawson once sought a change of venue because the local television stations lacked color facilities. Lost in the blaring controversy was the fact that Murray Blay Dawson was a fine lawyer, a fact that Alphonse Joseph Bressio respected deeply.

"Bressio. Al Bressio. So good of you to come." The voice was rich and strong and preceded Dawson into the reception room like a trumpet down a church nave. He strode into the reception room, his tanned majestic face agleam with beneficent smile.

"What are you doing out here, Murray?" asked Bressio. "I could have come inside as usual."

"So good to see you, Al. Are you all right?" said Dawson, shaking Bressio's hand while clasping the elbow up to the arm as though to prevent escape. Dawson's Saville Row elegance and stunning crown of white hair made the shorter, stiff-suited Bressio (no clothes ever hung on him well) appear like a peasant before a king. Bressio could feel the whole room stare at them both.

"I'm okay," he said flatly.

"I tried reaching you for the last two days, and then I heard about the tragedy of your cousin—"

"Oh, that's nothing, Murray. That's Jimmy Bugellerio. He's a twice-removed cousin. The funeral's tomorrow. In any case, it's not a big thing."

"I'm so glad you're all right," said Dawson.

"I think I should say no now instead of waiting for what you're going to ask," said Bressio.

Dawson's grip tightened, he forgot to smile and he tugged hard. "C'mon into my office. Let's get out of here."

Bressio shrugged and followed Dawson into the Dawson suite, which was protected by another receptionist who kept people from the private secretary, who was normally the last filtering link before Dawson himself. The suite was more like a living room with side rooms attached. There were no lawbooks or degrees testifying to knowledge; rather, a conference of expensive couches and soft chairs were set around a low elegant marble table. Just short of the walls was a deep bluish rug, and on two of the walls, expensive art dominated the room. Bressio remembered Dawson telling him he knew the Picasso from the Renoirs because the Picasso had funny eyes and the Renoirs had dots.

Ceiling-length white drapes blocked the windows and hid the bar, from which Dawson was now busily gathering things. Bressio plopped himself into a chair that had more character than most people and stretched his feet on the marble table. As always, they did not feel right there, and he lowered them as unworthy of the table. Dawson brought over a silver ice bucket, a bottle of Jack Daniels and two glasses.

"What is this 'no' shit, Al?" he asked. "What is it?"

"I didn't say no. I said I'd probably say no to whatever you asked."

"May I be privvy to your reasoning process?"

"Instinct. And you're too anxious. Basically it's my stomach."

"All instinct," asked Dawson, "or do I come off phony when I'm in the reception room? It was phony, wasn't it, Al? Right? I've got to work on that. Got to perfect being real."

"It was instinct. You came off real, Murray."

"I've got nothing against instinct, Al. I respect it. Especially in men I respect, but please use your head. Those people out there are paying clients. They come here because Murray Blay Dawson is not a man to be said no to. Not in front of them. If you want to say no, say no in here. Okay?"

Bressio nodded and took one of the two big drinks Dawson offered. The glass was crystal.

"All right. Let's stop this nonsense," said Dawson. "You're a rational man. You say no. I say yes, and I'm going to pay you, so don't give me this instinct drivel. I'm going to pay you for your stomach, which says stay out. Buy it some Tums. I don't need grief now. I have enough at home. I have enough all through the world. From you, Al, I don't want it."

Bressio leaned forward, his face screwed in confusion. "Am I missing something, Murray? I could have sworn I heard you make a contract between two people without one of them saying yes. It's like I'm not even here."

"Just listen, will you?" said Dawson.

Bressio hoisted a glass in salute to listening. Dawson took a gulp of his drink, and putting it down, leaned over the edge of the couch, fixing Bressio with his pale-blue eyes as he had fixed them on many a jury.

"First of all, let me congratulate your stomach on knowing something I don't know. I am not sure now I have a case, let alone am I sure what I want to do, let alone am I sure it is something either of us should touch. What I have is some confusion and I want to talk. Okay?"

"Okay."

"Do you believe me?"

"Of course not."

"All right," said Dawson, apparently ignoring the response. "See if you can follow this."

And Bressio listened to a summation that should have been presented in a classroom as a textbook example. It was clear, lean, and left but one logical verdict.

There was this woman who might be in danger of losing her life because she had helped a landlady. One simple act had set off a chain of events that only someone with Bressio's connections could unravel—Dawson believed. The woman and a friend had helped the landlady break into a downstairs loft because the previous tenants had moved out and changed the lock. The landlady, the woman and her friend found a pistol in the apartment and phoned the police, and their lives hadn't been the same since.

Bressio sipped the bourbon while listening to the evils that befell the woman. She began seeing visions: people following her; a red-haired man who smiled at her from subway cars; a man with a scar. Her friend was arrested in Arizona on a marijuana charge. He and a three-time loser had been stopped by a state trooper for speeding.

"It was a tip. I accept that," said Bressio, motioning with the glass for Dawson to continue. "These pushers stop in the middle of nowhere at four A.M. for a blinking red light."

"He wasn't even a pusher," said Dawson, interrupting his line of attack. "He's a drug-cult freak, artist type. Silly stuff. LSD, hash, ups, downs, in-betweens. You know, the harmless stuff."

"He's a pusher," said Bressio flatly.

"Not a pusher. He's into happiness drugs and sells enough to keep himself supplied."

"All right, Murray. A candy-store owner who eats his own candy isn't a candy-store owner."

Dawson shook his head sadly as though Bressio belonged among the invincibly ignorant of the world. He continued: "About a week ago the body of one of the tenants who had lived in the locked loft came floating up off the Fifty-ninth Street bridge." Perhaps Bressio had heard about it.

"The *Daily News* didn't let anybody not hear about it, Murray. She was a California beauty queen or something," said Bressio.

"It was a professional job, right?"

Bressio shrugged with a somewhat horrified look which said how would he know.

"You could find out, though, couldn't you?"

"Possibly. These things are touchy, Murray."

"Well, if anyone could, you could," said Dawson.

"What's the case, Murray, what are you leading to?"

"A few days ago I had one of my people check with the police and there is no record of their ever having investigated that loft building on 285 Pren Street. They are withholding evidence on something. Somehow the government—someone is doing danger-ous and peculiar things and I want to know why. Someone is fucking over this guy and I want to know why. Someone has killed the downstairs neighbor of this woman and I want to know why."

"I don't follow you, Murray. Where is the case you want me to help prepare? Guy? Woman? What?"

Dawson went to the curtains with all the formidableness of his six feet two inches. His hand went through the cloth and came out with a fat legal-size manilla envelope and just as formidably returned to the marble table. He threw the envelope on the table near Bressio's knees.

"That's seven thousand dollars in cash, fifty dollars an hour for a week of your time. Paid on twenty-four hours a day. Even for your sleep. Find out in a week for me what the hell is going on and if you do it in two days, take a few days on Dawson, Hemler and Burns. I'm mad, Al. I feel put upon by the U.S. government and I know I have friends who won't let them get away with that. I want to know what's going on."

Bressio looked at the envelope and felt Dawson's presence over him.

"First of all, Murray, I'm easing out of the investigative business, you know that. I'm moving more into the legal end of things. Consultations."

"Bullshit, Al. You need the money. The way you bet you always need the money."

"Secondly, Murray, old friend, I still don't know who your client is. Is it the woman? The pusher? Who?"

"The woman is my client. There's a custody case. I'm getting the child for her," said Dawson as though everyone should know this.

"What? What?" asked Bressio, struggling to somehow join another wild strand to a chaos of strands. "Let me get this straight. What are we doing with a child in this thing and what is Murray Blay Dawson doing in a custody case?"

"Winning it, I hope. Mary Beth Cutler—Cutler is the last name —Mary Beth Cutler is trying to get her baby back from her boyfriend the artist, who adopted the child legally with his wife. He was married when Mary Beth started going with him. Mary Beth had a child by him. I don't know her reasoning process, but I think she wanted the kid not to be considered a legal bastard. She had the couple adopt her and now she wants the kid back. Custody case."

"And the legal parents are contesting, right?"

Dawson shook his head.

"So if they're not contesting, Murray, you get the parents to sign papers and Mary Beth to sign papers. Your secretary could handle that, so why are you telling me this is a custody case?" Bressio knew very well why Dawson had brought in the custody case. It was a little detour to get away from what Bressio was approaching, a tactic like the repeating of the name Cutler, which sounded very familiar but which Bressio could not place right away. It might be that Dawson didn't want to discuss who the client was.

"So where is your big custody case?" asked Bressio again. Dawson appeared to be thinking deeply. He eyed Bressio, then the envelope.

"Take the money, Al. Don't give me grief. Get this whole thing untangled about the tip-off, the loft, the visions Mary Beth is seeing, and put my heart at ease. Okay? What do I have to tell you?"

"You'll find something."

"I feel hurt that you would think I'd lie to you, Al. Have I ever lied to you?"

"Sure."

"Not often."

"Only when needed."

"Take the fucking money!" yelled Dawson. "What the hell is the matter with you, Al? If I asked you to throw someone off the roof for seven grand you'd give it more consideration than this."

"If you'd ask me to throw someone off the roof, I'd know why there was so much money for a week's work. I wouldn't do it, but I'd know."

Dawson opened his hands in frustration.

"What do you want to know, Al? Ask. Anything. Ask it."

"Why did you really send for me?"

"How am I supposed to answer that? You don't believe anything I say. You just called me a liar," said Dawson, being unjustly accused. He interrupted being unjustly accused to pour two more drinks and sit down. He crossed his legs and folded his arms. The defendant.

"All right, Murray," said Bressio. "I see no rational cause for you to be interested in this thing. There's no notoriety that I know of. I don't see any great test of your skills, no chance to set precedent, nothing that would offer what I would consider a good reason for you to take the case. So let us explore the irrational."

Dawson nodded.

"Does this have anything to do with your one true love of the week, whoever she may be today?"

Dawson shook his head.

"Are you doing a favor for some actress or other?"

"I already answered no to that subject," Dawson said testily.

Bressio sipped his drink. Behind that hostile Dawson face, he saw a grin. Dawson was grinning at him. What small triumph was he hiding?

Dawson might just have asked him into this thing because Bressio might just be the one man to turn him down. Suddenly Bressio knew, and he smiled at Dawson and saw the hidden grin disappear.

"This boyfriend," said Bressio. "This boyfriend who got busted, how much does he have to do with your client's difficulties?"

Dawson shrugged as though the question were absurd. He looked at his watch.

"Would this boyfriend happen to be a one-time painter?" asked Bressio.

"Uh, yes, I think so," said Dawson with an annoyed tolerance.

"A one-time race driver?"

"He might."

"A time-to-time chef?"

"Not time to time. He still is."

"Does this boyfriend chew his water and drink his food and believe there is an organization called the Brotherhood of Acid-Makers which defends the purity and name of LSD?"

"He may."

"Does this boyfriend peddle around Greenwich Village on his bike with his drugstore in his knapsack, and has he been warned by you a score of times not to carry drugs around the city so brazenly?"

"He might," said Dawson, invincibly unhumbled.

"Might his name be L. Marvin Fleish?"

"It might."

"Then I have only one more question, Murray. Why did you

waste your time and mine by inviting me up here?"

Alphonse Joseph Bressio sat back in the chair, his annoyance balmed by the sweet oils of triumph. And had he remained firm in his refusal, he would have been spared a nightmare.

III

With cold rejection set neatly on the table alongside Dawson's seven thousand dollars immediate ready cash, which Bressio longed to bring into his life but not at the price of an L. Marvin Fleish, Alphonse Joseph Bressio listened to Dawson begin not mentioning things.

Among the things he told Bressio he would not bring into their strictly business conversation was Dawson's personally defending Bressio's late mother several years before in Brooklyn Supreme Court on a minor suit brought by a tenant. There were some people you represented, Dawson explained, even though professionally it was not your kind of case. You did these things for people who were important in your life and not to be dismissed and hurt like garbage.

Dawson was also not going to mention his firm's advancing Bressio money during several of his famous gambling streaks because Dawson considered these advances an investment in talent, even though Hemler and Burns had fought him consistently over the size of these advances and Bressio's fees.

Bressio and Dawson shared a close bond, the excitement and challenge of the law. Their friendship was far more important than some problems of a poor artist being overwhelmed by the U.S. government. Dawson understood why Bressio might unreasonably be afraid, and Dawson was ready to go it alone against the most powerful force in the world.

Above all things, Dawson didn't want their friendship to be ruined by Bressio's phobia about a harmless foul-up. All Bressio had to do was say no, and Dawson would never bring up the subject again.

"No," said Bressio.

Dawson would never bring up the subject again because it was impossible to reason with a dumb superstitious guinea. Impossible. "What the hell do you want from me?" screamed Dawson.

"Why don't we both do what we do best instead of messing around with a Fleish? What is this fascination you have with that guy?"

Dawson saw the problem not as his fascination but Bressio's unreasonable fear of a harmless artist. Dawson thought they should deal with that first, especially since Bressio was willing to risk a valuable friendship over it.

"You know why. You knew it when you started giving me details through the back door."

"Oh, that," said Dawson.

"That," said Bressio.

"He's a little unlucky for people. Okay. He's not a bad guy."

"His motives are immaterial to me, Murray. His results terrify me. For you, maybe it's an attraction. Sometimes you need that kind of nonsense in your life, I don't know. For me he's like looking into an open grave. He's going to get people killed. If not yet, it's inevitable."

Dawson sighed.

"No, listen to me, Murray. In little things and big, he's a disaster. He gets one chance at a Lotus Ford this guy invests his family fortune in, and L. Marvin cracks it up. He's been in at least eleven business ventures I know of that failed, one of them a marijuana farm that I hear and do not believe he tried to put in the soil bank . . . No, no, don't laugh, listen to me on this. He's bankrupted a half-dozen people at least, and who knows how many kids he sent to the funny farm with his drug, love, karma nonsense. He practically raped your latest wife."

"Not practically. He did. And we paid him for the portrait he was doing. You should see Bobo's face in that picture. It's hysterical. Angry?" Dawson laughed at the thought of his wife's grimace in oil.

"That's just it. I or even you would probably be long dead if we did anything like that. But with L. Marvin, nobody blames him.

Nobody. I'm telling you. Nobody except me. He's dangerous, and I don't think he's funny and I will not tie myself up with him in any way. He's all yours. I can't afford that in my life, not even at seven grand a week."

"You have Clarissa and I have Marvin, who has less viciousness in his whole body than that bitch secretary has in one of her unsheathed tits."

Don't mention Clarissa in the same breath with him," said Bressio, and saw Dawson step back. He did not realize how much anger was in him or that he had started to rise until he saw Dawson's face pale.

"Okay," Dawson said in a hushed voice, his face pallid. "Okay."

"I didn't mean to threaten you, Murray."

"It's okay, Al. I know how you feel about Clarissa."

"It's not okay. I'm sorry . . . it's, well, I don't feel that way about Clarissa. She's a good kid. Period."

"Sure, Al."

"I'm sorry."

"I said it was okay."

"Yeah," said Bressio, feeling hauntingly vulnerable because it was basic to his soul that people who did not practice violence should never be threatened with it, not even in the tone of voice. He did not like to see it in others and he abhorred it in himself.

"You know, Al, if it weren't Marvin in this thing, I wouldn't have offered such a high price," Dawson said with tenderness.

"I know," said Bressio

"And think about the hardship this Mary Beth Cutler had to endure living with Marvin. If you think his friendship places demands on me, can you imagine the life of someone living with that nut?"

"I can."

"And it's seven thousand dollars, maybe fifty-five hundred of it is what I call Fleish-hazard money."

"I know."

"And you'd be doing me a real favor, Al. I haven't had a fight with the U.S. government for months. I'm getting withdrawal pains."

Bressio smiled and picked up the envelope for what he at first thought was to reweigh the situation, but by the time his hands gripped the money, Dawson leaped from the couch in joy. It was all over.

"You want to hold the cash for a while or do you want me to deliver it directly to your bookie?" Dawson said, leaning down to fill the glasses while his feet danced around the table.

"I'll deliver it," said Bressio curtly. "Whose money is this?"

"Mary Beth's. Oh, boy, is she a piece of work. You think Marvin is bad? He's a deep-water Baptist by comparison. When you meet her, you'll know you've been underpaid. What a piece of work."

Dawson's joy was contagious, and despite himself, Bressio grinned.

"I knew I had you when you felt bad about frightening me," said Dawson, dancing the bottle to the middle of the room. He whirled to Bressio. "I'll tell you what I'm gonna do. Tell you what I'm gonna do. Because I'm feeling a little guilty about shooting fish in a barrel, and because I know how you feel about smack, and because I feel the same way myself . . . if you find that Marvin ever dealt smack, I'll drop the case."

"If this is the woman's money, then she's the client," said Bressio.

"And I'll tell ya what I'm gonna do, also. I'll say all right. If you can unravel this situation without helping Marvin, go to it. You filter out from a paranoid's vision what's real and what isn't, and you've earned your money. Work done—I forgot to tell you she's paranoid—completed. You can walk away from this thing free and clear and rich—until you reach your bookie, of course."

Dawson hummed a waltz and escorted the bottle around the office in a four-step which became a bugaloo. Bressio shook his head like a parent who cannot get his heart into disapproval.

"Just where can I reach Mary Beth Cutler?"

"You can almost never reach her," said Dawson, dissolving in laughter. "She'll reach you."

That evening, Bressio cleared his gambling tabs. Moochie said Bressio needn't have felt rushed. His credit was good.

"Yeah, I know," said Bressio and put another hundred on Chicago over the Mets and a hundred on Oakland over the Yankees.

"Anything new around town?" asked Moochie.

"No," said Bressio. "Make that five hundred on Chicago. The

Mets can't pitch Seaver two days in a row."

He was asked the same question at the Cedar Tavern on University Place and Eleventh Street by a bartender.

"Nothing new. Real quiet," said Bressio.

"Jimmy the Bug?"

"Nothing, from what I hear. He was complicating things and he was asked a few times not to and he wouldn't listen so I hear. He's being buried tomorrow from Fermio's."

"I know he was your second cousin or something, but I never liked him."

"Neither did I," said Bressio. "Relatives are like people you meet in the elevator. You don't have much choice."

"There was a funny-looking woman asking for you here about a half-hour ago. Said she knew you. Asked where you were. I turned my head for a second and she was gone."

"Did she say what her name was?"

The bartender shook his head.

"What do you think of Oakland for tomorrow?" asked Bressio.

"I think you should join Gamblers Anonymous is what I think of Oakland."

"Will you join with me?"

"I like Oakland very much," said the bartender.

Bressio reached his apartment building in the West Village five minutes before the eleven o'clock news. It was one of those pleasant New York City high rises that visitors always expressed a desire to live in until they heard the monthly rental. Bressio paid $650 a month for three rooms, plus $145 a week to the maid, plus $50 a month to the doorman to "keep his eye on things," plus $25 a month to the super "so that I don't have to go looking for you when I need you."

When he got off the elevator at the fifth floor, he noticed a figure disappear down a stairwell. Assuming it was a burglar's chickee, he double-locked his apartment door behind him.

The apartment was a semi-organized collection of old chairs and couches from his office and a table that almost matched the chairs and rustic lamps that matched nothing but gave good light. Clarissa had often tried to remodel it, even going so far as to give the furniture to the Salvation Army and ordering stylish replacements.

Bressio bought back his old furniture and gave the new tables, chairs, couches and lamps to Clarissa in lieu of a Christmas bonus.

Bressio opened a bottle of Jack Daniels and stuffed a frozen Weight Watchers dinner into the electric oven that was supposed to clean itself.

He turned on Channel 4 because sometimes the night news had either Dick Schaap or Jimmy Breslin, the only television newsmen he respected. To Bressio, the rest were actors.

When the actor announced Schaap would be on with a story, Bressio poured himself a tad more sipping whiskey and opened a package of dry roasted cashews. It was one of his cherished pleasures to watch a good professional work at anything. Long before, he had formulated a dictum that 85 percent of all the people in any given field did not know what they were doing. With Law, the figure touched 90 percent.

Schaap's opening cynical line brought an understanding grin to Bressio's face. He forgot all about his upcoming week of L. Marvin Fleish. Then the phone rang. It was the answering service. A Dawson client had been phoning every half-hour all day. Would Bressio take it?

"Yeah," said Bressio. "In ten minutes. Not before."

As soon as he hung up, the phone rang again.

"You're being followed," came a woman's voice.

"Is this Mary Beth Cutler?"

"Who are you?"

"I'm Al Bressio. This is my telephone number."

"Good. This is Mary Beth Cutler. Dawson spoke to you about me."

"A bit."

"What did he say?"

"I can't go through it all on the phone."

"Right. Good. The line may be tapped. Good thinking. Marve says you're a good man. He knows you. He says Dawson says you're a good man, too. I need someone I can trust."

"What's this following business?" asked Bressio.

"A real mean-looking guy came down your hallway about four minutes ago. About five feet ten, two hundred and thirty pounds. Well-dressed. Light summer suit, sort of crumpled. A real gangster type. I think he may be the one who's got a contract on my life."

"Was it a whitish double-breasted suit with white shirt and black tie?"

"That's the one. God, he was a monster."

"That's me, Miss Cutler."

"Oh, good. You're on our side."

"When did Mr. Dawson tell you I was hired for this?"

"This morning. He said he was going to see you later, that you didn't like Marvin, but he could get you to take the case. Marvin disagreed with him. Marvin says you like him very much, you just don't know how to show it."

Bressio was about to say something when Mary Beth Cutler unleashed a swarm of information. "Wait until you hear this," she said. "It's the most sinister trap ever devised and I'm in the middle of it. I saw the man with the scar again today, and it came right after the cars with the blinking lights. The police are in on it, too. I knew that for sure. The police are in on it. You've really walked into something this time."

"I believe it, Miss Cutler. What is bothering you specifically at this moment?"

"The whole thing."

"Well, look. Tomorrow morning bring the whole thing to my office. Do you know where it is?"

"The Woolworth Building."

"Right. Twenty-fifth floor."

"Uh-oh."

"What?"

"I think it's him again. Shh. No, he's walking past. Going around the block. I'm downstairs from your apartment in a telephone booth. Should I go back to my apartment or go upstairs to yours?"

"Look, do you have any money?" asked Bressio on the outside chance she really was being followed.

"Yes. I can give you money."

"No. You've given enough to Dawson for me. Do you have any money on you?"

"Yes. Should I tell you how much over the telephone?"

"Do what I tell you, Miss Cutler. Go into the subway. Any line. Go to Forty-second Street. They all go there. Take the shuttle back and forth until you're sure you're not being followed or until midnight, whichever comes first. Don't go on riding the subways after midnight. Get out. Hail a cab. Go to a major hotel. Check in. Lock the door. Don't open it for anyone. I'll see you at eleven A.M. in my office."

"Which hotel?"

"You decide when you get in the cab," said Bressio.

"The Biltmore?"

"Sure. Fine."

"What if this line is tapped?"

"I told you to decide when you get in the cab."

"Good. Good thinking. This is going to be great. See you tomorrow, darling."

Bressio hung up and sadly realized he had missed Schaap. He turned off the television. The phone rang again. It was Mary Beth Cutler.

"Was that eleven A.M. at your office?"

"Yes."

"Good. I'll be at the Biltmore."

Bressio hung up again and went to his window facing the street. He looked down at the phone booth on the corner. A thinnish woman in light tan raincoat and red babushka whisked from the booth down the street looking right and left. Mid-block she turned and rushed the other way. Bressio checked the street. He saw no tail.

He got his answering service on the phone and delivered some very special instructions. There would be something extra for the operator if the service were performed properly. He gave her Dawson's private home phone number.

"This is what I want you to do: Phone that number at four-thirty A.M. Get Dawson. Not his wife. Not his maid, but Dawson. Only Dawson will do. Tell him that Al Bressio has met the girl friend of L. Marvin Fleish. Got that? Repeat it . . . good. Perfect. Now, I will receive no phone calls from anyone until nine A.M. tomorrow morning. None. Under any circumstances."

"The standing Dawson call-through is out then?" asked the service operator.

"Especially the Dawson call-through."

At 4:45 A.M., Bressio was awakened by his answering service, which apologized but said his wife was dying at St. Vincent's

Hospital and he was the only one who knew her blood type, which could save her life. Could the answering service let the call through from the hospital?

"No," said Bressio sleepily. "If she hasn't taken the precaution to wear a blood-type badge, death will teach her a lesson."

The answering-service woman gasped. Bressio hung up. Murray Blay Dawson had just let him know he had gotten the message.

IV

Bressio woke up scheming how to avoid L. Marvin in the ensuing week. Perhaps L. Marvin would contract sudden cancer of the brain and die before noon. Bressio had been lucky before.

He put on a fresh gray silk suit, a white shirt and a dark tie. He switched off the television on the way out of his apartment as he headed downtown toward Little Italy and Fermio's Funeral Home on Mulberry Street, from whence his second cousin James "the Bug" Bugellerio would be buried.

He took a cab and then walked the last two blocks, remembering the early-morning summer smells of his childhood and how the ice would melt over the lettuce under canvas in the dark cool interiors of the vegetable stores. There were refrigerators and coolers now in these stores, but many of the good smells remained. He remembered dunking bread and butter into heavily creamed coffee, and running out to play before the sun rose high and made breathing a chore and life an oven.

It would be a hot day today, but not yet. Several storefronts had their windows painted over with thick green paint. These were the little gambling clubs, the meeting halls, the centers of business. Their occupants, who would arrive in a few hours, did not want strangers looking in. Hence the paint.

When Bressio turned onto Mulberry Street he saw a line of cars filled with men across from Fermio's. Some had cameras. Bressio judged there were at least six carloads, which surprised him, because at best Jimmy the Bug was worth only two cars of cops. He saw the early-morning sun glint off a large lens and stared into it.

The camera suddenly lowered, the plainclothesman looked away briefly, apparently regained the composure lost from seeing Bressio's face that close up, and began shooting again.

Bressio saw some men point to him and others take notes. He knew what they were doing. He only wished *they* knew what they were doing.

As soon as he entered the large aluminum doors of Fermio's, he said to the first Fermio he saw: "Who the hell are those bananas? Six carloads of cops to register the comings and goings of Bugellerio's mourners."

"They're new," said Patrice Fermio, a chubby but precise-looking man in black suit and black tie.

"No kidding," said Bressio. "They got a good front and profile of me. What are they doing, registering the world?"

"They're FBNC, Federal Bureau of Narcotics Control. Whole bureau is new."

"I know. I know. But this narcotics . . . Jimmy isn't narcotics. No one here is narcotics."

"They're new."

"They must have money and men to burn," said Bressio and headed toward the sounds of the professional mourners. Foolishness like that always unnerved him. Especially with people who carried guns.

At the entrance of the main parlor, Bressio blessed himself with holy water and walked solemnly along the dark carpet down the aisle between folding chairs to a rich bronze casket. He held his hands before himself as though approaching the altar rail for communion, as the sister had taught him more than a quarter of a century before at Our Lady of Pompeii School, down the street. Bressio leaned over the heavily cosmetized face of his second cousin, Jimmy, and kissed the cold, dark lips in formal respect.

The bullet hole in the Bug's temple was hidden by dark wax and a judicious addition of just the right shade of black thick hair, much like Bressio's. Fermio's was considered without peer in flower arrangements and bullet holes. Such was the reputation of Fermio's that people said you could give Genaro, Patrice's older brother, a fingernail and a photograph of the departed and he would produce your loved one almost as good as new. Sometimes better.

Alphonse bowed stiffly to the remains and stepped away to a flower-draped pre-dieu before the casket. He knelt there for a formal four seconds, crossed himself perfunctorily and rose to present himself to his mother's cousin, the grieving Philomena Bugellerio. She sat in the front row, with her other sons standing behind her. They were, as Bressio knew them, Billy, Sally and Joey, all in their late forties, all unmarried and living at home, and all aspiring to button man, hoping that seniority would accomplish for them what talent failed.

Alphonse kissed his mother's cousin dutifully on both cheeks.

"Blood," said Philomena, a scrawn of a leather-faced woman wearing severe black in contrast to the whitish powder on her cheeks. "Your cousin's blood has been spilled."

"Aunt Philomena," said Bressio respectfully, "I grieve with you in your loss. It was a hard business Jimmy was in."

"The spics got him. The spics did it to him, Alphonse. The spics spilled your cousin's blood." Her face whitened with anger.

The murmuring in the funeral parlor ceased. The mourners looked at a portly gray-haired man in a dark suit and then at Bressio. This was important. They knew that Philomena, having been rebuffed in her first bid for vengeance, was now seeking to transform a bad business experience into a race war. They also knew that despite many lucrative offers, Alphonse Bressio had always kept himself clear of family business. If he should change now, it would be of utmost importance to the portly gentleman, possibly to all five families of the city. Much more important than Jimmy the Bug's death.

"A hard business, Aunt Philomena," said Bressio and bowed courteously. The murmuring in Fermio's resumed and Bressio went back up the aisle past the official mourners, who not only added a dimension of grief but allowed others to discuss matters of the day, the essential grieving being taken care of.

"It is good to see you, Alphonse," said the portly gentleman, sitting first behind the official mourners.

"It is good to see you too, Don Carmine," said Bressio, bowing to brush his lips against the back of Don Carmine's offered hand.

It was Don Carmine Dursio, Bressio knew, who had allowed Jimmy's death. Everyone who mattered knew that, especially Philomena Bugellerio, but since she could not seek vengeance

against the man who fed her family, she had tried unsuccessfully
to elicit support vengeance against the men who merely pulled the
trigger.

Jimmy, as Bressio and many others knew, had been warned
twice to stop skimming from Puerto Rican numbers in East Harlem under the theory that if you took from people who had little,
they might be forced to fight for more. There were legitimate
complaints from East Harlem to Don Carmine, and it was ordered
that Jimmy be spoken to. But to his second cousin, Bressio knew,
anything less than a lead pipe across the bridge of his nose was an
invitation to proceed.

The hit man caught Jimmy from the side over a cup of bean soup
in a Spanish luncheonette as he was explaining to the finger man
responsible for setting him up that Don Carmine was only making
noises because no one could really take spics seriously. This was
how Bressio understood the incident.

"Come sit down beside me and tell me the good things that have
been happening, Alphonse," said Don Carmine. Immediately a
middle-aged man next to the don rose to offer his seat to Bressio,
who ignored him.

"Thank you, Don Carmine, but I must run. Business. I have an
urgent call which I cannot delay. Any other time at your conve-
nience I would be most honored and delighted to talk to you. But
I have a previous obligation."

"I hear your business is picking up. I am happy to hear that."

"Thank you," said Bressio.

"I have always said that if a man is happy, what can money buy
him?"

Bressio nodded respectfully. If his estimates were correct, within
five minutes of Moochie's receiving the money the night before, it
was made known to Don Carmine.

"With all due respects, I must go," said Bressio.

Outside, two cameras caught Bressio full face. He recognized
one of the men in a back seat as a New York City detective. The
detective shrugged, rolled his eyes upwards, and caught the nasty
glances of the rest of the men in the car. It made Bressio very
uneasy to think men like that walked around with badges and guns.

At the office Clarissa was frostily polite. "Are you ready to
communicate, Al?"

"I take it the medical files are on my desk."

"They are not."

"You wouldn't mind telling me why you did it."

"No. We agreed you wouldn't be a henchman for anyone any more. We agreed you were going to take the bar again. We agreed on that."

"I remember saying I would think about it."

"It was an implied promise, because you know I hate to see you do this sort of work—you could be a great—"

Bressio went into his private office, and when he had settled down he outlined the possibilities of avoiding L. Marvin in the coming week. He could check out what was going on at 285 Pren Street through Mary Beth Cutler's story, proving it unrealistic—which it probably was—or in the course of his investigation, find that L. Marvin sold or had sold smack.

What bothered Bressio was a very strong feeling this would not work. L. Marvin was in this somehow and in such a way that he would entangle Bressio and probably many others, leaving them that much worse off. Which was why he was being paid so much. Case closed. Get on with it. He needed the money.

At 11:45, Mary Beth Cutler had still not shown up. Bressio buzzed Clarissa on the intercom.

"Any word from a Mary Beth Cutler? She's Dawson's client."

"You would have seen a light buzz on your telephone if we got any calls."

"I thought maybe she might be in the outer office."

"You would have heard the door open."

"Thank you, Clarissa."

"Are you ready to talk, Al?"

"No."

"They're giving the bar again soon."

"You want to starve while I prepare to flunk the bar again?"

"Yes, and you know I would, Al."

"When I'm ready, I'll take it again. Until then, we'll eat."

"We could eat even better if you went to work for Carmine Dursio. I mean, if eating is what's worrying you."

"Replace the medicals."

"They were never really out. Just the dead wood, the doctors who didn't stand a cross-examination well and the ones who have been used too much. The ones you said to clean out a few months ago because the files were overwhelming us."

"So why the dramatics with the files open and the door open?"

"To get you to take a good look at yourself."

"Someone could have come in through the open door and cleaned out this place. Thank you very much, Clarissa."

Bressio heard the outer door open.

"A woman and a child. The woman looks a bit unwashed," said Clarissa.

"That's Mary Beth, I think. Send her in."

"A bit unwashed" was a kind description, Bressio thought. A grayish film covered her face as though she hadn't been near hot water in months. The tan raincoat looked fairly new but had yet to be graced by a cleaners. The hair appeared to be three shades of light brown, violent blond and black streaking out from the roots. Underneath the raincoat she wore what appeared to be a once-expensive blue print dress. She folded the raincoat and put it on her lap as she sat down before Bressio's desk. Her hands worked against each other as though in a contest to devour.

She did not respond when Bressio said he was glad to see her. Then he asked her to begin.

"I wanted to go to the Biltmore, but I thought it might be better if I went someplace else. I slept at the loft last night. Pren Street."

"Well, you're safe and that's what matters," said Bressio.

"I don't think the Biltmore is safe," said Mary Beth Cutler.

"Let's get to what's bothering you and who you think is trying to do you harm, Miss Cutler."

"Call me Mary Beth, dear. I didn't go because the Biltmore was crawling with them. I know you'll find this hard to believe but we've got a wing-ding of a case here. It's beautiful, dear."

"First, who's them?"

"The man with the scar is one. He appeared the day before yesterday at the supermarket and then again yesterday afternoon. I got into a cab right from the phone booth in case someone was listening to your line. I wanted to throw them off, make them think I wasn't taking the subway. Well, when I got into the cab, guess who was driving?"

"The man with the scar?"

"No, the red-haired guy who used to live downstairs with the woman who was murdered by the Mafia. They both came from Fire Island and moved in last December when I went to the candy store to—"

Despite himself, Bressio's pity rapidly succumbed to annoyance. "Whoa. Whoa. Whoa. Let's start with everyone who is following you. Then I want to know how much smack L. Marvin is dealing."

"Marve isn't dealing smack."

"Why did he stop?"

"He never started."

"Miss Cutler, I can't help you unless you deal with me truthfully. I'm working for you. You pay me. If you don't tell me the truth, I can't help you. I will not report Marvin to the police if you tell me the truth."

"Right, dear. Marve won't touch smack. He says it's not bad in itself, but that too many people bring too many bad vibes to it. They've infected an entire natural living organism by the bad vibes they've brought to it. Nothing wrong with smack in itself, understand, darling."

"You're saying he doesn't deal smack?"

"Never."

"Then why would all these people be following you around unless it was smack? Grass doesn't attract that kind of traffic," said Bressio, feeling slightly guilty for using her fears for his benefit.

"You're right. Murray said you were good, but I didn't know how good. Tremendous. You're great. Terry Leacock, that bitch. I bet she was dealing smack. She and her boyfriend. The redhead. That's what's causing it. Oh, you are beautiful, Al. You're beautiful. That's it. The whole thing in a nutshell. Isn't Marve wonderful. He said so too."

"About the dead woman?"

"No. The vibes surrounding smack. The first natural organic plant to be destroyed by man's ill thoughts of it. We have destroyed the goodness in the opium poppy. And we're paying the price."

Bressio took a yellow legal-sized pad from his desk and went to work with a well-worn pencil stub.

"Let's start with who's following you," he said.

Following Miss Mary Beth Cutler was the man with the scar, the red-headed man who had lived downstairs on the second floor and the New York City Police Department. On horseback, no less.

"Miss Cutler. If the cops wanted to tail you they wouldn't do it mounted."

"Al, dear, they follow me every time I'm near St. Vincent's Hospital. I know it. I wouldn't miss a horse. I mean, I'm not that crazy. You can't miss a horse."

"Miss Cutler, the police stables are near St. Vincent's."

"Then if they weren't following me, why did they stop when Murray went to the precinct house to ask them to stop?"

"Dawson went to a precinct house for you?" asked Bressio in amazement. This was going to have to be checked out with Dawson, and if the answer was yes, Dawson would have some very heavy explaining to do. Murray Blay Dawson didn't go down to precinct houses.

"Sure," said Mary Beth and Bressio believed her.

He tried exploring the incidents around the loft, and by the time Mary Beth was finished, he had three separate pieces of paper in front of him. One sheet was about the couple who lived downstairs in the loft. The other was their own loft. The third was incidentals like death lurking on the street.

The couple downstairs, as Bressio gathered, were young and attractive. The girl, Terry Leacock, came from a moderately wealthy family in Pasadena. The red-headed man had made a pass at Mary Beth which she rebuffed, a fact that no jury would believe unless it was established first that he had a record of peculiar tastes. All in all, however, her story matched what Dawson had told him she had said.

Bressio looked at the woman, at the three disjointed papers and then at his hands.

"You're going to have to do what I tell you to do."

"Anything, darling," said Miss Cutler.

"Do you know what your enemies are going to try to do?"

Mary Beth's eyes widened in excitement.

"They're going to try to prove you're paranoid so they can continue to get away with what they're getting away with," Bressio continued.

"Oh, my God. You know how they work."

"I understand what you're going through, Miss Cutler. We're going to cut them off at the bend. Head them off. You see, we can't let them dictate our moves. You've been letting them do that.

You've been reacting instead of acting upon."

"Murray said you were the best in the business but I didn't know you were this good. You're tremendous."

"What we're going to do is prove you legally sane before they can work that against you." Bressio's voice lowered into a drama of conspiracy. "We use our psychiatrist first, so that one of theirs can't get at you."

"Can we trust him? I mean, you know psychiatrists."

Bressio winked. "He's our man."

"All right," said Mary Beth but there was a note of hesitancy in her voice. "You do believe me, don't you?"

"You're paying me very heavy money, Miss Cutler."

"I know. Maybe I can't afford this man."

"Don't you worry about his fee," said Bressio, who had already made a mental note for Clarissa to bill Dawson for the first few sessions of the therapy. "He's on our side."

Bressio wrote down the address and telephone number of Dr. John Patrick Finney.

"He was once a priest. I hope you don't mind that."

"Hell, no," said Mary Beth. "We used to have all sorts of cardinals and bishops at Daddy's."

Bressio courteously ushered her to the door of his office and was surprised to see a very neat, very well-scrubbed little girl of about four sitting quietly at the far end of the outer office. Apparently it was Mary Beth's daughter. Her hands rested symmetrically on her lap and her feet were primly together. Bressio attempted to pass a little pleasantry with the child and got no response.

"Bobbi takes her time in getting to know people," said Mary Beth. "Brilliant child. Brilliant."

Clarissa was sending a signal with her eyes, but Bressio ignored her. He wanted to reach Dr. Finney before other business might delay the call and Mary Beth Cutler stormed in on Finney unannounced. Besides, it was that ten-minute-before-the-hour period when Finney would answer his own phone.

In another generation, Finney would have worn cassock and dispensed God's forgiveness. In this one, he wore suit and tie and tried to dispense the patient's own forgiveness. Bressio had been at Finney's parent's apartment when J.P. had informed his mother he had decided against the priesthood and would not return to the seminary, but would study psychology. She acknowledged the passing of her era with a wailing that would have done honor to a Greek chorus. She assaulted the heavens with candles, but J.P. remained firm in his resolve to participate in an even newer era of another faith. He was the only psychologist Bressio trusted because he often admitted doubts about the effectiveness of his therapy. These new psychologists brought fresh reality to the dogma of St. Freud. And Finney was one of their leaders.

"Hey, J.P., Bressio. A Mary Beth Cutler's going to see you. Give me a rundown on her, will you?"

"If she's coming as a patient, Al, I'm not giving you any rundown for court evidence. I won't do that."

"It's not for court, although she may tell you that. Just see her and use your own judgment. She's paranoid and I'm trying to figure out if there's anything to what she's seeing."

"Who are you to say someone is paranoid, Al? I thought I explained to you once it's a very, very broad term."

"I'm not looking for a lecture. Just see her, okay?"

"I've got a tight schedule, Al."

"It's important to me."

"All right. But don't go bandying around 'paranoia' like that, okay?"

"I will not use that phrase in vain again, Padre."

Bressio heard the door close outside and went to Clarissa to find out why Mary Beth hung around.

"You know she's Marvin Fleish's girl friend, Al," said Clarissa.

"Couldn't you tell?" said Bressio.

"Don't start with that code-of-the-jungle survival thing again. Marvin Fleish happens to be a very sweet person."

"L. Marvin stuck you for fifty bucks once, didn't he?"

"The deal fell through and he lost more money."

"L. Marvin tried to get into your pants rather forcefully one night, if I remember."

"He was honest and open and real about it."

"What did Mary Beth talk about?"

"You're not going to deal with your feelings about Marvin," said Clarissa, with the triumphant glare of one who has caught another in a psychological transgression.

"What did Mary Beth talk about?"

"It was nothing. Her landlady was killed this morning."

"At 285 Pren Street?"

"Yeah. Where she's living with Marvin. A loft building. Al . . . where are you running to now?" said Clarissa, watching him quickly dash into his office, take something out of his top drawer, and rush out again.

"Al, your safety strap is off your holster. Al, where are you going? Al?"

Clarissa's high-pitched wail followed him out into the hallway.

V

Before he reached Pren Street, Bressio snapped on the safety strap of his holster. He did not want it falling out, and although he never told anyone, he felt about it pretty much the way many women feel about their girdles. It was a reminder that his life was not exactly the way one wanted it.

There probably was nothing to the landlady's death, just as there was probably nothing to Mary Beth Cutler's fears. But now he could no longer delay checking it out. He was in it.

"Ecch," said Bressio as the taxi sped up First Avenue.

"Wha?" the driver asked.

"Nothing," said Bressio, and he reminded himself not to think of L. Marvin Fleish, for when he did so, he did not notice things with the acuity and perception that had not only kept him alive these many years, but made him financially successful.

Pren Street was a semi-commercial area set into a cusp of Little Italy about halfway between Canal and Houston Streets, a street of storage houses and darkened gray tenements where old grime ate into brick so the original color was only a suspicion until the wreckers arrived.

Bressio got out of the cab, his suit moistened by the hot muggy day that could make matches difficult to strike and most people give up moving around.

Down the street a car turned on its lights, then another and another. So much for the blinking lights following Mary Beth Cutler. They were near a funeral home.

285 Pren Street was a three-story building of graying cement

with very high and very wide unwashed windows. It was the only loft building on the block, so even without a number on the door he knew he was at the right place.

A half-century before, immigrants toiled in lofts like these, producing cheap garments, their own early deaths, and many successful and famous children.

Now people were turning these barnlike lofts into living quarters, installing their own hot water heaters and plywood walls. Commercial rents were cheap and the lofts spacious. This combination made a well-remodeled loft very valuable. Often a key to one of them, meaning the right to rent, went for several thousand dollars. Even a cheap rent in New York City was expensive.

It was Bressio's guess that L. Marvin had not only failed to improve his loft, but had probably run down its value. This suspicion was supported by the dust on the windows.

The street door was scarred metal with an ominously new Medico lock, stupidly set into a rotting wooden frame. Bressio tested the doorknob. Unlocked. The dark hallway smelled of old coffee grounds. From the harsh sunlight behind him, Bressio made out rising steps. He climbed, and as the door behind him clicked shut, he found himself in darkness, a black oven smelling of rotted garbage.

By the time Bressio reached the third floor, he was wet to his palms. He felt along the wall until he reached a door. Then he knocked.

"Who is it?" came a voice that turned Bressio's stomach to bubbling bile.

"Al Bressio, numb-numb."

"Just a minute. Boy, am I glad it's you, Al," came the voice.

"Is Mary Beth in there?" said Bressio through the door.

"No. She went to see you this morning."

The door opened, and in the blinding white light, semi-nude, stood L. Marvin Fleish.

"Ecch," said Bressio.

"Is that any way to say hello to an old friend?" L. Marvin was grinning. His strandy blond hair hung shoulder-length over his bare, pale shoulders. His yellow mustache shot from his upper lip like a brush run amok. He wore a loincloth and sandals. A small silver cocaine spoon dangled over his forty-year-old chest. All he needed to appear as a first offender in Arizona, thought Bressio, were needle marks on his arms.

"I said, 'Is that any way to say hello to an old friend?' "

"I wouldn't have you as a friend to cure cancer," said Bressio.

Fleish giggled. Bressio stepped past him into the loft. But for three soiled mattresses and litter the loft appeared unchanged from its original purpose. The windows were lathered with dust. Bressio looked back to the mattresses. Smoke rose from between two of them.

"I'm glad it's you, not Murray," said Fleish, scurrying to the mattresses set against a once-white wall now covered with revolutionary slogans in Day-Glow paint. Bressio smelled pot. Bluish smoke rose from the mattresses.

Fleish scooped up something at the base of the smoke, moving like a clumsy shortstop after a sizzling grounder. He almost stumbled into the wall but recovered his balance, laughing. In doing so, he kicked one of the mattresses, revealing a blue-black rifle barrel and the edge of a white shoulder strap on the wooden slat floor.

"What are you doing with a gun, L. Marvin?" asked Bressio.

Fleish grinned proudly. "It's beautiful, Al. It gives me protection without injuring anyone. You know I wouldn't leave a gun around where Bobbi could get it."

"Mary Beth's kid lives here?" asked Bressio.

"Sure. Where else?"

"L. Marvin, that is a gun."

"No, man, it's not. It's a groove. It's just some wood and metal. It's a Sea Scout training rifle for kids. But it looks like a gun. Even *you* thought it was a gun. Dig this, man, I'm into the heads of the violent ones. To them it's a gun. They'll respect it as a gun. To me, it's natural wood and metal from the earth. Good karma."

"Well, I'm certainly glad to see you've found another way to taunt death, L. Marvin."

"You think I ought to put it out of sight?"

"No. Take it on a midnight stroll down Mulberry Street."

Fleish took a deep drag from something minuscule between his fingertips. Holding his breath he offered the thing in his hand to Bressio. It was a joint. Bressio refused it.

"Don't tell Murray about the pot, okay?" said Fleish in a burst of breath.

Bressio shrugged.

"Let me fill you in on the Arizona bust," said Fleish as though he were going to reveal a wonderful sexual experience.

"Where's Mary Beth and her child?"

"She's split, man. Be thankful for small favors. What I have to go through with that broad. . . . She's going to kill me with that bail money she laid out yet. Look. Look."

Fleish pointed to a faint reddish blotch on his stomach. Bressio squinted attempting to make it out.

"I'm breaking out. Emotionally I cannot stand the woman and what she puts me through for a little bail money and the cost of your services."

"Go back to your wife."

"Harriet is worse."

"What's all this nonsense I hear about the loft downstairs?"

"A drag, man. Two squares."

"One of them's dead, and the other keeps popping up smiling at Mary Beth, I hear."

"Don't tell me your head is into Mary Beth's shit?"

"Your landlady was killed early this morning, wasn't she?"

Fleish took another deep drag on his fingertips. "Live chemically," he said.

"What about the landlady?"

"A downer. I was asleep. I heard Mary Beth yelling. I went to help. Mary Beth wouldn't stop yelling. She knows about the fucking rash, but she kept on yelling. I think she yelled just because of the rash, and I went downstairs and the landlady was at the bottom of the second floor. She was cold. She had never lived, man. I mean, she was never alive. You know, a walking zombie. A stiff. She was always after Mary Beth for the rent."

"How'd she fall?"

"Broken step. An accident. This place is a mess. She collected the rent right on the button, but never got around to fixing anything. Justice. It all comes back to you, and she got hers. I bet it was that fucking broken step she wouldn't fix and she didn't see it because of the lights she didn't have in here. The bitch. Look at this place. It's a garbage dump, and I won't put my love and sweat into it to make her rich—or her estate, that gross stupidity of capitalism."

Bressio watched as Fleish took a burning ash into his mouth.

"Waste not, want not," said Fleish.

"Anything special about the downstairs loft?"

"Same as this. No landlady repairs." Fleish shook his head emphatically.

"All right," said Bressio. "This is what you're going to do—"

"You're going to help me, right?" said Fleish.

"I want you to get rid of any smack you have around. Let me see you do it."

"I don't deal that heavy shit, man."

"L. Marvin, you can bluff your wife, your mistress, Dawson, my secretary, but, L. Marvin, you cannot bluff me."

"I don't deal horse, man."

"Forget it, rot in Arizona."

"I don't deal harm, man. I don't."

Bressio turned to the door and felt Fleish's hand gloriously and exoneratingly grab his arm. A legal assault. Bressio whirled and defended himself with two sharp open-handed smacks at Fleish's face. Fleish blinked. His cheeks flushed red.

"Tell Mary Beth to phone me or my secretary if you see her. I have a nice clean place for her and Bobbi to live. I don't want her or that kid spending another night here. She's going to stay with Miss Duffy."

"With Clarissa," said Fleish, and Bressio could have sworn he saw a big leering grin on that red-cheeked face. "She's going to stay with Clarissa?"

"Yes. She's my client, not you. Tell her I want her out of this place."

"That'll be nice. I hate living in this depressing atmosphere."

"You're not going, L. Marvin."

"I can help Mary Beth move. Who knows what Clarissa will want in her bedroom?" said Fleish, sharing a lewd wink.

Bressio reminded himself he had slapped L. Marvin twice already and his hand did sting. Then he reminded Fleish. "I did slap you in the face, right?"

"You didn't mean it, Al. You've got problems. I understand that. You didn't mean it."

"I knew I hit you," said Bressio. "That's right, I did."

And so disturbed by Fleish was he that when he left the loft he did not bother to check the stairwell or the downstairs loft or the candy store around the corner—a magnet for information—but just wandered out into the wet clammy heat, feeling his right hand sting.

By the time the sting was gone, Bressio had made two phone calls from a telephone booth. With any luck the calls could start the machinery moving that would clear up his obligations to Dawson within two days.

The first was to a headquarters lieutenant. Bressio wanted a rundown on anything to do with 285 Pren—specifically, did the police make any sort of investigation into a found gun, and what was the finding on a landlady's death that morning?

The lieutenant assured Bressio he would deliver the report personally, which meant he wanted cash on delivery.

Bressio's second phone call called for more tact and diplomacy. An old woman answered, speaking only Italian. Bressio asked about her health, her grandchildren, her other relatives. After a formal two minutes of small talk she put on her husband. In the same tongue, Bressio requested a luncheon meeting. The man said he would be honored to see his friend again.

For their 2:35 P.M. lunch, they met at Angelo's, a fine Italian restaurant near Fermio's and down the street from a tourist trap made famous by a recent shooting. It was generally considered that the victim lacked class eating there in the first place, recalling an old Sicilian saying about dying the way one lived. If the restaurant were respected, the contract would not have been filled there.

Angelo's had respect. As he walked past storefront athletic clubs bordering the street, Bressio received acknowledging nods from men lounging in front. When he entered Angelo's he found his guest waiting in the back room. The guest was a dark wizened man, in a pale-yellow suit with a stiff white shirt that lacked a tie but was buttoned to the neck.

Bressio ordered a heaping plate of scungili with a hearty side of lasagne. His guest had a bowl of vegetable soup, explaining his liver was bothering him. Bressio made a formal statement about the importance of one's liver and ordered a sweet red wine which ones liver ailments called for.

After his guest had begun his soup, Bressio noted there were matters concerning Bressio's business. He repeated twice that this was business and not a personal affair in which one might lose his head or take random offense. He also made it clear there was not a great deal of money involved, and that defined more sharply the parameters of Bressio's interests.

"There is something that might be of interest to me whereby I can turn a little profit," Bressio said. He watched the dark-brown eyes of his guest for any indication as to whether he was approaching matters that someone else might have a vested interest in. "It concerns a woman, Miss Terry Leacock."

The eyes remained warm. The guest nodded.

"She had an unfortunate accident."

Still warm.

"She is of no personal interest to me. There is no vendetta involved. Her accident was a circumstance of business, I believe, not connected with me. Her affairs touch mine only tangentially."

A narrowing of the eyes. Confusion.

"In some ways not very important to me she may have touched the life of one of my clients, from whom I am making a profit."

Warm.

"It may be the woman offended someone for a cause outside what I am concerned with. It is of business interest to know what injustice or transgression prompted her accident. It is of no concern of mine who she offended. I do not wish to know his name. Just why. I have no personal interest in the woman. Naturally these facts will require effort to gather. Perhaps there will be some risk involved to the person whose name or business is no concern of mine who amended this transgression. I naturally would not expect this service for nothing. I would be most happy to share a portion of this small profit I am making."

With great courtesy Bressio offered a folded fresh handkerchief across the table. It contained three hundred dollars cash. This was the retainer for asking. His guest would return with either a warning that the matter should not concern Bressio or he would return with the information and a higher bill.

The dinner guest thought deeply a moment and put the envelope in the interior pocket of his jacket. "I have heard of this woman who had the accident," he said in Italian. "I have read the papers.

It was not the sort of situation that was a warning or an outgrowth of troubles. It is not the sort of thing that is generally known, that is."

Bressio nodded.

"You are a man whose word is good, so it should be easier to ask, other parties not suspecting some foolishness of revenge and the like. I will see what I can do. You have my word."

Bressio assured his guest that he had faith in him and the guest noted that the young did not appreciate their livers. He was referring to Bressio, who was under fifty. Bressio accepted the advice with respectful attentiveness.

The lunch concluded, Bressio phoned Dawson from another outside pay phone. It smelled of urine. Bressio was put right through two secretaries.

"Whadya think, Al? Something to it, right?"

"Possibly. I doubt it. As I suspected, some of the information is going to be expensive. It was not an advertised affair."

"How expensive?"

"It could run three, four, maybe five grand."

"That's a lot of money, Al. That's a hell of a lot of money on top of what we paid you. This is a simple little grass bust in Arizona."

"You seem to be forgetting some incidentals which I don't want to go into over your line. I got one whiff of L. Marvin today and I want this thing cleared up fast even more than you do."

"I don't know if Mary Beth can get that kind of money, Al."

"If you're willing to go down to a precinct house for her, I have a sneaking suspicion that she can get loads and loads and loads of money."

"Oh, you know, then. I thought for a moment at my office yesterday you didn't."

"Know what?"

"You don't know then. You of all people, always talking about him like he was some kind of a saint."

"Oh, no," said Bressio and he leaned his head against the glass and wire mesh of the phone booth, not caring that it was greasy to the touch.

"Sure. William James Cutler is her daddy. Tight-fisted bastard, too."

"Hold on, Murray. You don't have any right to . . ." Bressio did not finish his sentence. Dawson was off the line and a secretary was explaining that Dawson would be back to Bressio in a moment. Bressio put in two more dimes before Dawson came back on the line.

"It's all set, Al. Cutler's going to fork over some more cash. You've got to pick it up yourself. He's got an estate in Old Lyme, Connecticut.

"Wait, Murray. Maybe I can swing the payment out of the fee you paid me."

"Nonsense. He's got plenty of money. You always said you wanted to talk law with William James Cutler. Now's your chance."

"Murray. You don't know what you're doing to me. I don't want to go to his place like this, like a hustler."

"He's probably the biggest hustler you're ever going to meet. He makes us look like tadpoles in a swamp. Come on, Al, he puts on his pants one leg at a time like you and I do."

"You had no right, Murray. You had no right."

"Hey, I thought you knew. I'm sorry, okay? If I weren't strapped for cash, I'd pick up the tab myself. I'm sorry. But it's no big thing, really."

"You had no right, Murray. You don't know what you did," said Bressio and hung up the receiver and waited a few moments in the stinking booth before he walked out into the stinking street.

VI

Bressio stopped several times on the way to Old Lyme, Connecticut, for coffee that ended up carefully balanced on the floor of the car, cheese and crackers that got stuffed in the glove compartment, and trips to the lavatory, where he stood useless before the urinals. He also got gas for the rented car.

"Fifty cents," said one attendant after Bressio had ordered him to fill it up. When he crossed the New York State-Connecticut line, he put the .38 police special in the glove compartment, since his license to carry was not valid out of the state. Naturally this called for pulling off to the side of the road and checking the glove compartment lock several times.

He thought of putting his shoulder holster in there also, but he would have needed to remove his jacket to unstrap the thing, and besides, who was he kidding? He was going to shake down William James Cutler, and he might as well have gone in with a lead pipe. That's how he was going to meet privately with William James Cutler, whom he had last seen that hot spring day the last time Bressio had walked on the grounds of Fordham University in the Bronx.

Bressio had worn a black gown and mortarboard with the tassel at ready to be swung over the doctoral corner. He had failed the bar after graduation from law school and had gone on to get his doctorate in law and had just failed the bar again when his doctoral thesis was accepted with the comment "brilliant." So there he was at the last commencement for the last degree he could get in law without the standard license to practice it, and William James

Cutler was one of the three speakers receiving honorary degrees.

Bressio's mother was in the audience, scowling at anyone who threatened to encroach on her seat and trying to catch Bressio's eye so she could signal her contempt for the whole ceremony.

Cutler, a former Under Secretary of State, a Princeton graduate but a school benefactor and a leading Washington lawyer, spoke of integrity and the law and civilization. He said that as scientists discovered animals that could use tools, animals that could laugh, and animals that appeared capable of love, their definition of man had to retreat from those previous boundaries. He offered one boundary which truly made man distinct, and that was the law. He said that he who served the law with integrity served the humaneness of man. Bressio was not sure, but he thought he might have seen his mother make an *obscene* gesture at that statement.

Bressio received his scroll of paper, flipped his tassel and later took his mother to a restaurant on the Grand Concourse. At that time he could not really afford it. "Eat, Ma," he said. "I got money."

"You got money," said his mother contemptuously. "You got paper. You could put it ina the batharoom, it belongsa there. You got money, you got ugatz."

"Ma. Willya please."

"Big shot. Professore. Doctor. Dr. Gavone. Pee Haich anda Dee Gavone."

"Ma, c'mon. I'll make money, but I'll do it my way."

"Your way. Pretty words. You alwaysa lika da pretty words. You thinka that bastid Cutler made his money with his words?"

"C'mon, Ma. Willya?"

"Them bastids bleed thousands. Millions. And then they gotta their money and they stand upa on thata stupid platform and say pretty words and a gavone like you believes them and don'ta take whatsa his. Take, Alphonse, take. That'sa what they do. You want a lawyer? Buya youself a Jew. They good at that. That's their business. Don Carmine'sa gotta them unda his rugsa and cupboards."

"Ma, I'm not going to work for him."

"Who paida for the roofa ova you heada, and da fooda in you mouth, and that fancy school with everyone looking downa they noses at you."

"You want me to end up like Papa, Ma?"

"You fatha was a good man. He had belly. He hada respect. What you got. A pieca paper. Big shot. Professore withouta piece of veal in you mouth."

"Papa was found in the trunk of a car parked off the Belt Parkway when the car started smelling too much, Ma."

"Witha respect. Ten blocks of cars wenta to the cemetery. Don Carmine himself paida his respects. You fatha had respect. He was a man."

"He went with his head blown off by a shotgun, and if Fermio's hadn't used a ton of wax and a gallon of perfume we would have had to put him away in a rubber bag. His best friend fingered him, Ma."

"Don Carmine avenged that."

"So fucking what. Another goddamned animal in a goddamned jungle. I don't want to be an animal. Weren't you listening to what that man said at commencement?"

Across the table Theresa Bressio slapped her son for besmirching the names of Don Carmine and God. Bressio felt the sting of the slap and felt the other people in the restaurant looking at him. He quietly ate his meal. Before he paid the check, he told his mother that some day he would sit in counsel with men like William James Cutler.

She responded in Italian that indeed her son may be at the same table with men like Cutler—with a napkin over his arm.

"Butlers don't carry napkins over their arms, Ma," Bressio answered in a petty observation reminding his mother that he was entering a world strange to her.

He offered her cab money home; she took it and promptly entered the IND subway.

Bressio, left without even fifteen cents for the subway, walked to his one-room apartment. He knew that in his mother's eyes he was committing two grave sins. One, not using his talents in the service of Don Carmine for which he would be well paid, and two, not living at home with his mother until a proper marriage could be arranged, whereby he would be passed on to another Italian woman.

Theresa died two years later of a heart attack from screaming at someone whose passing car had splattered her with winter slush.

At her funeral, Don Carmine himself attended, and she was given all the respect she could have wanted right to Holy Name Cemetery, where she was interred next to Bressio's father.

"A good woman," Don Carmine had said.

"Yes, a good woman," Bressio responded with the courtliness and formality he had always used with men like Don Carmine.

"And how is business, Alphonse?"

"Business is fine, Don Carmine," said Bressio and wondered whether under the ground Fermio's wax was the only thing that remained of his father.

He thought of his father and his mother and Don Carmine and his own young life as he entered the quiet stateliness of Old Lyme, and believed at last that he would never sit in counsel with men like William James Cutler but would always be what he had always been. There was no need to take off the holster. Al Bressio knew who he was and what he did for a living, and he would never pass the bar. He was the son of Salvatore Bressio, and brains and knowledge could not overcome it. He wasn't meant to pass it. He had always known that. Even before the first failure, he knew that.

But only in the bitter light of this Connecticut summer evening did he realize he had known it all along. "Thank you, L. Marvin," Bressio said in a rage so deep it sounded like a sob.

The Cutler estate had the grace of full green trees set with an artist's symmetry around immaculate lawns the size of meadows. The house was relatively small for the knoll it occupied, a white colonial house with green shutters and a small stone garage set off to the side. Bressio smelled the mild sweetness of the fresh-cut grass and lingered over the gravel on the driveway. But as he had to, he eventually reached the door, and since he did not feel like staring at the washed white paint, he rang the buzzer. At least he hadn't ended up in the trunk of a car on the Belt Parkway. Yet.

An elderly man with close-cropped white hair and a humble mien to the angle of his head answered the door. He wore a Hawaiian shirt and green Bermuda shorts. What a strange way for a butler to dress, thought Bressio.

"I've come to see William James Cutler," said Bressio.

"You're Al Bressio?"

"Yes."

"Come into my study. I'm William James Cutler."

The old man did not offer a hand. He straightened his head, and with a surprising firmness walked coldly into the house, leaving the door open behind him. Bressio shut it. How else should a man react to what is moral if not legal blackmail, he thought.

The Cutler who had appeared at the graduation had seemed taller and stronger, and the lines in his face were lines of strength. This man's face had lines of weariness as though he were waiting to die.

Cutler preceded Bressio into a room that looked as though it had been deep-polished twice a day for six hundred years. Of wood it was, dark and rich and shining with shelves to the ceiling beamed over by what Bressio judged to be oak. The windows were of lead glass with diamond-shaped striping. King James I of England would have been at home in this room.

"Will you sit down, please, Mr. Bressio. Am I pronouncing it correctly, Bressio?"

Bressio nodded and sat down in a chair he presumed was more suitable for a thane of Runnymede. Cutler used a high-back dark wodden chair behind a modest but solid dark-wood desk. The chair looked like a throne. Bressio found out immediately that William James Cutler was not a weak old man.

"I have spoken to Mr. Dawson, who represents a Mr. Fleish in a criminal matter and my daughter in a child-custody arrangement also concerning Mr. Fleish."

Well, that introduced it nicely. With a howitzer. Dawson was vulnerable because he represented two clients with possible conflicting interests. It had been a foolish thing for Dawson to do, but L. Marvin Fleish seemed to generate that sort of inexcusable and careless action.

"I believe another lawyer is representing Mr. Fleish in the custody matter," Bressio lied. By the time the papers were signed, Dawson or his secretary would get another lawyer in there somewhere.

"No doubt," said Cutler. "Mr. Dawson told me that my daughter may be in some serious trouble and that you are trying to unravel it. Is that true?"

Bressio leaned forward in a barely perceptible nod.

"He asked that I finance your further investigation. Mr. Bressio, have I been lured into paying for Marvin Fleish's legal fees in some manner?"

"Yes," said Bressio, surprising himself with the quickness of his honesty.

There was ringing silence. Bressio noticed Cutler's eyes for the first time and also realized he had been avoiding them before. They were sharp blue like a glacier pond.

"Thank you," Cutler said. "Well, I guess I have then. Perhaps, sir, you are one of those who consider Mr. Fleish amusing. But I, sir, remember my little girl. I remember a young, healthy, inquisitive, attractive woman who went to New York City to become an artist. She took my heart with her, sir. I did not stop her because you do not tether a young sapling when it reaches for the sky. You let it rise to where the wind can whip and lightning can strike, but where also are the sun and the breeze and the fresher air. When my daughter met Mr. Fleish, it was as though he poisoned the very roots. She was not always as she is now. Nor do I think she brought this sickness from her youth, although this flies in the face of what we know about psychology.

"I believe, sir, what she brought to people like Fleish was an openness. That openness proved tragic. Before this, I had believed that an open, inquisitive mind could deal with anything. I do not believe that now. I believe this chemical culture can destroy any human being. But I am of another age and another culture that seems as outmoded and useless today as the rack. Although I do appreciate some of the good new things, chemicals are not one of them nor is the irresponsibility of Mr. Fleish and his ilk."

Cutler had spoken with awesome control for the depth of his grief and Bressio could see the struggle for that control in the man before him. He watched Cutler withdraw a leather-bound book in which were loose-leaf pages of checks and with an ink pen first fill in the bookkeeping on the left and then the check. He tore it briskly out of the book and handed it to Bressio, who folded it and put it in his jacket pocket. The check was for $5,000, and Bressio knew then that Dawson had hit him for the maximum amount.

"Mr. Cutler," Bressio said as he was being ushered to the door. "I think I should tell you something. Sometimes when I know I'm going to run into L. Marvin Fleish I am tempted to leave my pistol home because I'm afraid I'm going to shoot the sonuvabitch."

Cutler looked startled. Then his chest heaved, his composure shattered, and he lowered his head. He wept, his arms stiff at his sides. Bressio wanted to put an arm around the old man, but he could not touch William James Cutler.

"I think I can help your daughter, Mr. Cutler. I mean, I *can* help your daughter, Mr. Cutler. You—you hang in there because . . . because, well, you hang in there. I can do things for Mary Beth."

Cutler's mouth opened and his head rose and his reddened eyes tried to express the gratitude his voice could not. Instead he embraced Alphonse Joseph Bressio and sobbed in his arms. Bressio enfolded the old man, and when Cutler was strong enough, released him.

"I'm leaving, and I'm going to phone you. And I'm going to phone you with good news, Mr. Cutler." Bressio turned from the old man quickly and left the house. At the New York State line he pulled over to the side of the road, put his pistol back in his shoulder holster, and cried.

He did not attach the safety strap, and that night he put a word out that both confused and unsettled those who thought it very important to know what a man like Alphonse Joseph Bressio was doing at all times.

VII

Bressio withheld his word lest he influence the information he was paying for. His dinner guest told a tale of misjudgment ending in death pretty much the way Bressio expected to hear it.

The killing of Terry Leacock was not the sort of hit that would accrue to anyone's respect. It was a nasty thing that had to be done. She was a beautiful young woman, and like many of her kind, thought her beauty entitled her to certain unreasonable privileges with a man who used his money to support himself and his family in Carona. She assumed, according to the dinner guest, that because the wife of the man was not beautiful, this husband would abandon his responsibilities and duties for a passing attraction. This proved to be untrue, since the man was of substance.

"How much?" said Bressio, referring to the Shylock's loan to Terry Leacock, who thought she could pay with her body for the cash she obviously didn't return.

The dinner guest had asked that question also and was not told the amount. But he did discover it was part of the financing for the narcotics operation that went sour. At the point where the guest told of the demise of this wanton who attempted to destroy the home of a good man, he smiled as a sign of justice done. It seemed Terry Leacock went into the East River screaming that her lover, this financier, would take care of her executioners.

But to show the perfidy of this woman, she was also living with a man suspected of being an undercover narcotics agent. Such was the end of such perfidy and thus was justice done.

"They lived at 285 Pren Street?" asked Bressio.

He was told on the second floor beneath a couple of no worth who were not married and did not respect themselves in dress or manner or condition of their home. Dirt.

"What was the color of this undercover's hair?"

It was interesting that Bressio should ask that, since the man's hair was flaming red. Did Alphonse have any pertinent information about the man?

"Possibly," said Bressio.

Another point of interest. The house on Pren Street was best kept away from, a lot of peculiar police activity there, so peculiar that the natural death of the landlady was kept hush-hush until the late afternoon. Naturally this aroused curiosity, and some people checked personally and found out it was a heart attack while walking steps.

Bressio nodded. His job for Dawson was done. He had all the answers about what was happening, and unfortunately even the reason L. Marvin got busted in Arizona and where the tip came from. Bressio wouldn't even need the headquarters lieutenant now.

Over zabaglione, a hot white rummy custard, he thanked his dinner guest. The agreed-upon price was $3,500, which Bressio noted was high even for such sensitive information, but since the guest was such a man of respect and since coming from him the information had to be true, perhaps it was even cheap at that price. Bressio went to the men's room to count out the last of Dawson's cash money, folded it in a handkerchief, returned to the table and gave the bundle to his guest with a warm handshake. Then he unloaded what he knew would be a shocker.

"The woman who lives on the third floor loft at 285 Pren Street, Mary Beth Cutler—I would appreciate you considering her as my sister and informing anyone who might be interested as to this fact. As though she is of my blood."

The dinner guest became suddenly effusive and apologetic for having referred to the couple on the third floor as dirt. Appearances were deceiving, he said. People should be allowed to live as they wished, he said. The worth of a person was not in what the eye could perceive, he said.

"Just the woman. The man is dirt. Just the woman and her child," said Bressio.

The dinner guest nodded deeply. Bressio knew he was very

curious why anyone should take an interest in this woman, but he would not ask and Bressio did not offer. How could he tell him about William James Cutler and the law being that special thing which made man more than a creature that walked upright? How could he tell him that in the chaotic whorehouse of the courts was that pure temple where man attempted to ascend to civilization, and for Alphonse Joseph Bressio the likes of William Cutler were its priests and its hope.

Bressio could no more explain these things to his dinner guest than he could have to his late mother.

It was enough that he knew and would pass on that anyone harming the daughter of William James Cutler would have a blood feud on his hands with Alphonse Joseph Bressio. Any assistance rendered her would likewise be appreciated.

In amounts, of course, to be negotiated.

Bressio knew Dawson's wife Bobo was having another one of her famous parties even before he saw the lights on in all three stories of the Dawson town house on East Sixty-third Street, an area so fashionable only one home had not been written up in *House Beautiful,* and that was because the owner was a hermit. Bobo's town house appeared not only in the home magazines but in *Life* when it did a series on famous bathrooms and in *New York* when she threw a party for the Black Panthers and Young Lords.

Bressio knew it was another Bobo party just by the manner of the woman who snatched the phone away from the maid. He knew from a telephone in the Cedar Tavern.

"Hi there, do you eat pussy?"

"Put Dawson on. I want to speak to him."

"Who are you?"

"Al Bressio."

"Are you a gangster?"

"If you can't get Dawson, put Bobo on."

"If you're a gangster, I'll eat you."

Bressio hung up and took a cab. He wanted to personally deliver to Dawson the wrap-up of the L. Marvin affair, the little key fact about 285 Pren Street that would explain why some people were really following Mary Beth and how L. Marvin had done it again. He wanted to show Dawson his commitment was over in one day.

He even had verification from the headquarters lieutenant,

whom he had met in a back booth in the Cedar Tavern, and whom he took great pleasure in watching squirm. The lieutenant had thought he had told him nothing and was becoming obnoxious about payment because, as he claimed, "I'm going broke in community relations. There's no money in it. Al, you gotta come across."

"I've always come across. You come across. What about 285 Pren?"

"I can't get to it."

"Whaddya mean you can't get to it?" asked Bressio, knowing exactly why the lieutenant was backing off, far, far better than the lieutenant. "You're at headquarters."

"Take my word for it. I checked with the precinct, they transferred me to a deputy inspector who started asking me questions, and I backed off. The money's shit since I got transferred out of Harlem to this nigger and spic sensitivity shit. But it's still a job and I don't want to lose it."

"Well, tell me what you know about the floater, Terry Leacock, who came up off the Fifty-ninth Street bridge."

"I'll check with homicide."

"She lived at 285 Pren."

"Okay. I'll check with homicide, but I'll need three hundred on this thing first."

"You check with homicide and you'll get what your information is worth," said Bressio, knowing that if the lieutenant did so, he would end up back on the same line with the deputy inspector.

"Look, Al. I need the money. C'mon. I've done you favors in the past."

"You want good-faith money, then."

"Right."

"Fifty bucks for good faith," said Bressio, dropping two twenties and a ten on the table like a tip.

The lieutenant stuffed the money into a worn billfold.

"Guinea cocksucker," he said.

Bressio smiled and went to one of the two phone booths near the bar. He dialed Clarissa's apartment. She had not been home earlier when he had called to see if Mary Beth was living with her yet. A voice answered that made Bressio want to take a piece out of the phone booth.

"What are you doing at Clarissa's, L. Marvin?"

"I helped Mary Beth and Bobbi move in."

"You move out."

"I'm leaving, man. When the going gets tough, the tough get going. Mary Beth isn't the only source of bread in this world, man."

"Put her on."

"You really want to rap with her, man?"

"You will get Mary Beth to the phone and leave that apartment, L. Marvin, or when I see you, I will break both your arms." Bressio hated L. Marvin for the naked threat, too.

Bressio heard L. Marvin laugh, assure him he was one of the funniest men in New York City, and snap his fingers.

"Hello," said Mary Beth.

"Are you all right?"

"Sort of. Did you break the case? Exciting, isn't it?"

"Mary Beth, you have nothing to worry about. Just stay with Clarissa for a while. Did you phone the doctor?"

"I couldn't. You see—"

"You'll do that tomorrow. No fooling now. All right?"

"Well, all right."

"And Mary Beth. Your father loves you very much."

There was a wooden clack at the other end as though the phone had been dropped and then Clarissa's angry voice.

"You bastard, Al. What did you say to her? She's crying."

"I told her I was going to put a contract out on her life, what do you think I told her?" said Bressio, and was in no mood for the nonsense he got when he phoned Dawson's house, and felt very much less pleasant when the cab took twenty minutes just getting to Union Square on a hot August night. It was in this traffic that Bressio noticed a black convertible maneuver with the cab, and make the same desperate side-street attempts to break out of traffic. Well, he had been expecting that. They should have been on him right from Pren Street. Perhaps in his anger over Fleish he hadn't noticed, although this tail was so inept it seemed like a waste of taxpayers' money to have it in an unmarked car.

The tail stayed behind the cab to Dawson's place, where Bressio tipped the driver, waved to the black convertible following him, and went up to the ostentatiously polished wooden door of the town house. He knocked the great bronze lion-head knocker and the door opened to a gust of noise and a haze of hash and marijuana that could turn on the Great Mojave Desert. Very bright, thought Bressio, for a lawyer who would be taking on the narcotics people very soon. He pushed through the crowded crush of bodies, noticing that the door had been opened by a woman now hiding behind it. She popped out, smiling. Her eyes were cocaine wide. She wore an alligatorlike sheath with high dark alligator boots. She focused on Bressio.

"A Mafiosi, a real Mafiosi. Make me an offer I can't refuse."

"Act puerile," said Bressio and mowed his way through some more beautiful people until he was in a large white domed expanse known in *Home Beautiful* as the "Dawson Downstairs Living Room."

"Murray Dawson!" yelled Bressio. "Murray Dawson!"

The noise subsided slightly.

"Alphonse Bressio," came a woman's voice about twenty heads away. Bressio saw severe black hair topped by, of all things, wide black sunglasses at this hour of the night. It moved through the crush toward him. It was Bobo Dawson in a faintly transparent black sheath. Her face was darkly manicured, accenting her elegant sharp features that looked as though they had fallen off an Etruscan wall.

She was thrice-divorced, and considering she was Dawson's fifth, the normal odds for connubial stability would have been almost nonexistent except that it was her money that paid for this house, the Hyannis house and the Ibiza house, and the two maids, the cook and the butler that went with them. She had earned this money from her first three vaginal investments, which reinforced Bressio's belief that marriage for a woman was a good contract, but for a man marriage surrendered riparian rights on his blood. It always mystified Bressio how a man like Dawson and many other good lawyers knowing so much about the law could get married so many times.

"Everybody, this is the famous Al Bressio I told you might be coming," Bobo squealed to her guests. "His father was offed in a mob war during the forties and he has connections with people you wouldn't believe."

"I saw him in *The Godfather,*" commented a man with a purse over his shoulder. Several others thought this high humor.

"Where's Murray?" said Bressio harshly.

"Upstairs in the den or bedroom. Go later. I want my friends to meet you. Tell them some stories about your growing up. Murray says you had a fantastic, simply fantastic childhood. I've told them so much about you, you've got to stay. You simply have to."

Bressio spun rudely from her, plowing through arms and shoulders.

"He's so beautifully brutal," said one woman Bressio banged out of his way with a forearm across her chest.

As he ascended the stairs, the Dawson house became less crowded. In the den, only a few people lounged among the giant plants under a Babylon of artificial lights.

"Dawson?" Bressio called out.

"Not guilty" came a voice from behind a giant fern.

Bressio found Dawson in a third-floor bedroom with a teen-age girl—both dressed. She sat on the large square bed and Dawson in a lounge chair, his legs crossed, his chin in his right hand giving the appearance of listening intently. This was his pose, Bressio knew, when he wanted to think about things privately while appearing to give audience.

"Murray," said Bressio interrupting Dawson's thoughts. The girl looked up at the intruding oaf, waiting for Dawson to put him in his place.

"Al, what's up?"

"Case closed."

"In a day?"

"I know the great conspiracy surrounding L. Marvin. It didn't follow him, he found it."

"I beg your pardon," said the girl. "But Murray and I were in a serious conversation."

"And we'll have to give it the proper time it deserves. A party is too rushed, too helter-skelter. Lacks the proper vibrations, dear. Some other time." The girl was out of the bedroom before she could muster serious indignation. Dawson plopped himself back into the lounge chair and began cleaning his nails. This was his real concentration.

"L. Marvin is living in a cool house," said Bressio. "Do you know what a cool house is?"

"Certainly. A place where they've got a stakeout on a narcotics stash."

"Two eighty-five Pren is undoubtedly a house with a stash and very definitely has a lot of undercover narcotics agents who tend to follow people coming in and out. Especially those who break into the apartment where I believe the stash is kept."

"Go on."

"Like so many out-of-town girls who are the prettiest where the competition isn't overwhelming like it is in New York, Terry Leacock tends to overestimate what she can do with her body. She finances a heroin deal through someone, a connected Shylock. He had to be part of one of the families or I wouldn't have gotten the information so quickly. She is living with an undercover narco at the time. This sort of cohabitation tends to ruin sales. She can't unload the stuff, can't pay back the money and pays with her life."

"Why can't she give the Shylock the heroin?"

"Some of them won't touch it. Besides, who is going to take smack from someone living with an undercover?"

"She could peddle her ass for the money."

"That's black stuff. You got the wrong group. Besides, what can she make—considering the competition—fifty grand in a year? Seventy in a year? I know the thinking of the guy who ordered her hit. It probably had a little bit to do with his personal pride, too, that he knew she thought she could use him. Now what happens to the heroin? Keep that question in mind as we run down this road. The landlady dies of a heart attack today. The cops keep it hush-hush. It naturally attracts interest. Some people check it out, and lo and behold, it really is nothing. Just a heart attack. L. Marvin and Mary Beth break into the second floor loft some time ago, after Miss Leacock is gone, and cops all over the place. When you or they check, lo and behold, nobody knows nothing. A headquarters lieutenant is denied information about the house today. And surprise, surprise, denying the information is a police rank that usually acts as liaison with the federals."

"You sure it's federals?"

"Pretty sure. This lieutenant is out of Harlem. They can smell it if it's local narcotics. He said nothing."

"Maybe he's holding out."

"All right, you want a definite on it. I'll go to 285 Pren Street and ask someone for a match. If he answers in a twang or a drawl, we got federals. New York in its municipal wisdom hires nobody but locals. It's probably this new FBNC that's been crawling all over the city."

"And Marvin?"

"You can ask L. Marvin yourself whether he offered to sell some grass to his friends."

"Entrapment," said Dawson.

"Speak to L. Marvin. If they suggested the deal, you got yourself entrapment. But I doubt it. I think these guys are after heroin, and they probably only passed along the tip to get him the hell out of Pren Street. Mary Beth's money brought him back. I'm assuming you used her money for his Arizona bail. He mentioned something like that today."

"Would they bug a place with millions of dollars of heroin around?"

"First of all, ever since the New York City police department got heroin stolen from its evidence safes, nobody is going to leave a million dollars of smack lying around. Nobody I can conceive of is going to be that stupid."

"You're right, but they would have bugs for what little amount they have there."

"I'd think they would, Murray. But we're never going to be able to get that into an Arizona court, not when they have a trunkload of grass against your boy."

"I don't like entrapment either."

"It's your case. Is your stomach at rest now that you've found out how your little genius got himself stopped in Arizona one fine night? Any loose ends I failed to tie up?"

Dawson shook his head. "Nice job," he said glumly.

"And you're in no position to go butting heads with narcos, not with the atmosphere in your living room."

"They're Bobo's friends, not mine. It's her house. I just live here."

"All for L. Marvin, what the hell's the matter with you? Enough is enough. What's with you and L. Marvin? Do you owe him your life?"

"Give me the Cutler money."

"Thirty-five hundred of it is mine," said Bressio, giving him Cutler's green check.

Dawson examined the check and handed it back.

"What's coming off?" he said.

Bressio looked at the check. It was made out to him; even before he had told Cutler his feelings towards L. Marvin, the check had been made out to him. And with his face, too.

"Well, Murray, it seems as though Mary Beth Cutler has got a little defense fund to be used for the benefits of Mary Beth Cutler. I want to put you on notice that we consider it highly irregular that you represent both her and the Fleishs in this matter."

"I hate sneaks," said Dawson. "Let's get a bite to eat."

The Dawson kitchen was one of the best in the city, but Dawson did not like using it. He could get neither baloney and mayonnaise nor delicatessen. Delicatessen to Dawson was Jewish delicatessen, and while Bobo had in the past years featured such a specialty at a party for Sammy Davis, Jr., Dawson could not regularly get the food into the house. The Swiss cook would no more allow it than he would baloney. In a concessionary move, the cook had offered exotic Middle Eastern dishes which to Dawson tasted like something left too long in the refrigerator.

"But that's real Jewish food," the cook had complained.

"Then give me some unreal Jewish food like I was brought up on."

"What you were brought up on, sir, was Eastern European cooking adopted by Jews."

"All right, that."

"They were—with all pardons, sir—peasants. Now the Rothschilds—"

"Fuck the Rothschilds," said Dawson.

An argument ensued in which the cook angrily declared Dawson had the palate of a peasant.

"You'd better believe it," Dawson had said, vainly searching for an ethnic insult that went with Swiss. Bobo had smoothed over the tension by saying it was impossible to find such a good chef equal to the one they had and such a good man equal to the one she had. Dawson refused to apologize to the chef or even negotiate a small portion of the refrigerator for himself, and thus Bressio knew that when Dawson said he wanted a bite to eat, it meant leaving the town house and walking several blocks down Lexington Avenue to the Star's Delicatessen.

At the Star's, Dawson was greeted with a "Hi, Murray. Having another party at your house?"

Dawson ordered a hot pastrami on rye and a cup of coffee, heavy with cream. Bressio, insisting he was on a diet, started with black coffee, then said he did not want Dawson to eat alone and had a pastrami with him, and threw in a couple of hot dogs with potato salad on the side.

"Side order of potato salad?"

"No," said Bressio. "Side order of hot dogs, put the potato salad on the hot dogs and give me a diet cream soda with it."

By mistake, the waiter brought French fries too, but since they were at the table already, Bressio ate them.

"What's with you and Cutler?" asked Dawson.

"The check?"

"And him telling me I should clear everything to do with Mary Beth through you. That's pretty fast company for a kid from Little Italy, isn't it?"

"Yeah," said Bressio.

"What did you say to him? I couldn't stretch a conversation twenty seconds with that guy, and I'm Murray Blay Dawson, and he phones me tonight talking like you're a junior partner of Mitchell, Walker and Cutler."

"What were his words?"

"That he was prepared to stand by any of your actions and that if I had any further reason to contact him I should do it through you."

"No kidding," said Bressio, not even ashamed of his big kid grin.

"Watch that guy, Al. You're better off working for Don Carmine."

"Do I hear jealousy, Murray?"

"Sure," said Dawson, dunking an end of the pastrami sandwich into his sugar-heavy coffee. "That's why I went to the precinct house for Mary Beth. I wanted to see if that guy was for real. Couldn't get near him. You go up to his place to shake him down and you're goombahs on the hello."

"I want L. Marvin out of Mary Beth's life," said Bressio.

"Listen to God," said Dawson. "How are you going to accomplish that?"

"I don't know," said Bressio.

"Don't hurt Marvin, okay? I mean, don't go out of your way to hurt him in order to separate them."

"For L. Marvin I go out of my way to go out of his way. I want those adoption papers filed."

"They're ready to go."

"You're not some lawyer talking to a client now, Murray. Ready to go and gone are two entirely different things. I don't want to be held up on those papers at the last minute because you want maneuvering room. I want them out. Now, you want money on that, you can have it. I'm cutting the loose ends between Mary Beth and L. Marvin."

"They're going to go. Don't sweat it. Consider them gone. Now I want your thinking on Marvin's situation."

Dawson mentioned several tacks he might take with the Arizona arrest. He had been right, he said, with his instinct that the government was involved, but it really didn't do anything unjust as he could see it. Perhaps it was even a good thing that Marvin had this experience before he got in any really difficult scrapes. Perhaps it would have a maturing effect. With this in mind, Dawson outlined how he would inform the new Federal Bureau of Narcotics Control that he knew of their cool house, but would not disclose it because he knew they were going to put in a good word for his client in Arizona, a situation they were partly responsible for. It was their choice—do they go after the hard-drug dealers or a freaky artist type who got in over his head on a first offense?

"A year suspended on a guilty plea," said Bressio, estimating the results of Dawson's actions. They left the delicatessen and walked back up Lexington Avenue, the day's garbage encroaching on the wealth of the neighborhood.

"Yeah, I think so. A year suspended," said Dawson. "This isn't a juicy fighting case anyhow."

"Especially since Fleish was probably guilty as sin," said Bressio.

"Probably?" asked Dawson in amazement. "They got him with a trunkload of grass. A whole car trunkload *and* he signed a confession."

"You didn't tell me about a signed confession."

"Well, he won't go around giving confessions any more. If he learns that from this experience it will be worthwhile for him. Just to learn to keep his damned mouth shut. Ninety-five percent of all the people who are in jail now are in there because of their mouths. One way or another their mouths do it to them."

"I know," said Bressio. "L. Marvin doesn't deal smack, by the way."

"See, see. You just may have misjudged him. Seriously misjudged him. You know, Al, the more I think about this bust, the more I think it may be just what Marvin needed. He's an artist, and he just may get back to some serious work. Some good, serious work. I'll miss the kid in him, but I guess everyone has to grow up sooner or later. For Marvin it came when he was forty. Gone is the beautiful, innocent, exciting child. Well, so be it. 'The laughter fades and the wisdom begins. There is a time for everything. In death there is rebirth.' "

Bressio listened to Dawson quote from St. Francis of Assisi and was deeply moved.

At the Dawson house, Bressio found out he didn't have to play God. The post was being filled. Beautifully.

A telephone was thrust into Dawson's hands as soon as he entered the house.

"Marvin . . . don't say anything on the phone. Marvin, just keep your mouth shut. Marvin, do not say anything to anyone. Not about anything. Just keep your mouth *shut* this time. Shut, shut, shut!"

Dawson slammed down the receiver. Bressio laughed. He laughed till tears formed in his eyes and he laughed to weakness. He laughed all the way to the Eleventh Street Federal House of Detention.

When Dawson pulled the family Rolls to the front of the fortresslike brick building, Bressio finally got enough control to quote St. Francis back at Dawson.

" 'And it is in dying that we are reborn.' "

"Shut up," said Dawson. "You didn't have to come. You filled your agreement."

" 'It is in giving that we receive and in . . .' "

VIII

A young man with swinging long sandy hair who wore a ruby coke spoon prominent outside his tie-dyed T-shirt signaled the Dawson Rolls with one hand while reaching for something in the hip pocket of his patchwork dungarees with the other.

"You can't park here," said the young man and opened a small, thin billfold showing the blue and white of the new FBNC cards.

"Who are you?" said Dawson, haughtily refusing to look at the card.

"Federal Bureau of Narcotics Control, suh," he said, with the syrup of Mississippi in his voice.

"I thought so," said Dawson. "Congratulations, Al."

"At the end there just beyond the hydrant, you can park," said the young man pointing down the street.

"But I see other cars parked in front," said Dawson.

"Federal cars. You can park down there. Not here."

Dawson shrugged and gunned the Rolls down the block, bringing the limousine to curb in one screeching swoop, which was quite a feat, for Rolls do not tend to make screeching swoops even under the heaviest foot.

"Who are they trying to kid?" said Dawson, red flushing up behind his ears.

"If they can get away with it, why not?" said Bressio. "A lot of those FBNC people around this city lately."

Dawson ignored the comment. "I am almost insulted they would pull that amateur shit on me. On me. On *me.*"

"It isn't pulled yet," said Bressio.

"It will be."

"So it won't work."

"But they tried it on me."

"What puzzles me, Murray, is them having L. Marvin for five minutes and not knowing everything he knows."

"He's at last learning to keep his mouth shut."

"I haven't had a chance to get to my book yet, Murray, but I'd be willing to lay odds."

"Drop dead," said Dawson and sprang out of the car, marching up the block to show the FBNC his contempt for it. Bressio followed at a leisurely stroll, and somehow they reached the iron door simultaneously.

The groovy kid who had shown them his badge let them in. Fleish stood in the disinfectant-scrubbed bare hall talking with a black who had corn-row hair topped by a black, green and red skullcap. A black liberation button was prominent on his gray leather shirt. Around his neck on a chain was a molded black fist. Any passer-by would take him for a black militant. Bressio and Dawson assumed he was a narco. To this narco, L. Marvin Fleish was talking away to beat the band. He saw Dawson and Bressio.

"Murray. Al. Hi. Am I glad you're here."

Dawson hardly noticed Fleish. He spoke to the black narco, who, oh, man, was he sorry nothing was open at this hour where Dawson could confer with his client.

"There are offices in this building. I've spoken to clients here in rooms set aside for lawyers and clients to exchange confidences in private. It's the law, you know," said Dawson.

"The law opens at 9 A.M., man. You want to wait?"

"Has he been booked?"

"He's here," said the black narco.

"The charge?"

"Conspiracy to sell marijauna. Look, man, I'd like to open an office for you, but it ain't my slammer, dig?"

Dawson dug. He exchanged glances with Bressio, who smiled tolerantly. Let them play their game.

Then, lo and behold, the black narco had an idea. "Why don't you dudes use a car outside? It's private."

Dawson said he thought it was a good idea and that he would use his car. The white narco entered the conversation by saying he couldn't allow that because Dawson's car was down the street and he was sorry, suh, but Mr. Fleish might attempt to escape. They were responsible, suh, for Mr. Fleish's detention and he couldn't allow that. With all due apologies, suh.

The black narco pleaded with his cohort, but to no avail. He even called his partner a racist honkie, such as in "What else could you expect from a racist honkie?" The least the white narco could do would be to let this poor guy and his lawyer use one of the FBNC cars out front where they could be watched from the prison. And surprise, surprise, the racist honkie said he would allow this, but only for a little while and only because his partner was losing his head over the whole thing.

L. Marvin followed the interchange intensely. Dawson and Bressio looked bored.

Outside a light drizzle began to form as gray emerged in the new morning sky. The street smelled of urine and wretched wine. The black narco agent pointed to a gray government car.

"It's unlocked."

"No kidding," said Dawson.

"He's the nice guy," Fleish whispered to Bressio. "The white guy is the bastard."

"That's usually how it works, L. Marvin," said Bressio.

"The white guy being bad and the black good?" asked Marvin.

"Whatever," said Bressio.

Dawson stopped Fleish from entering the car. He looked at the car, then at Fleish and the jail. The narcos, Bressio knew, would never dare bug a room in which a lawyer and client were supposed to share privileged information. The courts would crucify the department if they tried, and with a lawyer like Dawson it would be foolhardy in the extreme. Nor would they lightly go about bugging his personal car. But in their own car, for other purposes, what law did that violate?

Naturally, the information could not be used as evidence, but it could be used for leads. Was there something bigger Fleish was involved in? Bressio dismissed the possibility. Who would get involved in something big with L. Marvin? The narcos were probably just jumpy about the cool house.

"I'd like to do something for Imaru, the black guy," said Fleish. "For getting us this car and being so down and everything."

"When they burn your pink little ass, L. Marvin," said Bressio, "you'll probably find out that Imaru is probably Charles Smith with a degree in accounting from Purdue."

"Listen to him," said Dawson. "That's free advice."

"He's not working for us any more?" said Fleish.

"First of all, shut up, Marvin. Just keep your mouth shut," said Dawson, his voice sharp and scolding yet hushed. "Now we are going to enter this car, in which I do not want too much said. Just say yes or no to my questions. Do not volunteer any further information unless I ask for it."

"Cool, man. I dig," said Fleish his face a cool composure of calculating cunning.

"Do you really understand, Marvin?" Dawson repeated. The drizzle began working down the gracious crown of white. Bressio pulled up his collar. Fleish seemed impervious.

"Dig it," said Fleish. He winked knowingly.

"Dawson and Fleish got in the back seat, Bressio in the front. Bressio was smiling.

"Now to begin with," asked Dawson. "They know this is your first arrest, correct?"

Fleish narrowed his eyes. This man was telling him something confusing. Bressio knew Dawson was working for leeway. No matter how small, he had seen Dawson turn the temporary lack of knowledge of a previous arrest or something that minor into a major advantage. Even if it only lasted a day, this was a fighter who needed only that one brief small opening to connect. And with a Murray Blay Dawson one thing always could lead to another. What the narcos didn't know that dawn might be a help to Fleish.

"I'm talking about what they know. Do they know you're a first offender and—"

"Are you talking about the Arizona bust two weeks ago for the grass?" asked Fleish helpfully.

"Bup, bup, bup," Dawson hummed to the tune of "Three Blind Mice." Bressio examined the texture of the seat covers. Fleish waited for the next question.

"Did I say something wrong?" Fleish finally wondered aloud.

"Yes," said Dawson.

"Oh, they know about Arizona already. I told them because they knew everything already. I was just helping them with some minor details. They're groovy people. A bit square, but they tuned in fast. Especially the black guy. There's a richness in the Third World we whites may never understand."

"Shut up, Marvin!" Dawson screamed, red-faced. "Shut up, shut up! Up! Up shut! Shut, shut, shut, shut up that mouth!"

Fleish pressed his lips together, squelched.

"Good night, Murray," said Bressio, turning to the front of the car, resting his head on the back of the seat and closing his eyes. He heard the door open and felt Fleish and Dawson get out of the car. He opened his eyes. Whispering, Dawson stood with Fleish near the car. Bressio could not hear them. He saw the rain eat into the magnificent white crown of Dawson hair. As it matted and drooped, Bressio dozed off, dry and comfortable.

He was awakened when the morning sun was red in the east. He felt a hand on his shoulder. It was Dawson. Fleish waited in the middle of the street.

"C'mon. I'm done," said Dawson. His face was grim. His hair was a dull gray mat and he looked like a very tired and very old man.

Bressio yawned, stretched and got out of the car. It was hot and it was just dawn. It was going to be a scorcher of a day, but he did not mind.

"I'm taking the boy genius back inside," said Dawson.

Fleish was sullen. His shoulders drooped as though under the yoke of outrageous oppression. The brush of a mustache clotted against his face; his long blond hair was wet and stringy. Bressio smiled broadly at him, but Fleish only nodded, chastened. In that moment there was a touch of pity in Bressio's heart, but only in that moment. It disappeared when Fleish spoke.

"Oh, another thing. They want permission to search my loft. They can get it through the court anyhow, and I'd like to do the black guy a favor. I mean, he asked and he's a down dude, dig. If we don't help those people, who are we going to help?"

"Is it clean?" asked Dawson. "Nothing incriminating?"

"Clean like Mr. Clean."

"I didn't ask that. I asked, is it clean? Yes or no."

"Yes," said Fleish.

"Are you sure?" said Dawson.

"Absolutely."

"That mean's there's nothing there, right?"

"Right."

Dawson sighed. "All right. Why not? You've given them everything else."

Dawson drove Bressio to his apartment on Bleeker Street.

"I'm not giving up," he said as Bressio got out of the car.

"Please, Murray. This is beyond games. Cut L. Marvin loose. If it's your conscience, if you think you owe him something for some strange reason, pay some kid lawyer to waltz him around. Pay some good lawyer. I'll chip in if you cut him loose. Enough is enough."

"I'm not fighting for him any more," said Dawson. "It's for me."

"Against whom?" asked Bressio, truly amazed to the point of exhaustion. "Against whom, Murray? Against whom?"

"The laws of the universe," said Dawson and gunned the car down Bleeker Street, a narrow, tight road originally designed for oxcarts, not Rolls-Royces. Bressio looked at his watch. By his reckoning, Dawson hadn't slept for at least twenty-four hours. And he was a fifty-five-year-old man.

IX

As Bressio slept contentedly through the morning, several people in Old Lyme, Connecticut, and in the simple Brooklyn home of Don Carmine talked about him.

William James Cutler told his wife that for the first time in years he could honestly substantiate reasonable hope for their daughter. His wife disagreed, to the point of tears.

"We thought that before when she started seeing the psychiatrist, and we thought that before when she went to that special home in Switzerland and we thought that before when she agreed to come home and seemed as though . . . and seemed as though. Jim, it has always seemed as though."

"You don't know what I discovered about Mr. Bressio."

"I saw him get out of his car yesterday. He terrified me."

"In all this seamy business, he may be the first moral man I have met."

"That should tell you something about hopelessness."

"He phoned this morning to say things were beginning to work in Mary Beth's favor now. I'm going into the city tomorrow to meet him at my office. I think for the first time in years we're not powerless."

"I am sorry if I can no longer hope with you, Jim. It is too hard to hope when hoping is never nourished by success. Maybe you should return to your office tomorrow, but for business. Use your energies more productively. As for me, as for Mary Beth's mother, I cannot bear to hear of another plan that has failed."

"Did you know that Fleish fellow is in jail, dear, and Mary Beth is not? They've been separated, and Mr. Bressio has told me he is working on keeping them separated. If we can get her into some sort of program, get her out of that whole environment—"

"We can't even get to see our own granddaughter, how are you going to arrange these things."

"Mr. Bressio can. I know it."

"He's probably going to make a fortune off you, Jim, like the others. It is not an easy thing to say, Jim, but give up. We have lost our daughter. We are not the only parents in the universe this has happened to. I have my life to live, too, what little is left of it. I want to live it with you. Let the dead bury the dead. Mary Beth is dead and has been for years. And you know it."

"I know power. If there is one thing I know it is power. Bressio has power. I can feel it. He can reach where I haven't been able to. It's a perfect parallel to Vietnam. I was thrashing around clumsily with all the influence of a modern industrial state while what I really needed was someone who knew the jungles. Now we have him."

Mrs. Cutler enfolded her husband's face in her hands. "That's a perfect description, Jim. Vietnam. Let's get out."

"No," said William James Cutler. "I will not surrender Mary Beth. I remember her too well."

In Bressio's office, Clarissa was sorting the morning mail and preparing bills when the phone rang. It was Mary Beth Cutler. Clarissa forced herself to be polite, because as Bressio had reminded her in the 7:00 A.M. phone call, Mary Beth was a client.

"Al says he doesn't want you going back to the loft on Pren Street, and he means it, Mary Beth. Now get off that fucking tack. He told you to stay at my place, so stay there. You're paying him a small fortune for his advice—now take it. Stay at my apartment ... All right, see Dr. Finney. When are you going? Well, stay at my apartment until your appointment."

"Right, dear. Good," said Mary Beth, but when Clarissa phoned back a half-hour later to ask Mary Beth to check the freezer to see whether Clarissa would have to shop that evening, no one answered. Clarissa Duffy shuddered. What a creepy pair. And that daughter. The kid never said anything and did exactly as she was told, like a robot. And to top off the morning, one of Al's friends whom she detested so much phoned with one of those cryptic and complicated messages which did not need a heavy Italian accent to make it even more foggy.

"Youa tella Alphonse, Missy, that his dinna guesta lasta nighta says he was wrong abouta da house what dey talking, yes?"

"It's Ms.," said Clarissa viciously.

"Righta, Missy."

Clarissa tried to make a coherent statement from the man, but when she looked at her notes at the end of the conversation she saw only something about a house being a very bad place. And since the man was going to phone back anyhow, she promptly threw the notes in the wastebasket not knowing that that unclear message had a market value of approximately twice her weekly salary. Besides, she told herself, Al didn't need that sort of person any more. That's what was wrong with his life to begin with.

Murray Blay Dawson was also talking about Bressio. To his mirror in his office. The drapes were pulled back and he looked at himself revitalized by a half-hour's nap in the barber's chair where his face was freshened and his hair returned to its glory. He was a bit dizzy from lack of sleep.

"Murray. You're not going to fuck up your relationship with Al Bressio for Fleish. Bressio is too good an ally. He's really too good a friend. If you have any friends. So why, Murray, my dearly beloved love, are you thinking what you are thinking? I will tell you why, darling, because in some ways you have a lot of Fleish in you. You are really an L. Marvin Fleish with a couple of screws better mounted and fifty more points of I.Q." Dawson gave himself the famous Dawson grin. He rang his private secretary.

"Did you send out those adoption papers yet?"

"No, sir. You told me not to unless you gave the word. They're addressed to the court and waiting for hand-delivery. Should I send them over now?"

"No," said Dawson. He thought for a moment. Bressio needed those papers in his campaign for Mary Beth Cutler, whatever the dimensions of that campaign were. Dawson had promised the papers. Should he hold out he would have as an enemy both the famous Cutler influence and Bressio, perhaps his only friend, and if anyone could ever count on an ally, his best ally.

But in risking the offense, Dawson would also have some leverage against this awesome pair, and since Marvin's position was
virtually without any reasonable hope, that leverage might just be
the only slim chance Fleish had. To put it simply, Dawson would
be most assuredly facing great difficulty for a chance so slim it
might not exist. It just didn't make any sense.

"I'll buzz you in a second," said Dawson and went back to the
mirror behind the curtain over the bar.

"You know, Murray, if you sent out those papers now, it would
be the first sensible thing you've done this week. Bressio is right
about L. Marvin Fleish. You're paying a hell of a price. As your
legal counselor, sweetheart, I demand you file those papers."

Dawson rang the secretary again. "Hold the adoption papers
until further notice."

"Very good, sir."

Dawson went back to the mirror and kissed it. "I love you, you
crazy sonuvabitch."

In a Jewish neighborhood on Eastern Parkway, Don Carmine
was having lunch with a visitor. The man was a friend and an
adviser, known to a few people as Anselmo Felli and to almost
everyone else as Arnold Foster, president of Alpen Real Estate, one
of the larger property management firms in the city. Naturally, it
never suffered labor problems and had an easy way with zoning
restrictions.

The two men talked over lentil soup. They talked about Alphonse Bressio. It was this friend and adviser who had first noticed
the worth of Salvatore Bressio's son. The lad was fifteen at the time,
and in one of those incidents that will occur in life became involved
with three older men when his spaldeen bounced into their car
window. Now, this pink rubber ball, so common to New York City
streets, could cause little damage. But one of the men, to teach
Alphonse a lesson, threw it into a sewer. The young Bressio decked
him with a single punch. The other two men came out of their car
to avenge their companion. At only fifteen, the young Bressio sent
them both to the hospital. These facts were verified by the Dursio
adviser, who spoke to those who had seen it. And to make young
Bressio even more attractive, he did not have an undue temper,
nothing that would cause trouble without sufficient reason. He was

not just another talented hothead. Young Bressio had a mind, and when the adviser passed an afternoon's conversation with the widow Theresa Bressio, he found out further that the late Salvatore had taught his son early the skills of the gun.

"He's a young Sal Bressio, even better. He's smarter," Felli had told Don Carmine excitedly. But there was only one thing wrong with the boy. He would not make sensible use of the abilities God gave him. He had this crazy law thing in his head which everyone thought would leave when he grew up. But even in later years when he failed the bar, it did not leave.

Even the gambling did not bring him to seek the employ from Don Carmine, and the extensive credit shown him by all the Dursio books proved fruitless when he always paid.

"Someday he will come to his senses" was the word. "Someday he will realize that this is a hard world and a man should make use of what he has instead of chasing dreams which do not exist. Someday, and on that day he will be of immense benefit to whoever gains his allegiance."

But year after year the day did not come, so at lunch with Don Carmine, Felli told him the strange thing that was happening with Alphonse Bressio. He told him how Alphonse had passed the word along that an apparently worthless crazy person should be treated with the respect as if she were blood kin. Now here was the interesting part. The woman lived at 285 Pren Street.

"Alphonse is not involved in that craziness. I know it," said Don Carmine. He ladled himself some more soup from the tureen that his wife had put on the table.

"But if he is?" said the adviser.

"He would come to us first. Alphonse has a very good mind. That insanity is not his sort of thing. Still . . . we will have nothing to do with it. We have even better reason now not to be involved if Alphonse has interest in it. Which I doubt."

"He is said to be interested in the welfare of the woman as a business thing. Is it possible that is all he is interested in, a small business thing? Or in some way might it be a part of his dream-chasing?"

"That is possible. With Alphonse that is very possible." The topic switched to more pleasant matters such as FHA financing being arranged for a project. The family had a vital interest in its outcome. The adviser interrupted real estate talk to suggest perhaps that Alphonse did not know what was happening at 285 Pren Street.

"He has sources," said Carmine Dursio, and the subject was dismissed.

Bressio woke at noon and to celebrate the start of a beautiful day decided he would break his diet. He would eat breakfast, not just have a scrimpy cup of black coffee. He deserved a little reward. For his reward, he went to a luncheonette on Sixth Avenue.

"English muffins, toast and bagels, sir?" asked the counterman.

"Yeah," said Bressio. "Every diet should have a break." And he doubly deserved that break because he hadn't placed a bet the day before.

Across town, Murray Blay Dawson was wrestling with his conscience which for such a consistent loser had an awesome resiliency.

"Ah, to hell with it," he said and told his secretary to file the adoption papers.

"That final, sir?"

"Yes," said Dawson. "Ninety percent."

"Sir, that means file it, correct?"

"Immediately. I don't want to change my mind. You might not know it, but I am one of the most moral people you are ever going to meet."

When Bressio dropped in that afternoon, this feeling of morality had so overwhelmed Dawson that he was exuding joy to the whole world. Naturally Bressio was suspicious.

"What do you want now, Murray?" said Bressio.

"I want you to sit down and relax."

"Un-uh. On behalf of Cutler we'll go L. Marvin's second bail for the papers on Bobbi. I think that's a good deal for your client. He's going to get hit with $5,000 grand minimum, and with him being such a flake, he might walk. The bail for the baby. You're not going to do better, Murray, and if you try, I guarantee you a heavy dose of grief."

"If that's the deal you're offering, Al, forget it."

"Five grand is great for two signatures, especially since the kid is Mary Beth's natural-born and the father is facing two drug charges, and you've got a conflict of interest staring you in the face."

"I said forget it, Al. The papers have been filed. That was part of the deal. I'm not going to bargain for the life of a child. And I'm not going to leverage you. That you want those papers processed is enough. I personally think it's a good thing that Mary Beth is getting her child back legally and I only hope she is well enough to be a good mother."

"I missed something in there," said Bressio.

"You didn't miss anything. Mary Beth is getting her daughter back. She's the mother. I think she made a mistake having Marvin and his wife adopt it. I'd like to spend more time with you but I'm bushed. Haven't slept in almost two days, and I have a lot of work."

"Is something wrong, Murray?"

"No. If in the excitement I didn't get a chance to tell you nice job on unraveling the situation at Pren Street and its link to the Arizona bust, I'm sorry. Nice job, Al. It's a shame that you're giving up that kind of work. At that, you're an artist."

"You did hire me for a week," said Bressio, truly worried about the tiredness in Dawson's eyes.

"Or until the job was done. It's done. Well-done. Unfortunately even we can't overcome the self-destruct of our client. But that's life."

"What are you going to do about L. Marvin?"

"I don't know. I've got nothing to work with. Two, mind you, *two* signed confessions, and I don't even want to tell you the rest."

"What would you need to work with? I'm mean, I'm just asking out of curiosity."

"First," said Dawson. "You have got to hear how the boy genius got himself arrested for the second time. This you cannot miss."

The brilliant capture of L. Marvin Fleish by the Federal Bureau of Narcotics Control as told by Murray Blay Dawson to Alphonse Joseph Bressio:

Marvin, feeling obliged to help his accomplice of the Arizona episode, ventured into the only field he knew, importing pot. Through a local contact as yet to be arrested, he arranged to import into New York City fifty-five pounds of Acapulco gold (the best or right up there with the best) through a contact he had made in Arizona. Where in Arizona? In the Phoenix County Jail, no less, where the successful meet to plan even greater successes.

The finances were as follows: Marvin would purchase the marijuana from his Arizona contact at $150 a pound, resell it to the New York contact who provided the up-front money for $200 a pound, leaving Marvin with a profit of roughly $2,500, with which he would bail out his friend of the Arizona adventure. The financier, a pusher, could easily resell Acapulco gold at $45 an ounce, leaving him a substantial profit also.

It was in the best tradition of the free enterprise system that Marvin engineered the wholesaling. It also brought to mind a terrifying prospect. Out there in New York City walking around loose was a person who trusted L. Marvin Fleish with nearly $8,000 cash.

They were to meet in a hotel on Twenty-third Street, the Chelsea District. Room 17. The hotel was known for two things: actors out of work and pushers in work. Marvin showed a sense of tradition.

Marvin received a phone call from his Arizona contact. They were very clever, these smugglers.

"Do you have the package for Mrs. M?" asked Marvin from the hall phone on the second floor of 285 Pren.

"Yes," said the other James Bond. "I'm in St. Louis Airport. I'll get into Newark by 8 A.M. and I'll meet you you-know-where with the packages of Mrs. M."

"For Mrs. M," Marvin corrected, lest the United States government realized M stood for marijuana and it was packages of M.

"Yeah, for," said the accomplice.

The accomplice neatly made it to Newark Airport despite the dogs that can smell the stuff stationed at every major airport. He hailed a cab for New York City and was picked up on the Manhattan side of the Holland Tunnel and whisked jailward along with two suitcases. Exhibit A.

Meanwhile, intrepid Marvin was playing it cool. He put nearly $8,000 cash (Exhibit B) in a locker in Grand Central Station, the kind in which you insert quarters and get a key back (Exhibit C, the key). He made sure he wasn't tailed by hitting three bars and checking to see if any faces became familiar. None did, and he proceeded to the Elsinor Hotel on West Twenty-third Street where he cleverly asked the hotel clerk if a Mr. Smith were registered. There were seven Mr. Smiths, which one did he want? asked the clerk.

"The one in Room 17," Marvin told the first witness.

"Oh, that Mr. Smith. I'll check."

The witness then said Marvin would have to sign in on a visitor's pass. No alarms rang in the mind of the accused. He signed it J. Jones, leaving no traces but his handwriting on Exhibit D.

A young man with fashionably long hair, mustache, T-shirt and heavily patched blue jeans opened the door of Room 17 when Marvin knocked.

"Yeah?"

"Are you Mr. Smith?" asked Marvin.

"Yeah," said the young man, later to be identified as Agent Blake Van Sluyters.

"I'm Marve Fleish," said Marvin, finally feeling he had found someone he could trust.

"Come in," said Agent Van Sluyters, who shut the door behind the accused.

Marvin, having been burned once very seriously, did not rush into revealing his motives.

"You here for any special reason?" asked Van Sluyters.

"I might be," said Marvin casually.

"What are you here for?" asked the agent.

"Things," said Marvin.

"What things?"

"What things do you think?"

"I'm asking you," said the agent.

"I'm asking you," said the very wary and cautious L. Marvin Fleish.

"We gotta wait," said Agent Van Sluyters.

Marvin lit up a joint and handed one to the agent, who offered to pay for it. Marvin, from the goodness of his heart, refused to take money, thus foiling in a small degree the ever-tightening trap. They would not get him accepting money for drugs.

"But I insist," said the agent.

"Forget it. What is it, a buck?"

"A buck I'll be glad to pay. No reason why you should carry it."

"The day I can't share a joint," said Marvin, "is the day I quit using."

The agent put the numbered bills back in his pocket. He also told L. Marvin he would smoke his joint later, and he put Exhibit E in his blue jeans. Then he went into the bathroom and came out with a snub-nosed .38-caliber pistol and badge. He told Marvin to lie on the floor.

The United States Attorney was thus left with only fifty-five pounds of marijuana, the statement implicating Marvin from the young man who had the number of 285 Pren Street, a key to a Grand Central Station deposit box, the $8,000 in that box, Marvin's signature as "Mr. Jones," a joint, Agent Van Sluyters' testimony, which said Mr. Fleish asked specifically for a Mr. Smith at Room 17, identified as the name and room by the boy picked up with the fifty-five pounds of marijuana.

So Marvin filled out in his own words why he did all these things because the narco agents seemed genuinely interested and friendly, and besides, they knew everything anyway.

"Why do you think I was in the room?" said Marvin slyly when he knew the jig was up, "to jerk off? Of course it was my contact point. I wasn't going to bring the money with me because sometimes you can get held up. I was just going to give my contact the key."

The narcos probed for more than an hour as to who had thought up the locker safety device, but Marvin insisted it was his own idea.

Thus was L. Marvin Fleish captured and charged.

When Dawson finished, Bressio was rubbing laugh tears away from his eyes.

"So what would you suggest?" said Dawson.

"They didn't even need the confession," said Bressio. "Maybe the *Miranda* decision. We get the confession thrown out, maybe, but jeez, why bother?"

"I don't even think we can get the confession thrown out," said Dawson. "They offered him right to his counsel, but he wanted to get the confession out of the way first."

Bressio made a disdainful face, signifying everything was not as bleak as it seemed.

"Granted, a great case, but a weak charge. Lots of slip-ups in conspiracy. Now if we can do a job on the guy who brought in the pot, and somehow we can weaken L. Marvin's confession in court, and play the harmless marijuana before a jury and we make a deal down in Arizona to plead guilty but part of the deal is they hold sentencing until after the New York trial, and you bring in L. Marvin to the jury and judge clean with a job, and you show the contact who implicated him as vicious . . . Gee, Murray, we just might not bleed to heavily at all."

"Suspended in Arizona and a year, maybe two years, in Danbury," said Dawson.

"With time off for good behavior," said Bressio. "After all, it is pot, not smack or speed."

"I thought you thought all of them were the same."

"I'm talking for the court."

"You'll deal for him in Arizona and do a job on the kid, Al? Is that what you're offering free?"

"I suppose," said Bressio. "It's not free. I've been paid."

"So you, too, are becoming part of the Fleish mystique. He's exciting, isn't he? God's own foul-up."

"No," said Bressio. "I didn't like the way you looked this morning and I don't like to see you fight with your hands tied. I'm doing this for you, Murray."

Murray Blay Dawson, who could play an entire range of emotions like a piano keyboard, suddenly found himself confronted by real gratitude and affection within his breast and he did not know what to do with it. He looked around the room for some sort of prop or something to do, anything not to look at Bressio.

"Uh, Marvin's contact is a kid name Loring, Calvin Loring, a pre-med student at Prusscott College just outside of Des Moines, Iowa. He's nineteen and I think you'll have a tough time doing a job on him. Farm boy. Heretofore clean."

"You know he'll be no problem, Murray."

"Yeah. I know that. Uh, how's Clarissa?"

"She's fine, Murray."

"Yeah. Good. Well, here we are." Dawson was saved by a buzzing under the low marble table. The phone, Bressio saw for the first time, was connected to the underside of this table. He had never seen Dawson answer a phone in this office. It was a pearl-white Princess receiver.

"It's the U.S. Attorney's office, this guy Cartwright, who's handling Marvin's prosecution . . . Yes, hello. This is Dawson."

Dawson signaled Bressio for a pad and pencil. Bressio gave him a pen and the back of an envelope of a bill that had been in his pocket. Dawson began scribbling furiously.

"Yeah. Yeah. Yeah. Really, and . . . and . . . and . . . Anything else? . . . No. I'm not too disturbed. Why should I be disturbed? It's not me who's going to spend the rest of his life in jail."

X

Bressio got a receipt for his pistol from a clerk in the house of detention, and felt just a bit undressed going to the conference room where prisoners could meet lawyers and relatives. Dawson was too mad to see Fleish.

"This is too much even for him," Dawson had said. "You'd better see if this list is correct. If I saw that ninny again, I'd throttle him. I've got to come down off the ceiling first."

Fleish entered the room in pale prison green escorted by a guard. The harsh fluorescent light made him seem all of his forty years and then some. He slumped into a hard-backed wooden chair on the other side of a metal table dividing the room.

"This place is a bummer, Al," Fleish confided.

"I'm glad to see reality is creeping up on you, L. Marvin. Do you still think the world only requires that you be happy with it?"

"I'm a changed man, Al. I looked at those bars this morning and I said, if this is cool, I'll be warm. No more of this shit for me, man. Bad trip. Bad trip."

"It's a little bit late for that, L. Marvin. The U.S. Attorney's office phoned Dawson this afternoon. You know that Lestoil-clean loft of yours, the one you so freely gave them permission to search?"

"Yeah?"

Bressio took the envelope Dawson had written on out of his breast pocket.

"It seems as though they found fifteen tabs of LSD; a quart bottle of reds (Seconal); four dollies (methadone)—in state hospital packages, no less; seventeen footballs—dex and amphetamine combined, that is; fifteen DBM's—that's, as you know, faster-working LSD for people who don't want to wait thirty more seconds in reality; and five packages of white powder now being analyzed by the laboratory."

"Oh, that," said L. Marvin. He snapped his fingers and nodded knowingly.

"Those things are illegal, too, L. Marvin."

"I wasn't thinking of that. I was thinking of pot. There's no pot in the loft. They didn't find pot, did they? Because if they found pot, they fucking well planted the shit."

"They didn't have to plant pot with all the other goodies you left for them, L. Marvin."

"Yeah, but I was thinking pot when I said they could check out the apartment without a warrant. I wasn't thinking of the other stuff. I should have thought of the other stuff."

"Dawson wants to know what the white powder in the five glassine envelopes was."

Fleish picked at his mustache as though generating some mental energy which would enable him to analyze the envelopes on the spot.

"Glassine envelopes . . . glassine envelopes. Oh, yeah. I call it Consciousness IV."

"Do some other people call it heroin?"

"No, no, it's new, man. It's a wipe-out." His eyes twinkled and his hands began to move in a happy descriptive pattern much like a Gillette executive explaining a new miracle blade.

"You know how it takes maybe five seconds with DMB? You don't, huh? Okay. This is instant. I mean, instant. It's condensed DMB. You trip the minute it hits your tongue."

"Anyone ever live through it?"

"We haven't tried it out yet. I was waiting for the right vibes, man. I'm not tripping Consciousness IV until everything grooves. What with these hassles and everything, I wouldn't go near the stuff. No. I want a nice clear day with a good morning and maybe a joint, and a wooded stream and no air pollution, cops, hassles, hunger. A beautiful scene of love with someone I love. The way the world should be. *Then* I'll drop Consciousness IV."

"With all that, why would you need Consciousness IV?"

"To expand it, man. Expand it."

"I hope you learn to like jails, L. Marvin. Now some questions about Mary Beth."

Fleish stood up and exposed his stomach. "No rash. Look. You see. It was her that did it."

"What drugs is she on?"

"Speed. She's a speed freak."

"LSD?"

"Just a couple of times."

"Anything else?"

"No, just pot, hash sometimes. I don't think she was up to DMB."

"Regular, does she use this stuff?"

"Just the speed."

"That does cause paranoia."

"She was weird when I met her, man. I mean, she was a real package. She wanted to try everything all at once. You know?"

"And you helped her."

"I couldn't stop her."

"She's addicted to speed, then, correct?"

"Speed isn't addicting. Nothing is addicting, man. It's all nature. It's the bad stuff you bring to it. She brings shit to it."

"L. Marvin, I have heard about your proverbial luck before, but you have never been so lucky as you are now that I left my gun at the door. If we were outside, I would put a bullet in your face. Just sit where you are and I will turn around and leave. Say nothing. Do not even blink your eyes, for if you blink them I will take them out of your head. I am going to try very hard to leave here without killing you. I will need your help. Do not even say yes."

Bressio was still trembling as he walked out into the sweltering dusk of Eleventh Street. He noticed he picked up a tail on the way out and the tail dropped off at his office.

Clarissa was gone. She had left notes. The work was done. He saw the Cutler appointment was made for the morning at Cutler's offices. Good. He could not speak to the man now without depressing him, as Bressio was depressed.

So Bressio went to a singles bar on Second Avenue—commonly called "meat racks" by male and female alike—and bought several girls drinks; after finding one who said she found him fascinating, he took her to the Plaza Hotel for the evening, and in so doing effectively removed himself from his sources of information, who most assuredly would have reached him that evening. He did not wish information on anything. What he wanted was to have a painful hangover in the morning to take his mind off the tears that were perpetually behind his eyes for a young girl who had grown up in a home he wished he had grown up in.

"Why are you taking the bullets out of the gun?" said the blonde in the hotel room.

"Because I don't know you," said Bressio.

She flipped her bra over a sedan chair and poured herself a drink from the bottle Bressio had ordered sent up.

"It all depends on which gun you want to risk," she said, laughing.

"C'mere," said Bressio.

When they had exhausted themselves, the blonde said, "That was great."

"Bullshit," said Bressio.

"Well, it was okay," said the blonde. "At least you could get it up. You'd be surprised at all the guys who can't get it up. Talk, talk, talk. At least you're not talk. You want to go again?"

"No," said Bressio.

"Something's bothering you."

"Yes."

"Well, a little talk is all right."

"Maybe I don't know everything, right?"

"Sure."

"And who am I or some shrink to write off a human life, right?"

The blonde became nervous. She looked at the unloaded revolver on the bureau drawer.

"Where there's life, there's hope. And I'm only human."

"That's two clichés," she said.

Bressio poured himself a tumbler and worked it to the bottom. He put the bullets under his pillow, kissed the blonde good night, and went to sleep. In the morning she was gone, and he did not remember her name. Which was probably fair because she probably did not remember his. Thus did Bressio spend an entire night away from people who might have warned him about Pren Street.

XI

Clarissa had a bandage over her left eye when Bressio entered the office with morning coffee and Danish.

"I fell. It's nothing, Al," said Clarissa as Bressio unloaded a slightly sloppy white paper bag near her IBM electric.

"I didn't ask," said Bressio.

"You would. I see that Mary Beth Cutler is the daughter of one of our leading fascist pigs, William James Cutler."

"You don't know him, Clarissa."

"He was Under Secretary of State, wasn't he? Under Dulles."

"And Kennedy."

"It was his kind who started the genocidal Vietnamese war."

"Did one of your liberated boyfriends belt you or something?" Bressio examined the mail.

"Why do you say that?"

"Because you're trying to get me into an argument. You know how I feel about your childish use of the word 'genocidal.'"

"You had a one-night stand last night, didn't you?" asked Clarissa. "I can tell. I can always tell."

"Who was he?" asked Bressio, nodding to the bandage.

"Al, you've got an 11:30 A.M. appointment with Cutler. Do you know where the New York office of Mitchell, Walker and Cutler is? I'll get the address for you."

"Who did that to you?"

"I fell and it's none of your business; now get over to Mitchell, Walker and Cutler. The airline confirmed your reservations this morning made by Dawson's office. You have Phoenix, at 4:30 P.M.

leaving from Kennedy, and a 1:30 P.M. tomorrow from Phoenix to Des Moines. What the hell is in Des Moines, Iowa?"

"Who did that?"

"One of your goombahs called again with some kind of a message about a house—"

"Who did that to you?"

"He didn't leave his name. He called yesterday and today, saying he tried reaching you last night at your apartment."

"Who hit you, Duffy?"

"None of your fucking business because I've seen you settle my scores and I don't like seeing you that way and I don't like seeing you like that. Now, get out of here or I'm leaving. I'm not talking, Al, so forget it. Besides, what's the big thing with me? You went out screwing that trash last night." Clarissa attempted to open the container of coffee gently, but the cover gave with a start, spilling hot brown liquid on her hands and desk and the morning mail Bressio was returning to the desk.

"You're dumb," she screamed. "You're just so goddamned dumb, a big goddamn guinea. A big goddamn dumb guinea who can't even see what's in front of him. Fucking gavone."

Clarissa was crying, and since Bressio could not cope with her tears—he never could—he left the office. Mad.

He was still mad when he saw a white Eldorado power its way through the City Hall traffic on Broadway and cut off a Volkswagen at the curb. The Volkswagen driver poked his head out of the window to complain, saw the four men in the Eldorado, and pulled away quickly. The two men in the back wore white T-shirts. The driver wore a conservatively cut shimmering green suit. Seated next to him was an oaf of a man in a black suit with a white polo shirt underneath. All wore little gray fedoras slightly too small for their heads.

"Alphonse, Alphonse," called out the driver.

"Hello, Willie Knuckles, what are you doing out of the Bronx?" Bressio looked down at the thin, hard face with the scimitar nose and dark lips.

"I've come to talk with you and offer an indemnity."

"Talk," said Bressio.

"We have heard that you are concerned about a woman who lives at 285 Pren Street."

"Is she all right?"

"As far as we know."

"Then what's the indemnity?"

"That in a minute. We have concerns about 285 Pren Street. We wonder if you shared the same concern, you know."

"What?"

"There's a bit of smack there left lying around. A cool house, you know?"

"So?"

"So we wondered if, you know, you were interested in it, too? You know?"

"I'm not. Just Mary Beth Cutler."

"Okay, okay, okay. Good. It ain't much smack and it looks as though we can do it, and we just didn't want to cross wires, you know."

"The indemnity."

Willie Knuckles passed a white legal-sized envelope up through the open window. Bressio did not touch it. He saw the two men in the back seat slide their hands behind their backs. The man in the front seat reached into his jacket.

"It's for you, Alphonse."

"What's it for, Willie Knuckles?" said Bressio, apparently ignoring the reach for weapons.

"It's five hundred dollars, Alphonse. And could be more, you know, if you think it should be more. We ain't got no quarrel with you, you know. Yesterday I came to your office, police and all. Respectful, right, Carlo?"

"Right," said the man in the front seat, whom Bressio did not know.

"And I was real respectful and everything, you know. And I wants to leave a message. Just a fucking message, you know. Right Carlo?"

"Right," said the man in the front seat.

"And it was what I told you just now almost."

"Right," said Carlo.

"And I was polite."

"Right," said Carlo.

"And all of a sudden, like, I had done something, and I hadn't done nuthin', you know. Nuthin'. Right, Carlo?"

"Right."

"Your secretary, Miss Duffy, comes at me swinging and screaming like I don't know what. Like, I should get out of your life, you
know? That stuff she was screaming real crazy. And I ain't coming
here to get in your life, you know, Alphonse, not that I have
anything against youse or anything, you know. I'd drink with
youse and it'd be a pleasure. And she comes at me and I lift my
hand to take care of myself. That's all. Just lifted the fucking hand,
right, Carlo, and I—like, it was an accident—cut your secretary
over the eye. No hard feelings. Take the five yards. I didn't mean
no ways to do it."

"You hit Clarissa Duffy?" said Bressio, and he shrugged as
though this were no major event, not even worth indemnity.

"Yeah," said Willie Knuckles, smiling.

Bressio laughed lightly and looked around the block. The men
in the back seat put their hands on their laps, smiling broadly with
Bressio. So did Carlo, who took his hand out of his coat. Bressio
shrugged again and chuckled. They all smiled with him. Then he
pulled Willie Knuckles out through the window of his Eldorado by
the flesh of his cheeks and broke his scimitar nose against an
upcoming right knee, cracked his cheekbones and kicked him back
against the side of the car through the groin.

"Yeah?" said Bressio, sticking his head into the vacated window,
his right hand on his unsheathed gun. Hands remained on laps.
"You touch her, Carlo?"

Carlo shook his head.

"Any of you touch her?"

The two men in the back seat shook their heads.

"Evened out, right?" said Bressio.

"Right," said Carlo.

Bressio knew there would be explaining to Willie Knuckles how
no one had time to get to their weapons and how Bressio moved
too fast. He knew he would meet Willie Knuckles again on the
street and there would be formal acknowledgments that all was a
misunderstanding and everything was forgiven. He also knew that
if there were a contract out on his life, Willie Knuckles would be
the first to try to fill it. But there had been others, and that was life.
Besides, he would never let Willie Knuckles very close to him
again.

Willie Knuckles groaned as he tried to lift himself from the curb. A crowd of passers-by gathered, aghast.

Bressio kicked Willie Knuckles in the bloody face. It was not a cruel act as the passers-by surmised. It was merely to put Willie Knuckles away momentarily so that Bressio could turn his back on him and walk away. Which he did.

At Mitchell, Walker and Cutler, high above the fury of greed and fear known as the New York Stock Exchange, there was no waiting room. Which was the first thing special Bressio noted about the firm. People didn't get stacked up like planes waiting to land.

A middle-aged secretary was examining her typing at a simple, functional, gray metal desk, her glasses perched at the tip of her nose. "Yes, can I help you?"

"I've come to see William James Cutler. My name is Al Bressio."

"Oh, yes, we've been expecting you. Won't you come in, please."

She led him down a wide cork-floor corridor with widely spaced white doors signifying large offices. The white walls in between each had one modest print, more to break up the expanse of wall than to show art. Bressio judged that they had passed eight offices, and there was an equal number behind them in the other direction. A faint smell of stored paper, dry to the nostrils and somewhat numbing to the mind, reminded Bressio of the Fordham library.

At the end of the corridor, she knocked on another door, and Bressio expected to be ushered into Cutler's secretary's office.

"Come in," said Cutler's voice. The secretary opened the door, and Bressio was in Cutler's office. He had heard of hidden lighting before, but never hidden secretaries.

"Mr. Bressio. Come in, please," said Cutler, rising from behind a well-polished wooden desk. This was a law office. From floor to ceiling, in wooden bookcases, were thick high books.

He looked more like the Cutler at graduation in his dark suit and vest with the soft white shirt and the Princeton tie.

"It's so good of you to come," he said, shaking Bressio's hand warmly. "This is what I look like in working clothes."

"Yeah. I noticed the difference. You look more like I remembered you at Fordham graduation. I bet you didn't know that I heard you speak."

"You got a doctorate of law that day, according to what I've been told about you. Yes, I have had an investigation made of you. And let me say I am very impressed. More than impressed. I am grateful that you're willing to help me. You may be the only man who can."

"I'll do what I can do . . . it's—well, I'll do what I can do."

"Good," said Cutler. "Let's get down to cases. Fill me in on what Mary Beth has been doing the last five years. I know I have a grandchild."

"She's a pretty little girl. Very well-behaved. Her name is Bobbi."

"And Mary Beth?"

"I have her scheduled to see a psychologist I know."

"She's been to one of the best psychiatrists. If I'm correct, psychologists don't have medical degrees. I could afford a psychiatrist for her if you'd suggest."

"This guy is good. He's done some good research in drugs."

"I see. Can I have his name?"

"His name's Finney, but I'd suggest you not contact him. Let me say that I ask that you don't contact him."

"Done. Just tell me what I should do. I'm in your hands."

"There really isn't too much you can do, Mr. Cutler," said Bressio, taking an offered seat by a high wooden table. It was interesting that sitting catty-corner, the two men were in an equal conversation, but because of the height of the table they were always reminded of business.

"Then let me ask some questions about this Fleish matter and Mary Beth," said Cutler.

Bressio found Cutler's questions incisive, his mind always working toward clarifying and organizing even the most extraneous fact. Where Dawson might streak to the heart of a problem and seize its glowing essence to hold before the world, Cutler mined for it, exploring this possibility here and that one there. It was a method of eliminating what wasn't in order to find out what was.

He established that there was little possibility now of Mary Beth losing her child. No, neither Fleish nor his wife had any interest in Bobbi.

"Fleish appears to be somewhat at the mercy of those around him, but what about his legal wife? I would imagine she might feel differently."

"She signed the papers."

"She can change her mind and make a fight out of it."

"She can make a fight, but not a winning one."

"She can cause trouble."

"Yes."

"But you don't think she will, do you? Perhaps we should cut that one off at the bend, sort of act in the early part of the time frame. What do you think of offering this woman something? Hanging it in front of her like a carrot."

"I think we'd be putting ideas in her head."

"I think you're right, although I'd rather be more secure in this matter. I've never seen my granddaughter."

Cutler asked about the prospects of the Fleish charges, and Bressio was surprised at the rustiness of Cutler's criminal law.

"That would be double indemnity if they tried him again, because while those two charges are worded differently, they're really the same. They can't try a guy twice for the same crime, as you know."

"Of course. Of course. You know, you'll forget a lot of basic law, too, if you don't practice it. We just never had to use much of it in the important work in Washington. It was mainly knowing how Washington worked. Now if Fleish were involved in an antitrust action, ah, Mr. Bressio, then I'd be of a little more help."

Cutler also had questions about Dawson, starting with why he defended Fleish and then what made Dawson tick.

"God knows," said Bressio.

"Do you like Dawson?"

"Yes. I guess I do. Very much."

"I must admit a certain admiration for him myself. I always entertained a desire to practice criminal law, but I could never afford it."

"Dawson must clear upwards of $200,000 before his ex-wives could get to it."

"Hmmm. Yes. Couldn't afford it. Tell me, why didn't he put up bail himself instead of going through all the machinations to get it from me? I'm sure his time is more valuable than that. And if he trusted the client, he'd get it back. He's already devoting thousands more in free time for Fleish."

"You can't put up bail for a client. The bar association has it arranged to make it unethical, actionable before it, as a matter of fact."

"Hmmm. What's the logic behind that, as if I didn't suspect."

"Well, it's to save the lawyers telling clients no. Actually, they have given other reasons, but that's the real one."

"I thought so. What are the chances of Mary Beth waiting for Fleish to get out of jail and then returning to him?"

"If we get a few years, as I suspect we will, that time can be used in trying to help Mary Beth make a new life for herself. It's a chance, Mr. Cutler."

"A lot better than we had before. I can't even talk to her now. I haven't been able to talk to her for years, and when she had that baby out of wedlock, I—"

"It's not the kind of social stigma it used to be, sir."

"Would you marry her, Mr. Bressio?"

"Sir?"

"Would you marry someone like Mary Beth, knowing she gave birth to an illegitimate child?"

"I would marry someone I loved. I don't love her."

"Could you love someone like Mary Beth?"

Bressio felt his stomach tighten and his mouth go dry.

"You don't have to answer that, Mr. Bressio. The drugs, the goddamned drugs," said Cutler. He put his right fist silently into his left hand. "The drugs. They're a disease that must be smashed. People just don't understand, they don't understand how dangerous, how insidious they are, all under the guise of raising one's consciousness, instant happiness."

"On that you won't get an argument from me." Bressio rubbed the slight cut he received on his left hand when it scraped the Eldorado window pulling Willie Knuckles through it.

Cutler saw it, and Bressio suddenly discovered where all the secretaries were. Cutler's came in from a side door. Then Bressio saw a hallway, and realized that was the front door of Mitchell, Walker and Cutler. He had come in through the back door.

The secretary, a dowdy-looking biddy, applied first aid in the form of an unguent and dainty bandage. When she had gone, Bressio held up the cut hand.

"The cool house I told you about is slightly cooler than I

thought. Some small fry are sniffing around. Heroin will do it every time. That stuff is more liquid than money. Bad news."

"But it's under police protection. It's the bait in a trap, isn't it?"

"If I may ask, who will police the police? When heroin is stored as evidence in police headquarters, it walks. What about in a house? It's basic economics. If too much money is too easy to get at, people are going to take it even if you put a badge on their chests and call them something else."

"But this hasn't happened to cash evidence and stock evidence, if I'm correct."

"Money and stocks have numbers on them. They can be traced. Besides, you can't break them down. You can't make a thousand-dollar bill into two thousand dollars of five-dollar bills, but you can with pure heroin, and who's to say where it came from. You don't seem to understand, Mr. Cutler, that heroin is lighter and more valuable than gold, more stable than money, and less traceable than even broken-up jewelry—broken up meaning the stones sold separately.

"You can move a quarter of a million dollars of heroin in a woman's pocketbook if the heroin is pure enough. Did you know that? Now, you can do that with money, but only thousand-dollar bills with those cute little serial numbers on them, and try cashing a thousand-dollar bill sometime. You can do it with one big jewel, but try breaking a ruby down and it loses value.

"You take your cop on the beat. Or your narco detective, even the glorious young FBNC. They make a bust, they can always keep large quantities of the smack. The pusher isn't going to complain. It's grief for him when he gets into court, but let's say the bust is for a bank robbery. Well, the bank knows how much it's lost, and the sentences don't run heavier for a hundred thousand dollars than for fifty thousand—both of them being well into grand larceny —so the guy charged won't have any qualms about screaming that the arresting officer is a thief, too.

"But let's get back to our deadly little friend, heroin. Not only will the pusher not scream, but just for a little insurance toward that fact, the arresting officer will leave out some information so it's hanging there as a threat for quiet. He makes the collar less effective."

"Hmmm," said Cutler. "But I've seen news of massive heroin

arrests on television. They announce they capture a million dollars' worth of heroin here, a million there, a half million, one and a half million—rather substantial amounts, if you will."

"A. There are some honest cops. B. You don't know how much they find, only how much is left. And C. Look at the conviction rates on those big hauls. A lot of top people walk away from them."

"Hmmm. More insidious than I thought."

"It's weird stuff, Mr. Cutler. They just don't know how to handle it yet. Literally. They know how to handle money, but they don't know how to handle heroin."

Cutler thought a moment and then the fist went silently into the hand again. "What if the house on Pren Street is incredibly cool, so to speak? What if this new agency has decided to make the house a contact point for an incredibly big stash—let's say the results of several busts, as you call them. Draw out the major dealers. Spread the word of this massive amount. Draw them into a confrontation of major proportions, and in one blow, deal the heroin industry a setback it has never known. Sort of bring the pushers into a large-scale engagement instead of this guerrilla warfare thing that's going on now. Put some spit into the fight, so to speak."

"If I may say so, sir, that's an incredibly bad idea. For one, no established narcotics agency is going to risk it. They know heroin. For two, maybe this new FBNC might think of trying it, but it's got some men from the other agencies, I hear, and they'd be climbing the wall if they ever heard of anything so, well, so stupid."

"I don't understand."

"You put so much smack in any one place, you are guaranteed of men with money coming after it. That money which is a tool could wreck a whole department—guaranteed. There'd be so much money coming after that from so many sources it could probably take apart the FBI, which—I might add, sir—Hoover wisely kept out of that stuff when he could have gotten in."

"The government has done less wise things that somehow work out when it perseveres. I was Under Secretary of State for several years. I know."

"Well," said Bressio, "if there should be something as silly as this going on, I'd know about it. First of all, you'd see the family's structure start cracking at the seams as some people out of the territory went for it and others didn't. You'd see guys coming in from all over, and in an unrestricted market like that, you'd see a good many of them turning up as bodies."

"There was a shooting just a short while ago, in East Harlem, described as a gangland slaying."

"I know about that one. Nothing to do with narcotics."

"And that cut on your hand, did that come from someone in the Pren Street territory? I think it's territory, I don't know how you people divide up the city."

"Sir, I haven't divided anything into any territory."

"I'm sorry. You just spoke so knowledgeably that I thought . . . well, let me extend my apologies, Mr. Bressio."

Bressio signified with his hands that the remark was nothing, but his stomach gave him other signals, and they hurt to his very soul.

"To wrap this thing up, sir, the altercation was with someone from the Bronx, but he is such a small fry that I guarantee he was on a small errand. If there were anything big, he'd be squished like a grape. It would be out of his league, and I know these things because I was brought up in that shit. And I'm not a part of it."

"Yes. I know. And I am truly sorry I said 'you people'! There must be thousands of Italian-Americans who cringe every time someone with a vowel is shown to be Mafia."

"Millions."

The pain in Bressio's soul only eased when Cutler showed him to the front door. "Please don't use the back door again, Mr. Bressio. That's for secretaries and clerks and deliveries and I imagine for some of the younger lawyers. It's not for you."

"Doesn't make any difference to me, Mr. Cutler."

"The name's Jim, Al," said Cutler and he showed him through the front office, introducing him to Mitchell, a balding man with a hefty paunch who pointed out that the serious work of the firm was being done in Washington.

"This is just where we hang our hats when we're in New York City," said Mitchell.

"Very impressive," said Bressio.

"I hear you work with Murray Blay Dawson. Must be exciting," said Mitchell.

"Very exciting at times, sir. Yes."

"The glamour of the law," said Mitchell, chuckling.

"Sometimes," said Bressio.

"Often thought, although it would never happen, that I'd like to go head-to-head with a Murray Blay Dawson."

"Oh, I don't really think you'd want to do that, Mr. Mitchell," said Bressio.

"He might be right," said Cutler. "The intricacy and common sense of their strategy in a case I just heard about was rather impressive."

"You're rather impressive yourself, Jim," said Mitchell.

"I guess he didn't tell you, Mr. Bressio, but he was the one who got the health warnings on cigarettes."

"Don't go boasting around," said Cutler, chiding.

Bressio felt a tug on his arm. "I guess that was a good thing, but I don't see as how the health warnings really changes things very much," he said.

Cutler tried to guide Bressio out of the office, but Mitchell was launched. "My god, man," said Mitchell, shocked. "Without the concession of that meaningless little sign on the packs, we wouldn't have had a year more of television advertising, all advertising might have been outlawed, and—who knows?—it might have been another Prohibition situation. There was strong talk after that lung-cancer link of outlawing cigarettes. The whole industry faced disaster. That minor concession saved an industry, sir. An entire industry."

"We do some other things besides little packs of cigarettes," said Cutler, and with a hand at Bressio's elbow, guided him to the front door of Mitchell's office.

"Sales weren't even hurt in the long run," Mitchell yelled after them. "Go downstairs to the stock exchange across the street, and take a look at P. Lorillard and American Tobacco, if you think I'm exaggerating."

"The cigarette thing was not one of our prouder moments," Cutler confided. "But we had them as clients, and you know what a lawyer must do for his client. I was even a bit saddened at the poor showing of our opposition. I do not smoke and I do not think cigarettes are good things."

"Yeah, well—" said Bressio, and he was shown an empty office with a stately desk and stately chairs and empty white painted shelves.

"If you want to work out of here, Al, I'd be glad to have you."

Bressio was dumbfounded. Was that an offer of a job he had just heard? He answered more in shock than in a desire to refuse.

"Thank you for the offer, but I have to work out of my own office. It's sort of plugged in to all my sources, and I just can't afford to be away from where they know they can leave a message, Mr. Cutler."

"Jim."

"Yeah, Jim," said Bressio, and looking at his watch noted he had to rush to catch a plane to Phoenix.

XII

As Bressio's plane took off for Phoenix, Willie Knuckles, his head bandaged, his ears ringing, was directing his brother-in-law in the unloading of his golf clubs from his car on Bathgate Avenue in the Bronx when a sniper across the street sent a 30–30 slug through Willie Knuckles' brain, some of which clotted on the sweet spot of his Maxfli pitching wedge. The brother-in-law dove under the car. This was only the first killing among people maneuvering for what was in the house on Pren Street.

Sally Bugellerio, Bressio's second cousin, later that night, slipped under the wheels of an Uptown F train at the isolated Fourteenth Street station. Helping him slip were Johnny Tomasino and Alfiere (Al Donnelly) Donelle of Brooklyn, who kept pleading for cooperation as the F train roared in: "C'mon, Sally, you know you're gonna get it."

Tomasino joined Willie Knuckles and Sally Bugellerio the next day when he started his car and got a face full of engine parts and shreds of fire wall.

The *Daily News* screamed of gang war. The *New York Post,* which had lost the news break on Willie Knuckles and Sally Bugellerio to the morning *News,* but had a Tomasino exclusive, ran a sidebar on the meaning of the gang war, tying it in to every professional-style hit in the last two years.

"Silly, silly, silly," said Don Carmine, who normally read only the business section of *The New York Times* and the *Wall Street Journal.* He sipped coffee and ate buns with his friend and adviser,

Felli, in his Brooklyn apartment. "The world is run by fools. Fools. I am convinced of this."

"Does Bressio know? Is it possible he still does not know about Pren Street?"

"I do not see how," said Don Carmine.

"Perhaps his new associates on Wall Street have gotten to his head. Perhaps he thinks he is bulletproof? He worked over that Bronx nobody for no apparent reason, unless . . ."

"He did not kill that man, I am led to believe."

"If he is not involved in this silliness, then he is acting like some Calabrese," said Felli, using a Sicillian appellation of dim-witted, a reference to the people of Calabria, whose appellation "Siciliano" had connotations of untrustworthy and vicious.

"Perhaps, but he is not the biggest fool in this thing," said Don Carmine, who had a distaste for disorder that would shame Queen Victoria. "It is the narcotics people. Why do they not run their business properly? Why must they engage in such . . . such . . . silliness."

"It comes from Washington, I am told."

"And who tells Washington?" said Don Carmine. "Has Washington lost its senses? Has Alphonse lost his senses? I do not know."

In Mitchell, Walker and Cutler, Hedding "Puff" Mitchell looked in on his partner, who appeared to be in better spirits day by day. "How are you feeling today, Jim?"

"Much better. Much better, Puff."

"Things working out well with Mary Beth?"

"Much better. Much better."

"Say, Jim, I just happened to glance at the *Daily News,* I don't read it regularly, of course, but today I happened to glance at it and the Mafiosi seem to be going at it again. I was wondering if that fellow you have working for you now, Bissio, knows what it all means."

"Bressio."

"What does this fellow Bressio say about it?"

"He says don't believe what you read in the papers."

Mitchell thought a moment. "Say, I wonder if we can all have dinner at the club some evening?"

"I doubt it. Bressio is a loner."

"Well, if we can't have dinner, maybe he can work over the Securities Exchange for me," said Mitchell, chuckling at his own witticism.

"He may be a lawyer, Puff, if he gets over the bar. Many good men have trouble with the bar, some psychological hangup. I think that's what he wants."

"That's nice," said Mitchell. "Get them into law, maybe they'll stop littering the streets with their kin, eh?"

"We'd be lucky if one of those little sweethearts we siphon out of Harvard Law knew half the practical law of an Al Bressio," said Cutler.

"Sure, Jim. Sure. Can't judge a book by its cover. There's good and bad in all people. Michelangelo was Italian, wasn't he?"

"Yes, but they let him do the Sistine Chapel anyway, Puff."

"I see you're back in your same hostile form, Jim. Going back to Washington for some real work?"

"No," said Cutler.

"Oh, I thought you were working again, by all those Washington phone calls out of your private line."

"Go back to your *Daily News,* Puff."

"I don't read it regularly, just when the firm happens to have some possible interest," said Mitchell. "Maybe next week we'll be connected to porno houses."

"Then you'll have an excuse to read *Screw,* Puff."

"How do you know about *Screw?* Do you read it too?"

"No," said Cutler, wounding his partner, who when he returned to his private office phoned his wife to repeat what his great-grandfather had said about the Irish. "You can take the Irish out of Ireland, but you can't take the Irish out of the Irish."

"Jim Cutler push you around again, dear?" said his wife.

Mary Beth Cutler refused to lie on Dr. Finney's couch.

"Nothing personal against you, darling, but I don't know who's been lying on it before me, if you know what I mean."

"Does that bother you?"

"Oh, no. You know what bothers me. Al's told you, hasn't he?"

"You tell me."

"Well, today the strangest thing happened to me, and I'll get to the real good stuff later. Today I was in Little Italy with Bobbi, shopping, and these people started smiling at me. But not just there. That was where it started. Almost everywhere I go there's always someone who looks at me and smiles and nods and sometimes these men offer to carry my packages."

"Who are these people?"

"Well, first of all, they're all men and ..."

For the second time that day, Clarissa Duffy told the funny-sounding man that Al Bressio was out of town.

"Yes, he got your message. Now leaving him alone. You people leave him alone."

When Bressio checked in by long distance from a Phoenix motel room, Clarissa forgot about the messages when she heard that special tone in his voice, that guilty-as-fucking-sin tone. Oh, did she know that one.

"Everything is all right up here, Al. Fine ... No, nothing wrong with me ... No, I'm not mad. Why should I be mad? Bored maybe, sick of working for you maybe. Disgusted with you for being so incredibly stupid, but mad—no, Al, I'm not mad. ... What makes you think I think you met some stewardess on the plane? If an airline stewardess is your speed, Al Bressio, I hope you're happy. Enjoy your airline stewardess ... I didn't say you were having another one-nighter. I merely said forget it. When will you be back? ... No. No messages."

XIII

It was the grease for the hinge of the scales of justice. A thousand years of Anglo-Saxon common law, enlightened with older Judeo-Christian thought and influenced to a small degree by the legal order of the great Roman Empire—all of this came down to a brief haggle in Arizona and the grist for character assassination in Iowa.

And while it was not the kind of work Bressio liked, it was the kind he was very good at. When he saw the prosecutor's office in Phoenix, he knew there was no question of a plea bargain. He could get one. It was he who held the threat of trial, and all the concepts of due process were reduced to the reality of case overload.

The first indication was the prosecutor saying he had exactly half an hour to see Fleish's representative. He was on the phone when Bressio entered. The office was a neat air-conditioned cell stacked high with papers on the desk, a long table against the wall, and three of the four chairs. The fourth held a suit jacket. The prosecutor, a gaunt, balding man in his early forties with rolled-up shirt sleeves and loosened tie, nodded to the chair and with a twist of his head indicated the jacket should be thrown on the long table over the manilla folders. His name was James Andress.

"No," he said into the phone, waving Bressio to feel free to do what his head had indicated. "No. And don't phone again. The answer is no . . . Sure I'd like to discuss it, but I'd like to have time to sleep and breathe, too . . . No. That's final. Goodbye. Don't phone again." The prosecutor hung up.

"You're A. Bressio and you work for Murray Blay Dawson, correct? Sit down. Throw the coat anywhere."

Bressio folded the coat over what appeared to be the most balanced pile of folders. Then he sat down. Andress was impatiently drumming his fingers on a bare spot on his desk.

"I'm here about the Fleish case, as you have been informed. Mr. Fleish has been arrested and charged with—"

"I know. I know. I know. What do you want?"

"Possession simple."

"He had a trunkload of pot in his car. That's more than personal use. That's intent to sell."

"But, Mr. Andress, the state trooper didn't have a search warrant."

"He had probable cause."

"You say he had probable cause, and we say he didn't."

"A year," said Andress. "With intent to sell."

"He's a first offender."

"We hear he's got another indictment hanging."

"Hanging is not a conviction. It's all a question of where we're going to deal and where we're going to fight."

"I hear it's a federal charge. U.S. Attorney's office. They don't deal too easily."

"He's a first offender. Are you telling me we should take his first offense for leniency to the federal courts and fight you here?"

"Okay. You're in luck. His co-defendant yesterday made an attempt to break jail. I like that charge better. He's a real bad-ass, three-time loser, and this Fleish fellow is no pro, from what I gather. I'll give you the benefit of the doubt. Six months and a year suspended."

"Possession, and thirty days," said Bressio.

"That was a trunkload of marijuana."

"It may be inadmissible."

"And it may be admissible. That was a trunkload of marijuana. What do you want from me, Mr. Bressio? I didn't put it there. You don't smoke a trunkload. A year suspended is all I can give you."

"I don't want a felony. Can't use it. No way."

"If that trunkload of marijuana holds up, he's doing five, I promise that, Mr. Bressio."

"A year suspended for possession simple or we go to court. Otherwise you're giving us nothing."

"Okay. A year suspended on possession. You're lucky his accomplice made that attempted break and we can put that bowser away for good. Otherwise I couldn't give you possession simple."

"*Consumatum est.* Done," said Bressio, and as they shook hands, the phone rang. Bressio got a cab to the airport and thought about such things as a man being innocent until proven guilty, a man's right not to be forced to testify against himself, his right to face his accusers, and all the other rights learned painfully through centuries of human mistakes. And it all came down to a busy prosecutor who would lower a charge and let a judge know that the state thought a year suspended was adequate punishment. One did not need a Harlan Fiske Stone or the Supreme Court for that. This kind of law Bennie the fence back in Brooklyn could practice.

Bressio was in Des Moines by 3:45 P.M. If plea-bargaining was unpleasant for him, this was downright gruesome. And at this, it was said he was an artist.

It was not exactly character assassination. It was simply the gathering of testimony or other evidence that when introduced into court before judge and jury would make anyone in their eyes seem less reputable and hence diminish the testimony of that person, make it less weighty if not downright inconsequential.

In all his years, Bressio had not found anyone against whom some convincing person or evidence could not make seem dishonest.

He who steals my purse steals trash, but he who steals my good name . . .

Bressio put that thought out of his mind and got a cab from the airport to Pruscott College. Some investigators would unearth heaps of garbage about a person's past, some of which might be admissible. They tended to confuse gossip with evidence, morality with law. Bressio was known to produce evidence both effective and admissible from the most fragmentary material. He knew his law.

Calvin Loring, Fleish's accomplice in the second arrest, appeared from the thumbnail sketch Dawson had given Bressio to be the perfect all-American boy. He was nineteen years old, of farmer stock, a pre-med student at the college. According to the U.S. Attorney's office, Loring had no previous criminal record.

Dawson, in a conversation by phone just before Bressio's plane departed, called Loring "Andy Hardy, the bastard. He's going to kill us if he shows up with those pink cheeks of his."

"Don't worry," Bressio had said. "He's human."

"He's not fucking human, Al. The sonuvabitch was Four-H, Christian Youth, a Freedom Foundation winner for some article I got here on responsibility being the cornerstone of freedom. We can't let our boy genius go into a conspiracy trial with a guy that clean. They'll convict on impairing the morals of a saint without ever charging him with it. I've seen it happen before, even without a jury, and I want to use a jury on this one because basically our case is a pile of neatly packaged shit. You gotta do a job on Andy Hardy."

"It'll be done, Murray. It's a nice way to learn how to hate yourself, too."

"Hate, shmate. We got nothing else. By the way, I laid the law down to boy genius. No more Mary Beth, Okay?"

"Okay," Bressio had said. "Good. In fact, good."

Who steals my purse steals trash, but he who steals my good name steals . . .

Bressio got a Pruscott catalog and a map from the administration building, a red brick and aluminum structure that was an exact replica of a sewage disposal plant Bressio had once seen on Long Island. He went to the student union, another lifeless brick structure, and phoned back to the administration building. He knew the effect his appearance had on people even when he wasn't carrying a weapon. His voice didn't frighten.

He was looking for an old friend who went to Pruscott, a pre-med student, Cal Loring. Would the operator be so kind as to help him? After several transfers, a secretary of the dean of students told him that Loring lived at Fayerweather Hall. Bressio said Loring might not be there now, could she give him Loring's class schedule. As he listened, he opened the catalog and began marking. Loring was taking five courses: Chemistry 301, Biology 417, and World Civilization 2, which included the Laws, History, and Arts of Mankind.

Bressio phoned the chemistry professor and got a pleasant, efficient-sounding secretary who told him information on a student's activities would have to be cleared through the dean of students. A good secretary bucking the situation away from her boss. Arts of Mankind was the same. And no one answered at Biology. But at History, Bressio got what he wanted.

"I'm awfully sorry, but I'm busy. You just can't call up and expect that sort of information like that. I mean, who do you think you are? There's enough work here for five girls. Hold on . . . Yes, are you still there? The answer is no."

Bressio located the History building on the campus map and strolled over. If he had more time he might have made a broad vacuum-cleaner-type approach to Loring, one that explored many possibilities. But he did not have the time, so he would have to penetrate, following any opening offered. He didn't have to make Loring appear like Al Capone. He just needed enough to drag him down to the human race.

A grieved secretary was always a good beginning. This one was in her early forties with graying hair curled in a style of twenty years before. Her face was tense and puffy, and she moved hectically, like energy in conflict.

She looked up at Bressio, who saw the trace of fear in her eyes that ordinarily would make him feel bad.

"Did I frighten you? I'm sorry," said Bressio.

"Oh, no. You didn't frighten me. What do you want?" The voice carried the flattened twang of Iowa.

"I came to apologize. I . . . I phoned earlier," said Bressio softly. "And I guess I was out of place asking all those questions seeing how busy and, well, frankly, overworked you are."

"That's all right. Everything is crazy around here. No apologies needed. I should apologize to you. I guess I was abrupt."

"Who wouldn't be?" said Bressio in a most sympathetic voice. "I can't seem to find a thing around this campus. The people around here seem to believe that the students and professors are some sort of angels, saints—gods if you will. Not like us ordinary people."

"You spotted it right away, didn't you?"

"How could I miss? At first I thought it was because I came from New York and I talk funny. But as I looked around, I began to see they look down on everyone who isn't part of their special clique. Many people think the students are angels, but they're not. Some of the students are downright dangerous, and no one around here seems to appreciate that fact."

"You can say that again," said the woman, her curled hair

bobbing in righteous agreement. "You're the man who phoned about the student, right?"

Bressio nodded like a good little boy.

"I'd like to help you, but it's probably against one of their rules."

"Oh, I wouldn't want you to break a rule," said Bressio. Delighted to hear it was one of "their" rules and not one of "our" rules, Bressio leaned over her desk, glanced around to make sure no one was listening, and in a hushed conspiratorial tone revealed he was on a legal investigation.

"We suspect some very serious things about one of your students, Calvin Loring." Bressio gave her one of his cards with the neat lettering, the law degree and the New York City address. It did not call him attorney-at-law, but for this woman it made no difference.

"What did he do?" asked the secretary.

Bressio could see the spark of joy in her eyes. He hesitated, appearing to wrestle with the decision of disclosing his mission. "Calvin Loring has been arrested in New York City. I don't know if I should tell you . . . Ah, to hell with it. Calvin Loring has been arrested for conspiracy. Drugs."

"Conspiracy. That's awful," said the secretary, whose day—possibly week—had just been made into something more alive.

"We just want some background on his grades and professors. Nothing confidential. Nothing that isn't public record. I guess I'll be here a week until someone can find a record around here. I guess I shouldn't say it, but the administration here is rather short on competence."

"Short? There isn't a pointy head in this place that could park a car straight," said the secretary. And did she show that surprisingly nice man from New York City. She showed what one competent secretary could do in ten minutes. Without any fancy degrees. Just a good simple basic high school education and some plain old common sense. By phoning secretaries who worked in other departments, she learned that Loring had a C+ average across the board, with an A in World Civilization, but a very significant C in biology.

"Would have taken you two weeks to a month by the system they have here put together by all those pointy heads," said the secretary proudly. But Bressio only pretended to be listening. He was already hearing Dawson cross-examine Loring. *"You say, Mr. Loring, that you intended to go to medical school. But your average is C+. Would you please tell the jury what medical school you intended to be accepted at with a C+ average?"*

"Well, I sort of planned on improving my grades."

"You planned on improving your grades ... Isn't it true, Mr. Loring, that no medical school would take you with your current average?"

"Well, you see—"

"Yes or no, Mr. Loring?"

"No."

"Then it's a lie, isn't it, Mr. Loring? You have a lot of people believing you're going to be something you're not. How many people have you used like that before, deceiving them into thinking you're just some sweet little innocent ... All right, your honor, I withdraw the question. Let me rephrase it."

It would not be enough to shatter Loring, but it would do as an opening wedge. Bressio expressed amazement that one secretary with a few phone calls could do more than an entire administration with doctorates. He had to give her something for her troubles. Yes. Don't say no. He wouldn't hear of it. It would have cost him a week's wait and hundreds of dollars in time to get what she had gotten.

Well, if he insisted. A fifty-dollar bill? She couldn't take that. Why, that was half a week's salary right there.

Bressio listened to how little they paid her and explained his problem further. He insisted also that she put the money in her purse immediately. That's the least she could do for being so helpful.

"You sit right down. I'll really show you something. It's drugs you're interested in, right?" said the secretary.

She phoned a friend in administration, a luncheon companion at World Civilization, a cook at the student union. Did she show Bressio!

According to the grapevine, Calvin Loring wasn't one of the big users, but he was one of the fellows who hung around Rebecca Hawkins, who was. Becky Hawkins had contacts all over the country, it was said, and what was worse she lived with a professor,

William Winstead, at 47 Clover Lane, although no one could prove anything.

"The drugs?"

"No, the sex," said the secretary.

Bressio insisted she take another fifty. This time there was no fight.

If she worked where stocks changed hands or in a trucking terminal where goods were shipped and some of the people back in New York knew her nature, this woman would be owned. They would get her addicted to an extra income, and then she would go looking for them with information. It had happened so many times.

Bressio remembered hearing an uncle laugh about a young cop. "He comesa arounda now. Heh-heh. You see hisa face. Heh-heh. Now we cut him off ana wait for something good. You see. He finda it. You no thinka that funny, Alphonsey? You funny kid."

Bressio listened to the secretary's last complaint about her job and could not tell her how lucky she was that no one wanted to own her.

Who steals my name . . .

Forty-seven Clover Lane was a modest little bungalow of a house with a white picket fence, mowed grass and green flower boxes in the window, the kind of house Bressio once thought all Americans outside of New York City lived in until his father took him to Troy, New York, a gray slum of a Hudson River town. Bressio found out later in his teens that Troy was the layoff center for the East, and his father was not taking him on a summer vacation but using him as a gesture to show the people in the area he was not there on business. The morning after they left, a tavern owner was found with four bullets in his head on the floor of his car parked on River Street. Bressio's father had been fond of extolling the use of the commonplace.

Bressio knocked on the door, expecting a breath of fresh rusticity. What he got was Greenwich Village. A thin man in his mid-thirties with an Indian headband around his long brown stringy hair blinked into the sunlight. Brightly colored love beads bobbed to the oversized buckle on his faded and patched blue jeans. He wore sandals and his feet needed washing.

"Peace," he said.

"William Winstead?" asked Bressio.

"All of me."

"I'm a representative of a lawyer involved in the Calvin Loring case," said Bressio, which was technically correct, since Fleish and Loring were both on the same charge of conspiracy.

"Case?"

"Loring has been arrested in New York."

"Bad," said Professor Winstead. He nodded Bressio inside.

The living room was a flowery-old-lady sort of dwelling with rosebud covers over the sofa and chairs and knitted antimacassars set like a desperate defense over those portions of furniture that would encounter hair or arms.

"Becky, Cal's been busted in the Big Apple," yelled Winstead.

"Oh, no. Just a minute. Damn." The voice was young and fresh and hostile. Becky Hawkins appeared in the kitchen doorway and demanded to know, pointing at Bressio, "Who's he?"

She was barely plump with last baby fat, a rather attractive young woman with fresh red cheeks, clear blue eyes and long sandy hair. A thin, faded blue T-shirt enticingly covered her rather large young breasts and her blue jeans bulged with a fresh hello.

"He's a representative of Calvin's New York lawyer."

"Let's see your identification," said Becky.

"I have a card," said Bressio, giving her one of the cards he had given the secretary in Physics.

"You a lawyer?"

"No."

"You represent Calvin Loring?"

"No. I represent the lawyer who represents a party charged with Calvin in a marijuana situation."

"What's the charge?"

"Conspiracy."

"So they're not exactly on the same side," said Miss Becky Hawkins. "Will, go upstairs and turn on or something."

"But Becky, honey."

"Get out of here, Will."

"You can be a mean down bitch, Becky," said Professor Winstead.

"Move it."

Becky Hawkins plopped into a sofa and motioned Bressio to the overstuffed cushion next to her. Bressio sat a good arm's length away from her.

"Was Loring caught with anything?"

"Fifty-five pounds of Acapulco gold," said Bressio, watching her eyes closely.

"Does he have a lawyer?"

"I believe a public defender. I'm not sure."

"And you represent Fleish, Fleish is his name?"

"L. Marvin Fleish."

"Uh-huh. And you're out here to do what?"

"You know what I'm here for, Miss Hawkins."

"For dirt on Loring, right?"

"Pretty much."

"And you want me to hand him up, right?"

"And you will," said Bressio.

"Oh, really now. I'm going to hand up a boyfriend just because you come to Pruscott with that tough Mafia face to tell me so. Really."

"No. You're going to hand up Loring before he hands you up as the engineer of the deal."

"You have something?" asked Miss Hawkins with contemptful curiosity.

"The U.S. Attorney's office will if it doesn't already. People feel pretty lonely without good counsel. Or maybe Loring tried to reach you and couldn't. Or maybe many things. But little old Calvin Loring got busted all alone in the big city, and he didn't reach the person behind it. Why? And do you think the U.S. Attorney's office is going to stop with a little messenger like Loring? Think about all these things, Miss Hawkins."

"You're fishing in the dark."

"Not at all. You deal on campus. I know that. You know Loring. And you were very concerned with what he was caught with, as though you had a big investment. You didn't seem all that bothered with his plight. I wish you could have seen your eyes when I said fifty-five pounds of Acapulco gold. They were something, Miss Hawkins. And you yourself told me you didn't know whether he had a lawyer, which means, as you know, Calvin is feeling very much alone right now."

"And you know and I know, ugly face, you can't prove it."

"I'm not the one who's a danger to you, Miss Hawkins. But let's say I get a deposition from you and you come to New York City to testify that Mr. Loring was a heavy drug user, dealt in all sorts of drugs, big, and then he turns around and names you, there isn't much of a case against you."

Becky Hawkins wiggled a scrubbed forefinger signaling she wanted to hear more.

"Of your own volition. Why, any good lawyer could show any Loring accusation was just his attempt to discredit your testimony, that is, *if* your deposition gets in first, and is followed by your testimony in court. Wowee. You're clean."

"What if Loring's lawyers move against me? Send someone like you out here to find out things about me?"

"He has a public defender, Miss Hawkins."

"Are they like they are here?"

"It makes you want to vomit to watch them work."

"Hmmmm. Who's the prosecutor?"

"U.S. Attorney's office. They're good."

"They're good enough to have the FBI or someone check me out real heavy here."

"It would be the FBNC, but I might add, Miss Hawkins, they don't have any special love for Loring or hate for Fleish. I don't think there would be all that much reason to. But consider this: If someone kind enough to testify for his client got into trouble with the law because of it"—Bressio paused to give a stage of silence before the magic words—"Murray Blay Dawson would defend her."

"Spit and damnation. Murray Blay Dawson? The guy in the magazines? The guy who wrote the book? The lawyer who appears on these night shows? That one?"

"That one," said Bressio.

"Fleish must be a rich sonuvabitch, huh?"

Bressio smiled. After all, why tell a lie now?

"Dawson was married three times, wasn't he?"

"Five."

"He's a sexy-looking stud. Does he look that way in real life?"

"Better," said Bressio, with the mental reservation that Dawson in person didn't look as phony as he did on television.

"The Big Apple. I wonder if I could afford the airfare?"

Bressio assured her that would be taken care of. Another good point was that if the inconceivable happened, a first offender as Becky was, with Dawson behind her, would only get a suspended.

"And I'm nineteen, too," said Becky. "They don't put you into the slammer if you're white, nineteen on a first offense. I wouldn't even need someone like Murray Blay Dawson for something like that. What sort of a house does he live in?"

"Houses," said Bressio, checking his watch to see how much time he had to while away until his evening flight to New York City. He had made three reservations just in case he would find two like Becky Hawkins. He didn't need another.

XIV

When Murray Blay Dawson saw the blossoming young girl in the print dress, he crossed his legs and focused intently on Bressio. He brought in famous cases to explain the Fleish situation. Bressio tried to catch Dawson's attention while Dawson was staring at him, but to no avail. Bressio glanced at the girl, looked directly into Dawson's eyes and shook his head, signifying "no, no."

Dawson, oblivious, continued on his tack. Yes, this reminded him of a similar problem they had with Dr. Dorsted and the killing of his wife, and the killing of those people in San Diego. The problem of which trial to attempt first. There was a difference in the Dorsted case. The first acquittal couldn't help but influence the second trial because of all the national publicity. You just couldn't escape the cameras sometimes. They seemed to pop out of the walls. But Dawson was boring Miss Hawkins with all this talk, wasn't he?

"Not at all. Not at all," said Becky.

"You're boring me, Murray. Can we talk alone?"

"Certainly. I just didn't want Miss Hawkins to think there was anything mysterious about some Park Avenue law firm."

With gracious courtliness Dawson explained to Becky Hawkins that Al Bressio was not only someone he hired, but a friend, too. The more famous a person gets the more he realizes how valuable real friendship is.

"That's so true," said Becky Hawkins.

"C'mon. C'mon," said Bressio impatiently. When Becky's fresh bouncy duff was on the other side of the door, Bressio gently grabbed Dawson's ears like a schoolboy. "Hey, Murray. Stop the nonsense."

"What are you talking about?" asked Dawson, appearing surprised.

"Becky Hawkins. You don't want to mess with her."

"Me, with a kid I'm going to use as a witness, and Bobo on a jealousy kick again and Bobo the only woman I've ever been able to live with? What do you take me for, Al?"

"I know you, Murray. I'm running over half the country for one of your peculiarities. So don't use illogical as a defense, especially when it comes to broads."

"I'm a middle-aged man, Al. She's just a kid."

"At least don't marry her."

"Al, I can look after myself. What's with Fleish?"

"We got a year suspended possession simple, and best of all, no trial date."

The Dawson mind began to churn. A little smile formed. "If we get the New York charge into trial right away with a guaranteed year suspended at the other end, I am thinking that you are a very beautiful person, Alphonse Bressio."

"And Becky Hawkins has got a tale of woe to tell you how Loring is the big pusher on campus, perhaps even the boy who started poor little her. She's gonna dump on Andy Hardy so heavy he'll never surface. Our little pre-med, by the way, has a C+ average."

Dawson examined his nails. "Al, if you get out of this end of the law, it's a crime against genius. You know what we have? A client we made into a first offender after pleading guilty on what could have been—should have been—two felony charges. It's like striking out in baseball and working the averages so it doesn't show as a time at bat. Al, I don't know what to say. We might get him off with three, maybe four months, when he should be doing five to fifteen years. You know, we might, if the U.S. Attorney's office gets just a little bit lazy—"

"Stop dreaming, Murray. They're not getting lazy with you as counsel."

"Yeah. I suppose so, but there's a little play here. Wowee. I feel young again. Bring on that little broad."

"The curse of L. Marvin is upon you. I am clean, over, and moving on."

"By all means, Al. And thanks. Thanks, really. I appreciate what you've done. By the way, there's a mob war on since you left."

"Who says?"

"The papers."

"Oh. Hey, I'm dealing expenses through Cutler now, but we're holding you to keeping L. Marvin away from Mary Beth. That's the price."

"You don't seem very impressed by mob wars."

"I am. I'm not impressed by newspaper accounts."

"Another distant relative got it, a Bugellerio."

"Oh, really, which one?"

"Salvatore."

"That's too bad. Don't forget the deal, okay?"

"And a guy named Tomalino."

"Might be some sort of thing. Watch your step with Hawkins. She is not nice."

"And a Rugerrio Posolimo, alias Willie Knuckles."

"Oh, Jesus Christ Almighty," said Bressio slapping his forehead. "Holy Mary, Mother of God."

"What's the matter, Al?"

Dawson had known Bressio was supposed to be fast, but he was shocked at the speed with which the incredible chunk of a man fled his office. Who was Posolimo to him? Well, no matter. Dawson would never fully understand Bressio, his confusion of loyalties and principles that ran searingly deep.

But he was right, very right about playing around with a young girl who might possibly be the witness who could show Marvin Fleish was an innocent bystander, practically, dragged into this affair by the cunning of that master pusher, Calvin Loring. That was still a guilty plea. There had to be a not guilty in there somewhere, but every time Dawson's mind began reeling out possibilities it always ran into the snag of L. Marvin Fleish, his confession and his actions of the night of his second arrest.

During one of these reeling out of possibilities, Dawson fleetingly saw his hands on the young plump breasts of Miss Rebecca Hawkins and remembered she was waiting outside. He would have to talk to this witness and explore ways in which to juggle this Fleish thing. Perhaps fondle it from a different angle.

Al Bressio was slapping his forehead in the back seat of a taxi whose driver didn't quite understand the instructions.

"A block this side of Pren Street. Two eighty-five. You know where 285 is?"

"On the corner of Demster, I think."

"Right. Well, a block before that block on the corner stop."

"I don't understand."

"Look, I forget the name of the block before it. Wait. Turn right at Houston on Pren and I'll tell you when to stop. Don't stop suddenly, just a normal slow casual stop. Very easy."

"Hey, what's going on?"

"What's going on is I've been very stupid. Now listen to me and you'll get a good tip. Just slow down and stop when I tell you too. Stupid. Not you, me. Stupid. Stupid. Stupid. Stupid. Gavone." And Bressio slapped his forehead again with the heel of his hand.

And the cabdriver was very nervous.

On Pren Street, Bressio could feel what he already knew would be there. You could tell it by what was not visible. People did not lean out of their windows in the hot summer afternoon. Children did not play stickball on the street. Men did not lounge in undershirts on the stoops. It was quiet. Dead quiet and still on a sunny Thursday afternoon. Bressio tipped the cabdriver five dollars.

He walked very slowly to 285, not pretending to be casual because no one who mattered would believe that now. He did not look up to windows or scrutinize draperies for movement. They were there. And who knew what a direct glance at some frightened young gunman would set off.

At ground level, curtains moved in the warehouse opposite 285 Pren Street. Bressio couldn't help but notice, but he did not look. A car drove slowly up the street from behind him, and when it passed, he saw two men in the back seat and one up front driving.

He felt an itch under his left armpit near the holster, but he dared not touch it. Perspiration soaked his shirt and came into his eyebrows. With an exaggerated slow far-out reach, he wiped the perspiration from his eyes with his left hand and then returned the hand to his side in the same circular motion as though taking down a very slow salute.

His lips tasted salty and he felt there was not enough air in the air. He breathed deeply once, then entered the unlocked door of 285 Pren. The hallway lights were still not working. The door shut behind him, sealing him in darkness. He waited, listening, his eyes made useless by the bright street. He took two sure steps into the blackness and waited. There was rustling down to the right, probably in the basement stairwell.

He could taste the garbage stench of the hallway. His shirt was soaked now. He moved two more steps and waited. He was at the stairs. By two steps and wait, he made it to the top of the first flight. His eyes adjusted and he realized no one could see. He wiped his right hand dry on his jacket and slipped the .38 police special from the holster, releasing the safety as he did so. With the thumb of his gun hand, he carefully scratched the itch.

He felt along the wall with his left hand. It was oily wet and he cut a finger by going through a paint chip too rapidly. His fingers stayed on the wall until he felt the doorframe. They hurdled it and made it across the door to the knob which, as Bressio suspected, felt cleanly polished, glaringly free of grime, a perfect receptacle for picking up fingerprints. He waited. No sound. He turned the doorknob. It was locked.

With his cut left hand, he fished his American Express card from his wallet without removing the wallet from his jacket. He waited. Nothing.

He pushed the card edge vertical until its side was flat against the inside of the doorframe. He wheedled the card between frame and door, and felt the card pressured flat toward the door. The frame overlapped the door. No good. He eased the card out, and with his left thumbnail felt the wood of the frame. The nail dug in. The frame was old and rotted. With the pads of his fingertips he gently felt horizontally across the frame until he reached an indentation. He checked the indentation with the thumbnail to make sure it was not just part of the design of the molding. The thumbnail penetrated. He ran it up and down. It was the right spot. He slid the card into the crevice and worked it down until he felt the tongue of the lock. He angled the card so the forehead of the card became the pressure point, and then, increasing the pressure, he pushed down. The door clicked open and Bressio simultaneously moved out of the way of the glaring light that sent a thin, vertical, door-tall beam of white light against the far wall he had felt along. He waited, listening. Nothing.

He reached out the card hand and pushed the door the rest of the way. Nothing. With gun brought forward he moved, ready to shoot into the second-floor loft where a month before L. Marvin Fleish had barged in as a favor to a landlady, and come out alive and unconscious of his incredible good fortune.

The sunlight came through a dust-lathered high window at the right and made the loft bright enough to hurt Bressio's eyes, but not so much so that he could not see the loft was empty. He checked behind the door by pushing it gently until it hit the wall; then he closed it behind him.

The slatboard floor was bare but for some crumpled papers that appeared like food wrappings. It smelled of old oily rags. There was no reason to assume the loft was laid out any differently from L. Marvin's upstairs. The walls were plaster and Bressio could see no fresh plaster, so what he looked for was probably not in the walls. Bressio looked at the floor, a good half-century old with no ruptures in the worn wooden slats, probably the same floor immigrants toiled on.

It had to be the bathroom. He stepped into the center of the loft and saw an old blue painted door at the far end, beyond where the hallway would have had its boundary lines.

He heard the slats groan under his feet, and with finger light at the trigger he tried the doorknob of the bathroom door. It was unlocked. He opened it with a swift pull, ready, half expecting to see the barrel of a shotgun even though he had heard no breathing inside. It was empty. The room was six feet long and four feet wide. A chain hung from a wooden box above the toilet and the small bowl of a sink was yellow with age. It could not be the box above the toilet. That wasn't big enough for the death of Willie Knuckles, the Brooklyn guy, and Bressio's second cousin from downtown, Sally. Wars weren't started over something that small.

He should have known right from the beginning. If he hadn't been so riled by L. Marvin that first day, he would have sensed the tension in the street and checked it out. If he hadn't been so riled with Willie Knuckles he would not have accepted the explanation of the little thing he was after, and would have checked it out. Yet never would he have expected this, this quantitative change that made a qualitative change.

Nor would he have expected his dinner guest to feed him misinformation. Perhaps from the original source, this misinformation came. Yet by now the dinner guest surely should have known. Everyone must know, and by not telling him, the dinner guest had committed an offense against Bressio that was akin to a stiletto between the ribs. Undoubtedly he had been paid to misinform Bressio. Undoubtedly. Otherwise, he would have been the first to warn him. The very first.

But what it came down to, the real reason he had not known was all too simple. It was just too viciously stupid to be believable. Bressio looked down at the bathroom floor, where a new tarpaulin covered approximately four and a half feet from walls to toilet base. There it was. It had to be there. He listened. Nothing.

He knelt down and with his left hand pulled back part of the tarpaulin. A green plastic bag the size of pepperidge Farm stuffing was wedged against where the floor had been sawed through. He pulled farther. Another plastic bag. He pulled the tarpaulin a third of the way back. Stacked side to side like little fat green missiles were plastic bags. Bressio pushed a hand down between two of them and felt another layer. Farther down there was another layer, and another.

"No," he whispered softly. "No. No. No."

There was another layer, and another and when Bressio's cheek touched the top bag, his arm fully extended, he felt the top of another layer. It just kept going down. He smelled the stale base of the toilet, and his stomach jumped in little curlicues, and his breathing was very rapid. Sweat dropped onto the top bag at his face, and when he pulled his arm out, the top bag was wet from his face, and he was shaking his head.

"No. No. No. Why? The idiots. The idiots. Oh, goddamn them, the fucking idiots. What did they think they were doing?"

He re-covered the stash with the tarpaulin. Bait. Who knew how much? Wasn't there anyone to tell these people that when you have enough bait, it is no longer bait, but an achievement? The three deaths were just the beginning, and out there on the street were people who could not conceive he was not desirous of what lay beneath that tarpaulin. Someone, undoubtedly the FBNC, was offering as bait an empire. That was what was at Bressio's feet. An economic empire. Wars between nations had been fought over less than what those, those, gavones had stuffed beneath the flooring of a bathroom.

There was running on the stairs. Bressio heard it. He backed out of the bathroom, and was behind the hallway door when it was kicked open. Bressio caught the door with his face and his left hand so it wouldn't bounce back. Two hippie types ran past him, guns at the ready. One had red hair. They only had to see the bathroom door partly open to fire into it, slamming it closed with wood splinters flying.

They got off seven very fast and very loud rounds between them. It was just the kind of situation in which they would shoot if Bressio yelled out, "Hold it!" If either of them turned, Bressio was going to shoot first and worry about the courts later. The pair was just that jumpy.

"All right. You in there. Come out," yelled the redhead. They had the sick, frightened look of men who thought they had just killed. They waited, guns forward, crouching. Then the redhead saw Bressio and the gun forward.

"Drop it," said Bressio softly.

"Oh, my God," said the redhead. His partner, a wide-eyed towhead in blue denim overalls and jacket, also saw Bressio. He started to turn and Bressio was about to squeeze off a bullet into his chest, when the lad let loose his pistol as though it were scalding his hand. It made a dull clunk on the wooden floor.

"You, the redhead. Drop it," said Bressio softly.

"Yes," said the redhead.

"Hands up," said Bressio with gentle coaxing in his voice. "Up, up. Over here. That's right. Over here. Very nice."

Bressio circled the approaching narcos and got them between him and the open door. "Good. Very good," said Bressio in the same reassuring voice.

"We're FBNC officers. We have identification in our pockets."

"Yes. I know. I know who you are. Just do what you're told. I'm not after the stash."

"You couldn't get out anyhow," said the redhead.

"I know. Just stay where you are, that's right. Very good. Very good."

"We are federal officers."

"Shhhh," said Bressio.

More running up the steps. Three officers, two in blue jeans and one in white summer shorts, crowded the door with guns pushing ahead of them.

"Hold it," said Bressio loudly. "Just stay where you are. Trigger-happy idiots. This is just what happens. Get the twenty-seventh precinct on the phone."

"You a cop?" said one of the men in the doorway.

"No. Get the twenty-seventh precinct on the phone and get them over here. Now."

"We're federal officers."

"I know. Don't come in and don't shoot or your buddies are dead. I said stay there. No fast moves. You're gonna get us all killed. Now send someone to phone the twenty-seventh precinct."

"No way, man," said the narco in the white shorts.

"Redhead. What's your name?"

"Clyde Forrest."

"Who's in charge? Which one of those guys?"

"I am," said Forrest, his freckled face dripping sweat. Bressio could see his stomach tremble under his T-shirt. "Do what he says."

"Tell them to ask for a Sergeant Philosophus Jones. He's got sense and he's on days."

"Ask for the guy, Willie. Ask for him," said Forrest.

"Drop your gun," said the narco in the white shorts.

"Are you kidding? With you cockamamies running around?" said Bressio.

"We can get you for resisting arrest. We're federal officers."

"Willie, he knows that," sobbed Forrest. "He fucking knows that already. Get the damned coon sergeant from the locals."

"You know Jones, then," said Bressio.

"Tell you what, fella," said the narco in the white shorts. "You drop your gun and we'll all go to the twenty-seventh precinct together. All of us. Okay?"

Bressio shook his head at that foolishness. He was not about to go unarmed with these people around.

"I'm ordering you, Willie," said Forrest. "Get Jones *now,* or so help me I'll fucking have you on fucking report for fucking everything. Now do it."

"You want to bring the locals into this thing?" said Willie angrily.

"Yes, yes, yes!" said Forrest.

"Tell Jones Bressio is here," said Bressio. "Trying to stay unkilled amidst narcos with guns."

"Look. You put your gun away and we'll put our guns away," said Willie.

"This gun doesn't holster until there are police around."

"Will you do what he says, Willie, Jeezus. Do it."

"All right," said the narco in the white shorts. "I'll keep the fat guy covered. Johnson will get the locals, but you'll have to answer to upstairs, not me."

"I'll answer. I'll answer. Put your gun away."

"But he's got a gun."

"I'll take that chance," said Forrest. And he waited with his hands up, looking up into Bressio's gun.

Bressio heard Jones's slow labored trudge up the steps and thought the sight of his heavy black face under policeman's blue was very comforting. He flicked the safety on his gun, put it in his shoulder hoster, and snapped the safety strap closed around it. Forrest lowered his hands in relief. So did sidekick.

" 'Lo, Alphonse. I seen you met the new crusaders against narcotics."

"Yeah, Phossy. That I did."

Gathering his nerves, Forrest turned on Bressio with threats. Bressio was in trouble, he said. Bressio had threatened the life of a federal officer, he said. Bressio had attempted murder of said same federal officer, he said. He had corroborating witnesses, he said.

"So charge me," said Bressio.

"I'm not sure what I'm going to do with you," said Forrest, jiggling his hands to get circulation back in them.

"Let's all go down to the station house," said Jones wearily.

"Through the back way. I don't want to blow this thing," said Forrest intently.

"Blow this thing?" said Bressio incredulously. "Oh, God have mercy on us all."

"There might be some people across the street watching this house."

"Might be?" said Bressio, and he shook his head sadly.

Bressio rode in the back seat of the patrol car with Forrest, who stared angrily at him, a menacing look on his young face. Sergeant Jones drove, the black sirloin rolls on his neck appearing to support the prim police hat which bobbed when he chuckled.

"Beautiful. Beautiful. Beautiful," said Jones. "You people are just beautiful."

"I can consider your comments a lack of local cooperation," said Forrest.

"You just do that little old thing," said Jones. "Beautiful."

"Incredible," said Bressio. "Incredible."

"You betta watch yoself, Al, this narco here gonna charge you wif murder. Heh-heh."

"I don't know how we'll handle this man," said Forrest.

"Good luck in your attempts," said Jones. "The New York City Police Department is here to assist you in whatever assistance you should deem necessary within the law and especially regarding the rights of the individual under the Constitution."

"Don't get official with me, Sergeant."

"I wouldn't get anything but official with you, sonny. With you people and that house it's CYA all the way. Cover Your Ass. You people want to shoot up a door. I'm going to report a door shot full of holes. They want to bury it upstairs, fine with me."

"We have good reasons why we consider that house a maximum sensitive area."

"I know when guns is shot off, I gotta make a report. You give any answer you want, sonny. I'll just put it between them little quote marks. You want to say you shootin' at King Kong, I'll put that down too, 'cause I am here to assist you in whatever assistance you should deem necessary within—"

"I am not at liberty to disclose, especially in front of a prisoner, why that house is maximally sensitive. Nor do I wish to discuss it with you, Sergeant."

"You a real winner, sonny. You ain't gonna talk lest Alphonse Bressio find out what's going on in New York City. Oh, you are beautiful. Beautiful."

As the patrol car reached the baroque cement architecture that marked the twenty-seventh precinct house, Bressio tapped the wire mesh that separated front from back of the patrol car.

"Keep going, Phoss. I want to speak to this kid," said Bressio.

The patrol car passed the station house as though it never intended to stop.

"Pull in. I'm going to charge this man," said Forrest.

"Keep going, Phoss."

"Sergeant. I order you to let us out here."

"Take us to Gino's," said Bressio.

"Am I being abducted?" demanded Forrest.

"Right. In collusion with a sergeant on the New York City police force, I am abducting a federal agent," said Bressio.

"Now I really have you," said Forrest, grinning angrily.

The car stopped in front of a small, dark coffee shop in the West Village. There was a large polished espresso machine in the window.

"Thanks, Phoss. I'll take care of you later," said Bressio. "You just heard a bribe offer, kid. C'mon."

"And you heard it accepted, too," said Jones.

"C'mon, kid. I want to tell you about some economic facts of life and why you are in very serious trouble."

Bressio got out of the car and waited. Forrest looked at him suspiciously. "You're an ambitious young man, and you want to save your career, don't you?" said Bressio.

Forrest looked like a fox sniffing poisoned meat. He leaned forward, drumming his fingers on his faded blue jeans. Bressio noticed his hands were freckled also.

"Kid, I'll even tell you why all the experienced men left you with that disaster back on Pren Street."

Forrest pointed a shaking finger at Bressio. "I'll give you five minutes, wise guy, and then I'm going to throw your ass in jail so hard your spine won't stop ringing till you're fifty," said Forrest and scrambled out of the patrol car. Bressio's quick hands saved him from stumbling, and he guided the lad around a fresh pile of dog droppings, lest he step in it.

XV

Bressio ordered two cannoles, a coke for Forrest, and espresso for himself. He played with the wax drippings of the candle on the checkered tablecloth as he talked. He would be seen from the street talking to this man, and the word would be out that Bressio was trying to reach the narcos to make a deal. It was the nature of people to see only their own motives in others. So be it. It was too late now to do anything but try to save his own life and keep his friends and associates out of the crossfire. He was in it and he would not be safe until the disaster was resolved. He could stand on street corners proclaiming his innocence, but the people most likely to kill him would be the last to believe him.

Forrest refused to drink the coke or eat the cannole and sat across the table with his arms folded. As Bressio's finger's molded the wax he remembered being lifted up to the coffin at Fermio's to kiss Papa goodbye, and seeing that it wasn't Papa, just colored wax, he started to cry, and they thought he was crying for Papa, but what he was crying about was that it wasn't Papa in the box but wax with Papa's hair on top, and when they went to the cemetery, his heart was broken when he saw them put the body in a deep hole. He wanted to tell all the grownups that they shouldn't bury the box deep so maybe when the grass came up again in the spring somehow Papa would return.

And as he grew up he found out how many men his father had killed. Bressio thumbed the wax into the base of the candle at Gino's and tried to explain to this young man whose voice carried a sharp twang the economics of the five families and why what was happening at Pren Street could get them killed.

Numbers and gambling, the hijacking at the docks and air terminals were stable things. They earned a regular amount of money within easily definable territories. There was shylocking also, which was rather stable and financed a goodly part of the fashion industry and some entertainment enterprises. On these things was the economy of the five families based.

All of these enterprises needed an orderly market, so to speak, with politicians and police being reached, no raiding of one another's commerce. There was what one might call a monopoly, which was the real base of power of the families. If one wanted to enter these fields, one had to be part of the system or the system would crush you.

"Do you follow, Forrest?"

"I'm waiting," said Forrest.

The system was good for the workers, too, because it provided a more stable income. This was the base of the power of the rackets, or the mob, or the Mafia or Cosa Nostra or whatever Forrest wished to call it. The leaders held their power through the resources of capital and manpower. From time to time, fools would try to reign by terror, but these reigns never lasted. The system thrived because everyone, and Bressio meant everyone, wanted it to survive.

Enter narcotics. Unstable because anyone could get into it. It required no extensive connections in politics; unlike gambling it could be hidden easily and did not require a base of operations, unlike shylocking you didn't have to have an enforcement body for payments, and unlike hijacking, one did not need extensive cooperation on the docks and in the terminals. Anyone could do it. It created an unstable market. Why should someone for three, maybe four or five hundred a week toil in the vineyards when he could make five years' income in a week. This was the real reason many of the important people opposed narcotics, not because of public outrage.

"You through?" said Forrest.

"No," said Bressio. "I want you to understand the framework you're working in." Bressio noticed Forrest's right arm twitch. Apparently he had a gun under the table. If this would make the lad feel more secure, perhaps it was not so bad. Bressio then explained the nature of heroin, its incredible liquidity. Despite all this, there was a generally orderly market in New York City, with an occasional connected person or so being punished for some transgression.

But then came 285 Pren Street, and what Forrest was sitting on was something else altogether. It was of such proportions, such awesome wealth that it created a new empire unto itself. There was enough capital sitting out open in 285 Pren Street to be worth the while of a small army in attempting to take it.

Forrest cocked an eyebrow and sat back, a bit more comfortable in his chair.

"And you're thinking, Forrest, that's just your strategy, right?"

Forrest shrugged.

"Well, I heard that same kind of silly thinking from someone who doesn't know anything about your business, and it was so absurd I thought it couldn't be."

Bressio could see confidence surface in the young man's face.

"Well, we just do our job," said Forrest. "You did pull a gun on me after I had identified myself as a federal officer, and from where I sit, Mr. Bressio, I think you're the wrong person to be lecturing anyone on anything."

"You can't protect that smack," said Bressio. "There is no conceivable way that heroin is not going to walk. It is of such value that men with money who know how to use that money are after it. In your brilliance at FBNC, you have created something that is worth any risk to get. You have done this knowingly, I see now, but what you do not know is that men willing to risk money and their lives, so many men, so many people, that they will succeed. You will be destroyed in your attempt to do the impossible. My god, Forrest, they couldn't even hold heroin as evidence in New York City police headquarters."

"That's New York City police," said Forrest. "We haven't had the time yet to become that corrupt—if we ever will."

"What do you think New York City police are made of? You think they're Martians or something?"

"They are of a culture, Mr. Bressio, that tends to tolerate moral laxity."

"Where are you from, Forrest?"

"Troy, Ohio, near Dayton. I don't see what that has to do with anything."

"Well, Forrest, you think of who has the major political jobs there and how they're passed around, and you out there think it's all very harmless and not really serious, but that's only because there isn't enough temptation to make it look serious. You're the same people out there that you are here. You are no different, Forrest. Believe me. You're dealing with people. And people are greedy and short-sighted. I guarantee that already some of your people have been reached. Guaranteed. No question about it."

"Mr. Bressio, what do you want from me?"

"I don't want the smack is what you're thinking, right? You were thinking that, right?"

"I would not have been surprised."

"Okay. J. Edgar Hoover kept his bureau out of this thing, this sort of thing, right?"

"It is not under the jurisdiction of the FBI."

"That's what I'm saying," said Bressio."

"Well, it's not because Washington says so. We have different agencies for different national functions."

"And you don't think Hoover could have gotten the FBI into narcotics up to its armpits if he wanted? You don't think narcotics could fall in his jurisdiction, coming in from overseas and crossing at state borders? I'll tell you what Hoover did before he died, he got it shoved in the laps of the CIA foreign and the Treasury Department local until your FBNC came onto the scene with flags flying to show everyone else how it was done."

"So?"

"So, why is it a kid of your age is heading up this cool house with all that smack there? Don't you think that if there was any potential for career advancement, senior men would be in there? Don't you think you've been set up? Hasn't that crossed your mind?"

"I don't know why I'm telling you this, but there were three men who had this house before me. One got an infection of some sort, one got transferred, and the other took a real early retirement. Ruined his career."

"All those men working for you who have not reported being offered bribes have either been reached or are thinking of making a deal," said Bressio. There was a flatness in his voice now. No pleading for understanding. "The connected people—Sally Bugel-lerio, Tomalino and Willie Knuckles—were killed because of the unrestricted competition for what you're sitting on."

"The papers called it a gang war because of the shooting in that restaurant a couple of years ago."

"That is not so, Clyde Forrest."

Forrest sighed deeply. "Well, quite frankly there's nothing I can do but hang in there and hope it works out. So I'm taking you in, Bressio, because it's the right thing to do. I think you're right, if you want to know the truth, but there's nothing I can do. I got to do what I got to do. Dumber things have worked out just fine."

Bressio felt the barrel of Forrest's gun press against his testicles underneath the table.

"Don't move, Mr. Bressio."

"You think you've got me, right, Forrest?" said Bressio.

The redhead's chin was almost in his coke.

"Deed I do."

"Would you believe me if I tell you you don't really understand the gun? It's not magic. It just fires a projectile which can kill." Bressio cracked into the hard shell of his cannole with a fork, lifting out a glob of white sweet paste from inside.

"That'll do, Mr. Bressio."

"It would do *if* I agreed that your gun at my balls was something I should be most afraid of, Forrest. But there is a minor problem with that move you're making. I got to be part of it."

With his excellent reflexes, Bressio shifted quickly and ever so slightly so that the gun was suddenly pinned between his buttocks and the chair. Forrest's freckled nose was in his untouched can-nole. Bressio put the fork prongs underneath Forrest's left eye, which had a very close view of a salt shaker. What had been Forrest's threat was now his trap.

"So now which is more deadly? A fork that can take out an eye or a gun that can shoot off the fatty part of my ass?"

"Okay. Let go," said Forrest.

"How can I?" said Bressio.

"Just get up."

"And then you'll have me. You haven't really left me much choice."

"What're you going to do?"

"I'm gonna finish your cannole, for one," said Bressio.

"Hey, I look queer with my hand down there. I feel stupid."

"Both of us maybe have fifteen minutes to live if one of anyone of maybe fifty people out there decides to do a job on us, and you're worried about how you look. You frighten me, Forrest. You're unreasonable."

"I'm reasonable as hell. Let me go."

"I can't," said Bressio. "Let go of the gun."

"I can't. I can't get my fucking fingers to open. You got muscles in your ass, you bastard. I thought you were mostly fat."

"We're gonna have to do this together, Forrest," said Bressio. He put down his fork, and with both hands grabbed Forrest's gun arm.

"Now you let go of your gun when I release my weight, okay?"

"Release your weight first."

"I can't do it."

"Okay, I promise. Jeezus, we look stupid," said Forrest.

As he jumped up, Bressio threw Forrest's gun hand away from him. The pistol went flying across the tile floor.

"I told you I was going to release. You didn't have to do that with your hands," said Forrest. "Can I get my gun?"

"Yeah. Yeah," said Bressio. "Do you understand what I'm talking about now, kid? If you understand what I'm talking about, you can better my odds for getting out of this thing alive and even saving your career."

Forrest got his gun from underneath a far table. The coffee shop was empty but for three couples, two of which were staring at him with extreme nervousness; the third was involved in a conversation of its own. Forrest stuffed the gun into his shirt and Bressio looked for the cannole. Apparently, the shoving had knocked it off the table. The checkerboard tablecloth was soaked with Forrest's coke and Bressio's espresso.

"You want something to eat, kid?" asked Bressio.

Forrest shook his head. Bressio ordered two rum cakes in case Forrest changed his mind and then explained what he needed from the young man. He also told him about himself and why he was now a target because those "people let out of their cages by your smack look at everyone near the place as competition."

Bressio had to know how this thing started, when he was

thought by Forrest's people to be involved, the connections with Fleish and Mary Beth Cutler, and if anything even zanier was planned by the new FBNC. In return for this, Bressio would show Forrest how to save his career.

It began, said Forrest, with a little success. He explained how he had been living with Terry Leacock, known to be involved in getting financing for heroin operations. Forrest had even been there when Terry had shown the heroin to some purchasers. He was her gun, she thought. What Terry had invented was a new system to sell the stuff. Bidding, like a commodity market. Did Bressio know that Terry's father was in commodities in a small way?

Bressio shook his head.

Well, all of a sudden, Forrest knew the names and whereabouts of maybe eight pushers the FBNC did not have any line on. Terry was killed possibly by one of the pushers, Forrest didn't know. But the interesting part was that dealers were coming out of their holes looking to buy. So it only followed logically to add some more to the stash and see if there were bigger dealers interested. There were. Well, one thing led to another, and the FBNC kept increasing the ante by shipping into the cache all the evidence of busts made around the country.

"But you can't do that with evidence," said Bressio. "It won't hold up in court if you have it wandering across the country. Any good defense lawyer will use its shipment to undermine its credibility as evidence. Was this the heroin seized? Was it another package? Maybe another package didn't really have heroin, but sedlitz powder. Do you follow?"

"Well, we were gonna get it all back without anyone knowing. I mean we got twenty, maybe thirty guys in the basement of 285 Pren and in surrounding buildings. Like upstairs said, we've got some spit into this thing now."

"Yeah, spit," said Bressio. "You know, if you should get that smack scattered back around the country to different trials and whatever the evidence will be used for, you'll have to have a whole department lying itself blue in the face to get a conviction on those little cases."

"Well, they won't know."

"Do you know?"

"Sure."

"Do at least four other people know?"

"Yeah. I would imagine. Maybe twenty or thirty."

"Do you know it is a proven fact that five people cannot keep a secret? But go ahead."

Well, the cache started building, and Forrest got a promotion because he was first in with the Leacock thing, and then the first guy running it bugged out and then the second and just yesterday was the third and here he was. And the funny thing about it was sometimes at night he thought about Terry and believed she really loved him. Did Bressio understand that?

Yes, Bressio did. What about Fleish and Cutler?

Two loony tunes, according to Forrest. Fleish was bothering everyone. Not really coming down into the basement or anything important.

"Why was the basement important?"

" 'Cause that's where most of us were. He'd stop some of the other guys on the street and because we dress like this, he'd insist on rapping. He gave us everything on both busts both times. Sometimes I even felt sorry for the people he dealt with. But after he broke into the second floor loft, upstairs wanted him the hell out of the way. So we tipped off Arizona and made the bust ourselves up here. We had no choice. We weren't into grass, but that dumb Jewboy brought us into it. Funny. Till I came to New York City, I always thought all Jews were smart, or at least not stupid. But that's not so, you know."

"And Cutler?"

"Oh, she's a freaky one. We couldn't figure her out. Thought she was pushing for a while, but that's not so either. She loses tails real good, just like a pro. And then you and that Dawson fellow were the worst part of the whole thing. When we found out Dawson was defending Fleish, wowee. Upstairs went out of its gourd. We were certain for a while that this Fleish was really into smack big. I mean, otherwise why would he have someone that expensive on his side, right? We thought you were an emissary from the Brooklyn don until we finally found out you work for lawyers. Yeah. We've had a tail on you, Alphonse Joseph Bressio, forty-two, Caucasian male, five feet ten inches tall, two hundred and forty-five pounds."

"Two thirty-four," said Bressio. "Got a pencil?"

"What for?"

"We're going to save your career. I got what I want. I don't like
what I see, but I see the pieces fit. So now for you."

Forrest found a ballpoint pen in a hip pocket and Bressio gave
him a napkin. He dictated a memo. It was to Forrest's superior.
There were to be two carbons, one to Forrest's superior's superior
and the other to the head of the FBNC.

"This is kind of risky," said Forrest.

"You like what you got now? Take my word for it, kid, all the
animals have been let out of their cages. Somebody farts loud on
Pren Street, it's gonna be a shooting gallery. And you people are
outgunned. That is, if the smack is still there now."

"The original goes to my boss?"

Bressio dictated a somber-sounding bureaucratic message warning about the insecurity of enough heroin to supply the East Coast
narcotics trade for eight months. The use of the house on Pren
Street was called a danger to the nation and to the department. In
Forrest's view there was no good that could come of it, and he
regretted going over his superior's head, but he felt for the good
of the department and country, he had to do it, since the three
verbal warnings and the memo of last week apparently had no
effect.

"I never warned him and never sent a memo."

Bressio smiled.

"This means I'm putting him on the spot," said Forrest.
"Wowee. Well, he put me on the spot. At least it will get that
disaster on Pren Street back out where it belongs."

"No it won't," said Bressio. "It'll get you shipped to Washington
with a label as an untrustworthy schemer."

"Well, that's not doing much for my career."

"When that heroin walks, you're gonna look great, kid. They're
gonna promote you with fanfare and by the time the dust settles,
it will look like your point of view was your agency's all along and
only a few misguided fanatics were for it. But the agency will be
in the process of weeding them out."

"But that didn't happen in Vietnam," said Forrest, wise for his
twenty and some years.

"Too many people on public record. It happened too slow. This
will be fast and obvious. In this stupidity, you're going to come up
as the wave of the future."

"I'll say I sent two memos. Yeah."

"Don't forget the carbons of those memos as proof. You got a typewriter in that basement fortress of yours?"

"Yeah. And loads of electronic stuff, too."

"Don't let anyone see you at work."

"I got a couple of buddies—"

"No, you don't," said Bressio. "Not at all. You got no one. Look out for yourself, okay?"

"Sure will," said the young man. "And when I'm the wave of the future, you'll have a friend at the FBNC—that is, if you don't deal narcotics." Forrest smiled.

"Yeah, the future," said Bressio and he picked up the candle that had fallen from the table when he released the young man's gun hand. He molded a loose piece of wax to the base of the candle, and shook hands goodbye, certain they were being watched and certain that those watching would calculate he had just made a deal for the heroin. It didn't matter. He knew how their minds worked. They were sure of that already. He cleaned the wax off his fingertips and left Gino's.

XVI

Clarissa was adamant. How should she have known the message from that old geezer was important. She hadn't seen Bressio around the office for three days. He was running around like some private detective, probably peeking into motel windows if not privately occupied by himself on the other side.

"You through, Duff?" said Bressio.

"Reasonably," said Clarissa, making the last preparations of the day to close down the office, which included unraveling Bressio's expenses which ended with the plane arrival at Kennedy Airport that morning.

"You're leaving town," said Bressio. "I need some work done for me in Montreal. Get a plane this evening and wait in Montreal for my phone call."

Clarissa stopped adding the bill for the new Cutler account. "You're in trouble, Al. You don't need me in Montreal. You just want to get me out of town. What's wrong?"

"I think I'm going to be killed," said Bressio.

"Can you tell me what it's about?"

"No. It's better that you don't know."

"It's got something to do with that old man who kept leaving messages, doesn't it?"

"Yes."

Clarissa covered her mouth with her hands. A horrible thought terrified her. "Did my failure to relay that old man's messages have anything to do with it?"

Bressio shook his head as though the messages were such a minor thing they could have nothing to do with his life.

"I did get you in this. I did. Oh, my God. I did. Oh, no."

"Now listen, Duff. I said you didn't. I will have a great deal better chance of surviving if I know you're safe somewhere."

"That's beautiful, Al," said Clarissa. She reached for a Kleenex and blew into it. She was crying. Bressio felt incredibly uncomfortable.

"I mean, I won't have you getting in the way and fouling things up."

"Oh, shut up, Al. You're beautiful." Clarissa blew strong into the Kleenex.

"So you're gonna leave tonight, right?" said Bressio.

Clarissa shook her head and blew strong again into the Kleenex.

"I got my pride, too, Al. I mean, you've got to respect my pride, also. I won't leave you now. You can use me to answer the phones here for a checkpoint. You can't trust your answering service. There isn't a girl there who wouldn't sell you out for a sawbuck. You need someone you can trust. You can't send me away from this like some kid. I'm a woman. I want to stand by you now. I've got a right to this."

It struck Bressio as terribly unjust that the only compliments he could think of were in masculine terms. So all he said was "Okay, Duff. Okay."

He wrote down the address of a small farm in Mount Carmel, New York. Clarissa was to take Mary Beth and Bobbi there, then return to the city. She should rent a car. If she found herself tailed, she shouldn't try to lose the tail. Just keep going around, stop and talk to some cop or state trooper about the weather or anything. Tails tended to lose themselves after a few hours anyway. No fancy driving.

"Maybe we could phone the police? I mean, why not? You're an honest citizen, Al, so am I."

"It is the nature of this situation, Clarissa, that the cops have probably been reached already, very heavily reached, and anyone rendering us assistance is going to be reached, heavy. I know these things. There's a lot of money out there."

"After this will you cut yourself off from that business, Al? Will you?"

"Don't you think I would if I could? I don't want to die, Clarissa. I'm afraid," said Bressio. "Maybe because of my looks there are a lot of people who think I shouldn't be scared. That's bullshit. You can be ugly, tough and afraid. I didn't ask for this face. If I had a choice, don't you think I'd rather look like John Kennedy or even Roddy McDowell? I got feelings, very tender feelings, that I don't think anyone cares about because of the way I look."

Clarissa Duffy placed her hands on Al Bressio's cheeks and kissed him gently on the lips. "You're the most beautiful man I know, Al."

"I don't think I could live if they got you, Clarissa."

"You take care of yourself too, huh, Al?"

"Betcher ass, sweety."

"I don't like that word," said Clarissa.

"Betcher ass, Duff."

"That's better, handsome."

Bressio hung his head like an embarrassed little boy. He was blushing. With a big stupid grin all over his face he was blushing right out there in the open.

"Big tough man," said Clarissa teasingly, and she punched him gently in his ample stomach.

Suddenly her phone rang, and when she went to answer it, a second light underneath the phone buttons lit up, signifying a second call.

"It's for you. Mrs. Dawson," said Clarissa. Bressio took it in his office. Even Bobo could not achieve annoying him now.

"Hello, Al. I thought you people looked down on pimping."

"What are you working at now, Bobo?" said Bressio.

"That chippy you imported for Murray this morning. Miss Sunnyville Farms."

"If you're referring to Rebecca Hawkins, she's a nineteen-year-old witness in the Fleish defense. You know, Marvin whom you find so funny and entertaining."

"Oh, they're calling them witnesses now," said Bobo.

"I don't have time to talk, Bobo."

"Just a minute, Al. I've got some great news for you. Cuthy Dempster of The Dempsters is interested in you."

"Never heard of her."

"You met her at the party."

"Don't remember."

"She said you were definitely interested in her and she returns the sentiment. She says she wants you to phone her. I have her number. If her husband answers, ignore him."

"I don't know who you're talking about, Bobo. I have never known a Cuthy Dempster and only vaguely remember hearing of The Dempsters. That's not my crowd."

"Of course not. The Cutlers are. If you move with the Cutlers, why step down to a Dempster?"

"I'm doing some work for William James Cutler."

"More than that, from what I've heard. You've had an invitation to join Mitchell, Walker and Cutler. Murray couldn't get into that firm with a crowbar. Don't kid me, Al."

"Me working in Mitchell, Walker and Cutler? Goodbye, Bobo," said Bressio. "I've got another call hanging."

Bressio popped the second lit button. It was Dawson.

"Al, I'm glad I reached you before Bobo did. Don't tell her about Becky."

"She already knows, Murray."

"That woman has radar in her head. Incredible. Fleish has got his pretrial tomorrow. I know you like to watch me work."

"You're not going to appear yourself, are you? You'll draw a crowd."

"I got one of the kids representing Marvin officially. He's on the docket. I'll substitute at the last minute."

"But what's a pretrial? You're not going to do any work at a pretrial that any of the younger lawyers couldn't do for you."

"Becky wants to see me in action. I thought she'd like it. You know, sort of a thrill for a country girl. Phone my secretary tomorrow morning. She'll give you the judge and court."

"I know what court," said Bressio. "What's the matter with you?"

"Nothing, Al. I'm finding out the meaning of life."

"You know, sometimes I think you and L. Marvin have a lot in common, Murray."

Bressio heard Dawson laugh and hang up.

He went out to Clarissa's office, but saw no one. She was gone. A note was folded beneath the bar of her typewriter.

Al,
You keep yourself alive. Don't worry about me. I'll be back in the morning with mission accomplished. You are a very beautiful man.

Love,
    Clarissa.

Bressio smiled and tore the note several times. He dropped a few pieces in Clarissa's wastebasket and out in the hall, and dropped a few more pieces in the garbage. He deposited the last of the note in the street. She would have to stop leaving things like that. If the stash at 285 Pren disappeared, as it had to any day now, someone coming across that note in the typewriter or on Bressio's body would assume she knew something. Too many women thought to know something had their nipples burned off with lit cigars.

If he and Clarissa were married, everyone would know she would be kept unaware of such things, partly for that reason. But as his secretary—well, secretaries and mistresses and whores had a rough life in the business of the five families.

The prostitutes who had once testified against a don during the 1940's had had Draino forced into their vaginas. It was not a nice business. A woman without status during times of trouble was open game.

Bressio felt depressed. Perhaps the beating he gave Willie Knuckles might help. Maybe they would think of Clarissa differently. A wedding ring, however, would have been more effective. Would she marry him? Could he keep her out of the office? These were things to be resolved if he were alive to resolve them.

On Chambers Street he picked up a tail he didn't recognize. Ah, well, he would have liked to have kept the note. He ducked into a bar and got change for the telephone. By staying alive, he was Clarissa's best insurance. Who knew what the animals were thinking and doing? Any sort of horror was possible when the natural order of commerce was disrupted. Then the lunatics took over. It eased his mind little that he could think of no don or underboss who had authorized sadistic torture on women, nor did these things happen often. They were, as Don Carmine called them, "regrettable sicknesses." Still, they happened. And in times like this they happened most.

Bressio dialed Connecticut information, hoping Cutler would not have an unlisted number. He didn't.

"Let me speak to Mr. Cutler, please, this is Al Bressio . . . Hello, Jim, I'll take that office you promised, but only for a couple of hours. I need it tonight. Is there any way you can get me a key? . . . No, you don't have to open it yourself. As a matter of fact it would be better if you didn't . . . Yes, dangerous . . . Yes, Mary Beth could be in some sort of trouble, but I think I can keep her out of it. I'd rather not talk on the phone. How long would it take you to get in from Old Lyme? . . . All right. Just circle your building. I can't stay any one place for a long time . . . I'll be there but not waiting. I'll bang on the side of your car. Gotta run. Thanks."

Bressio left the drink he had ordered on the bar and walked out. He went to City Hall Park and sat on a bench as the traffic went by. A car with three men parked in front of him. He waited five minutes, then cut back through the park and was picked up by another car. It was probable people just wanted to know where he was all the time. He turned into a one-way street, lost the car and picked up two walkers. He stepped down into a subway, got a token, and went to a phone booth. He dialed the number of his dinner guest. The two walkers waited by a gum machine.

The dinner guest was out, said his wife. Bressio said he would call again and he wished the wife would relay a message. She said she did not have a good memory and knew nothing about these things. Wise woman. Bressio did not stand near the edge of the subway platform. When an uptown local came in, he took it. So did the walkers. He got off at Forty-second Street and went upstairs to the street. He hailed a cab. It got stuck at a light. His two walkers got in a second cab. By the time the taxi reached Rockefeller Center, there was the cab and a Lincoln following him.

"You want to go through the park?" said the cabby at Central Park.

"No," said Bressio. "Take the East Side Highway downtown. Leave me off at the Staten Island Ferry."

At the ferry he got another cab.

"Wall Street," said Bressio. "The Stock Exchange."

Bressio told the driver to stop a block short of Cutler's building. The Lincoln behind stopped also. When he saw a gray Cadillac

limousine with Connecticut plates circle the block ahead, he gave
the cabby a ten-dollar bill, told him to keep the change and to catch
up to "that car over there."

Bressio was out of the cab and running and banging on the side
of the limousine. Cutler opened the rear door, slowing down.

"What's going on?" he asked.

"I'll tell you in your office. Park in front of your building."

After they had signed in with a pathetically old night watchman
and were riding up in the elevator to Cutler's office, Bressio told
him that what he thought could never happen, happened.

"About how much worth?"

"You name it," said Bressio. "Thirty, maybe fifty million dollars' worth of pure heroin. You can't really fix a price on it. Like
stocks. If someone were to dump a few thousand shares of General
Motors on the exchange in an afternoon, the price would go down,
so what's it worth? Pick a figure. A lot."

"That's a small fortune," said Cutler.

"Yeah," said Bressio.

"Is Mary Beth safe?"

"Probably," said Bressio and explained that because of his interest in her that he had made known in an effort to afford her some
small protection from the vicissitudes of life, people now believed
that he was interested in the stash at 285 Pren Street. It was a
question, Bressio explained, of people only being able to see their
own motivations in a situation.

"Is there a contract out on your life, is that the term?"

"I don't think so," said Bressio, looking nervously left and right
as they left the elevator. "They want to know where I'm at all the
time. Of course, if I sit down and wait, somebody may decide it's
a lot cheaper to kill me than to watch me."

"I have some very good relationships with people in Justice. I
think we could generate some protection for you in some way."

"What would they do, identify the body and then file a report
on man-hours to show they tried? Dead is dead, Jim."

Cutler let them in through the front way and went searching for
lights. As he explained, he was not used to this—the lights always
being on when he needed them.

Bressio used a secretary's phone. He got his dinner guest's wife.
She said her husband would come to the phone. All right, he had

obviously checked around and was coming to the phone with marching orders. Bressio explained that it was only this day that he got his message. He wanted to talk to him to explain his position in this matter. The dinner guest suggested a place of meeting, which Bressio refused. He gave him Cutler's office address, where he knew nothing had been prearranged for him.

But what of the risk to the envoy? asked the dinner guest.

"What risk?" Bressio countered angrily. "Don't tell me this silliness has affected you, too? Why should I wish to harm a bearer of messages?"

Yes, Bressio assured the man, he knew they were strange times. He hung up, found Cutler in his office, and thanked him for the use of the office that evening. He could go now if he wished. Cutler refused.

"This is Mitchell, Walker and Cutler. I'm not abandoning it to some threat of thugs. If one paper is moved by those people I can virtually promise the entire weight of the U.S. government coming down on their heads."

"And what if they're not bright enough to realize that, Jim? A threat is only as good as its recipient's belief in it. I don't even know who's outside waiting for me. What could the government do to them?"

"Apply pressure in the areas of shipping, gambling, things like that."

"Which would be fine for your dealing with people like Don Carmine. With him you'd get along fine. Unfortunately, this is the time of the zanies. The damn—the goddamn stash on Pren Street has let them out of the woodwork. A silly thing. A silly, silly, silly thing," said Bressio. And he shook his head slowly.

"It could work out for the best," said Cutler. "I know some people at the FBNC. Our firm has done a lot of *pro bono* work in narcotics legislation. They're good people at FBNC. Got iron in their blood. They just may tough this thing out. Most great victories occur when times look most perilous."

Bressio looked at the conviction in Cutler's face. He couldn't believe it. But he did, and Bressio had wanted to sit in counsel with this man, held him up in a dream of what was good and worth striving for, and all he was with all his power and fame and influence was a man who got a health warning on a pack of cigarettes.

His claim to fame was engineering something that purposely didn't work. There was no more to him, Bressio saw it now.

"Maybe, Mr. Cutler," said Bressio and asked to use a private phone.

"You're still working for us, for Mary Beth, aren't you?" said Cutler seeing a strong change in Bressio's face.

"Yes, I promised to try to help," said Bressio. He explained that Mary Beth was safely on a farm outside of New York City so she would not accidentally be involved when the shooting started at Pren Street. Dawson had had the adoption papers filed for Cutler's granddaughter, and L. Marvin Fleish had been given a warning to stay away, which he would probably follow. Bressio's rates were seventy-five dollars an hour on an eight-hour day.

"It looks as though we're in a reasonable position," said Cutler.

"Very reasonable," said Bressio. "You think it's reasonable, then it's reasonable." He glanced down the hallway through Cutler's open door.

"Don't worry about anyone breaking into Mitchell, Walker and Cutler. Only the office manager, Mitchell and I have keys to the New York office. We changed the locks several years back when some important papers were missing."

Cutler's rock confidence was somewhat shaken when he and Bressio heard a key in the outer door. Bressio stepped out of the sight of the hallway and drew his gun.

XVII

Bressio stood, back to wall, gun loose and ready and pointing at the open door to Cutler's office, listening to the footsteps in the hallway designed to muffle footsteps. There were several men.

Cutler, as Bressio had ordered, remained at his desk, appearing to work on papers, an executive spending a late night at the office. Cutler looked up from his work. He was supposed to be surprised, stand up and back away. Hopefully this would draw whoever it was into the room.

But Cutler did not look surprised nor did he stand up, nor did he back away. He smiled, a big grin of relief. "Farnsworth. What are you doing here?" he said. "It's all right, Al. It's my landlord, the president of Alpen Realty. I said it's all right, Al. I know him."

Then Cutler saw confusing things happen. Al Bressio did not lower his gun, and the president of Alpen Realty stopped in the hallway and the two men with him, both apparently businessmen, in suits and ties, drew revolvers.

"Hello, Alphonse," said Farnsworth. "Have things gotten so bad that you would hold guns in my presence?"

"His men have guns," said Cutler with a good deal of courage, for when he said this he was looking into the barrel of a snub-nosed .32.

Bressio's free hand made a short wave of the fingertips signifying he knew and that Cutler should stay out of it. "Hello, Mr. Felli," said Bressio. "It is not from evil in my heart, but from apprehension in these troubled times."

Cutler was both amazed at the florid eloquence emanating from

Bressio, and the force. What force in the man! So this is what the
dossier meant when it referred to him as a man of respect. But why
was he calling Farnsworth "Felli"? And Farnsworth was respond-
ing to that name. Funny, thought Cutler, he had always thought
Farnsworth had changed his name from Feldstein or Feinberg or
something like that. Farnsworth had acted so, so Jewish.

"What is there to fear from me? I come to negotiate," said
Farnsworth. "It is I who have apprehensions about you, Alphonse."

"Fear and guns are conducive to harm, Mr. Felli. This is an
unfortunate fact of life."

"We will put ours away," said Farnsworth. "You do the same.
As a sign of trust."

"Instead of putting them away," said Bressio, "let's lower them
and I will step out and you will see my lowered gun and I shall see
yours."

"These men have none of your high skills, Alphonse."

"I'm stepping out anyway. Your guns should be lowered."

"You know that would be a provocation," said Farnsworth,
standing between his two gunmen, a tanned, immaculate little man
with a pleasant but slightly fleshy face.

"Damnit," said Cutler, "can't you people even negotiate coming
around a corner? You there, to the left of Mr. Farnsworth. You
come in here with your gun lowered and then the others will follow
and then you can all put your guns in their holsters. Satisfactory
to everyone?"

Bressio nodded.

"Both of you agree then," said Cutler.

Farnsworth looked to the man on his right, who took a reluctant
step forward, then lowered his glance and would move no more.
Farnsworth shoved him angrily, but the man went only as far as
Farnsworth's shove. The other gunman, seeing this, edged away
from Farnsworth, shaking his head.

Farnsworth looked at the two men contemptuously. "I will
come forward," said Farnsworth. "I carry no weapons at all."

Cutler admired the man's courage and felt some small empathy.
He too knew what it was like to see employees fold under pressure.

"Here I am, Alphonse," said Farnsworth. He looked at Bressio's
lowered gun sadly. "Is this what we have come to?" Farnsworth

looked back to the hall and yelled, "You can put them away. He won't bite you. I said away. Come in here and look at a man. See what one looks like," yelled Farnsworth.

The two gunmen holstered their weapons, looking nervously at each other, drawing some strength from each other in the knowledge that each was not alone in his fear. They entered Cutler's office, eying Bressio as though he were an uncaged tiger. Cutler noticed that when Farnsworth signaled them to sit down, they did not take their eyes off Bressio. Nor did they stop looking when Farnsworth nodded Bressio into the hall and Bressio went with him to the far end out of hearing distance. Cutler saw them enter what he knew to be the smaller conference room. Naturally Farnsworth would know where all the rooms were. He owned the building. Funny, Farnsworth being a Mr. Felli.

One of the gunmen crossed himself. The other sighed with relief.

"Would you gentlemen care for something to drink?" said Cutler. They both shook their heads.

"Well, I can use a good stiff one, I'll tell you that." In a way he could not explain, Cutler felt a certain sense of exhilaration and pride that it was not a Mitchell, Walker and Cutler employee that had backed down, but these men, a reinforcement of the idea that quality always came to quality, no matter what the sphere. It was an amusing thought.

In the smaller conference room, which was only a neat, painfully bare table surrounded by floor-to-ceiling lawbooks, Al Bressio was not sharing amusing thoughts with Anselmo Felli. He had known the man since childhood. It was always Mr. Felli who had come when Mama needed some extra money, always Mr. Felli who inquired about young Alphonse, always Mr. Felli whom Mama would boast with pride that she could see if ever there was any trouble with city government, especially with building inspectors coming around the apartment building she owned.

"If you in any trouble, Mr. Felli take care of you, understanda, Alphonse," his mother had said, but even as a young man Bressio knew better. He knew Felli hadn't shown all that great an interest in him before he had to take care of himself with those three men. He knew what the gold watch was for at high school graduation or the offering of the car when he got out of law school. He knew what it was all about, but it was so much more practical to continue the charade of friendship.

Now, sitting in a conference room of Mitchell, Walker and Cutler, he saw the charade end after so many years. In a way, it was a relief.

Felli sat down at the table and rubbed his hands, examining his highly manicured fingertips. He wore a big diamond pinky ring on his left hand. "We want to know what is coming off, Alphonse," said Felli. He looked up from his hands.

Bressio noticed how cold his brown eyes seemed now. Yet in the coldness was reassurance. He was not dealing with a fool.

"There's been an accident of misinformation. My interest in 285 Pren Street was never what it holds, but was with the woman Mary Beth Cutler, who is the daughter of the man who owns this firm, one of the owners."

Felli nodded.

"The reason why this information—misinformation—blossomed was I was out of town on legal business and did not get word from our mutual friend, who has told you I was here at this office. I might add if you check with him he will verify that he gave me misleading information, information I paid for in good money and in good faith."

"He told you what he knew to be true," said Felli.

"I know that. Because of the nature of the size of the material at 285 Pren Street a source of his was willing to incur his wrath with misleading facts. This I understand. I am not a little boy. My only interest in this is the safety of the woman Mary Beth Cutler. She is a client, a valued client."

"What you say makes sense, Alphonse. Except that you are taking extraordinary risks for a client, even a most valued one. For days no one knows where you stand. You even disappear. When you are seen again, you are seen in that house. Shots are heard in that house, and during a tense time, a very tense time, you do not know how tense it is, when those shots are heard. You are seen later talking to, making a deal, with a narco. Now what can we believe?"

"I went to Pren Street to see for myself. I could not believe, even as I believed it, that a mistake of such monumental proportions could occur. I had to touch and feel the stuff for myself to see it's dimensions. And whether you believe me or not, Anselmo . . .

Anselmo," said Bressio, repeating Felli's first name to indicate that there should be no waste of time in presumed friendship and respect, "it is the truth, what I have told you."

"I believe you," said Felli. "But so what? I know you, but so what? These are very troubled times. This thing is like an avalanche. People making new alignments right within the most reliable regimes. And not just within our families. There is so much pressure it is driving all the top people in the families into thinking of new arrangements, some of which will not be so good for us or others. But that is my problem. Your problem is none of us feel we can afford to safely let you go wandering about without knowing what you were doing.

"All right. You say you do not wish to be involved. I say that is a smart thing to wish, Alphonse. I say that is a very smart thing. We do not wish to be involved either. But we are up to our balls. You want to go to a fancy school and think you're too good for us, all right. All right. You want to buy favors, all right. You want to have a special life to yourself, all right. You carry that gun around that all of us know you can use so well and you do not wish to use it in our service, all right. That was then. Those were the good times. There are no good times any more, Alphonse. No more kissing Don Carmine's hand and showing all the bullshit respect. You gotta take a side now. That's why I am here."

"You make it sound like there are only two sides, Anselmo. There is another side. Look at this office. You know what they take in a year? Legal? Without ducking to the botton of a car when they hear a loud noise? They can spend all their money right out in the open because they don't have to sweat the IRS asking them all those questions about where they got their money. It's a good life, Anselmo."

"I don't see no Cannigliaro, Bensi, Giordano on no names here, Alphonse. They got some lace-curtain Irish, a German Jew cause he's a fucking genius, and the rest are all their kind. This is their business, Alphonse."

"I've had the kiss," said Bressio, meaning he had been given an invitation to join the firm, which was untrue, but he had his special reason for saying it.

"What are they gonna let you make here, Alphonse? You're a smart boy. How much can they cut you in for with what you can

do? A hundred thousand a year? You ain't gonna see bread like
that. There are three guys here making that kind of money. And,
I might add, much more. But everyone else is lucky to see fifty
grand. This isn't any Hebe outfit where they go spreading it
around. They don't have to here. They're WASPS. Everything is
kept right here," said Felli, patting his chest. "On the other hand,
there is a silver lining to our situation. A lot of things are going
to be opening up. A lot of areas. A lot of new people will have to
be replaced. You wouldn't be just some soldier who'd leave me out
in some hallway with nothing but my suit between me and a gun.
You'd be a valued asset, and you'd be treated as such. You'd be
a very rich man, a very rich man. Real money. I bet I got more
money than that Cutler fellow out there."

"How much are you going to spend walking into people like me,
Anselmo? I made my deal. I got a good deal going with his daughter. Real money. I'm not going to throw it away to get my ass
blown off in one of your wars."

"It's 'your wars' now. I see. Well, maybe you think so and maybe
that Cutler guy thinks so, but nobody else thinks so and the only
question, Alphonse Bressio, is whether you get into this thing with
allies who can help you, or you go it alone with no one. No one.
Alone."

"That's the way it's really always been, *Mr. Felli.*"

"I hope they burn your balls off, Bressio," said Felli, his face
contorted in a sneer that revealed his gold bridgework.

Like a striking snake Bressio's left hand reached out to Felli's
painted tie, and handling him like a stuffed teddy bear Bressio lifted
him from his seat.

"Don't forget who I am, Felli," said Bressio. And he spit full in
the older man's face. Then he spit again and released Felli, who
steadied himself on the table and stood erect, not bothering to wipe
his face dry but letting the spittle run down his cheek.

"I will convey your respects to Don Carmine," he said.

"Please do," said Bressio. "I hope the summer is finding him
well."

"I am sure he returns the sentiments."

"Good day, Mr. Felli."

"Good day, Mr. Bressio."

Bressio ushered Arnold Farnsworth to the front door and signaled to his men to follow. They jumped from their seats and trotted up the hallway past the many staid and private offices of Mitchell, Walker and Cutler. At the door, Bressio pushed them out, stumbling into Felli, who suddenly unleashed his anger on his subordinates who had failed him. Bressio shut the outer door of Mitchell, Walker and Cutler to the sound of faces being slapped.

Cutler was at his desk, drinking a half-tumbler of sherry. The bottle sat on his blotter.

"Well," said Cutler. "So that's the terrible, terrible Mafia. They don't look all that tough to me."

"Yeah, well," said Bressio and could no more explain what fear was about to a man like Cutler than he could tell Felli. They just don't know, these people. "Look, while I'm working for you on your daughter thing, I'd appreciate your spreading the word or at least answering if someone asks you, I'd appreciate you telling them you're going to make me a member of this firm. I've got my reasons. I want to keep some people hopefully unsure."

"How did you know?" said Cutler.

Bressio cocked an eyebrow.

"I said how did you know I was planning to bring you into Mitchell, Walker and Cutler?"

"I didn't," said Bressio.

"Well, I've given it some thought and I've seen how your mind works, and I am sure that when the bar comes up again soon, you will take it and pass it and then join us."

"Wait a minute. Even people who are super experts at reaching people haven't been able to get to the bar yet. I know."

"Well, it's not really a question of slipping someone an envelope or anything that crude. You'd probably have to do some heavy preparatory work, but I feel rather confident that we can reasonably assure you on becoming a lawyer."

"That's a hell of a carrot you're holding in front of me," said Bressio.

"I was wondering what your price was," said Cutler. "You know, I'm what one might call an expert at determining a person's area of maximum concern. This is very important in our business, and I couldn't figure out yours."

"You still haven't," said Bressio. "Can I use a private line? I want to phone my bookie."

Cutler blinked and cleared his throat.

"I don't think I heard what you said very clearly, Al."

"You heard," said Bressio.

"Can I ask why? This comes as a considerable shock to me. You know who we are. I known you know who we are."

"Yeah. Yeah. I do."

"And you're still interested in law, I know that. I've heard you right here explain how you and that fellow Dawson plan to use the courts. No one can hide that sort of excitement from me. I know the law is where you're at."

"That's very much true, Mr. Cutler. It's been a long day and it's going to be a longer night for me, so just point me to the phone. I'm drained."

"Anyone on any of those secretaries' desks in the main hallway. The front," said Cutler, dumfounded.

"Thanks," said Bressio and as he sat down near a typewriter at one of the secretaries' desks, he thought about the note calling him a beautiful person and he wished again he could have saved it.

Clarissa would understand what Felli and Cutler could not. The Law. With all its whore judges and lawyers who knew more about collecting bills than the First Amendment.

In the law, there was what separated the men from animals, and while it was not perfect, in it was perfection. In it was the way out of young men being held over a coffin to kiss a wax face. In it was the way out of fear. Maybe not this generation, but maybe the next.

If he had told that to Felli, if he had given that as his refusal, he would be as good as dead. To show fear to a man like Felli was to die. Alphonse Bressio could not allow himself that luxury if he wanted to stay alive. He had to remind the close adviser to Don Carmine that he had not gone soft, that it was best to reconsider before any precipitous moves. Alphonse Joseph Bressio was not a man to be trifled with. Nor was he a man to devote a life to getting a useless warning on a pack of cigarettes.

The law was out there even if a William James Cutler did not practice it as a young graduate thought he did. There were Harlan Fiske Stones and Cordozos and Marshalls. They were beautiful people. As was Alphonse Joseph Bressio. Sometimes.

XVIII

Bressio arrived late at Federal District Court on Foley Square across the park from his office that he could not go to. Nor could he spend the night in his apartment. He had lost his tail on Forty-second Street and had spent the night sleeping in a Trailways bus to Trenton and back. All he had to do was keep moving and stay alive until someone got to the stash, as someone had to.

There would be a blood bath, and blessedly he would be out of it. They would all go after the people who got the stash and he would be out of it. Then it would be apparent he was no competition.

The heat wave had broken with an early-morning shower and Bressio felt cool tripping up the steps of the courthouse. He had washed and shaved at the Port Authority bus terminal that morning, phoned Clarissa, heard her beautiful alive voice, told her not to leave any more written messages, heard that Mary Beth and Bobbi had reluctantly gone with her to the farm in Mount Carmel, and told her he was fine and on the move. He also told her to bill Cutler with the clock running twenty-four hours a day.

Dawson's private secretary told him the Fleish pretrial was scheduled for 9:00 A.M., and it was 9:30 when he phoned. It was possible he would miss Dawson in action, but he doubted it.

Federal District Court was as good a place as any to spend a couple of hours, and he liked to watch Dawson work. Many young lawyers would make futile grandiloquent motions for dismissal at these proceedings and some of the older ones would go up to the bench tired and bored and let the prosecution dump on their clients, just not to be delayed in court any longer than they felt they had to.

The pretrial was the scut mechanics of the law, hearing defense motions for change of venue or lowering of bail or delayed trial date and often for dismissal of the charges, which rarely occurred. Here the defendant pleaded guilty or not guilty, asked to avail himself of a jury or not. Here the prosecution presented the grand jury's indictment to the judge. And right here was one of the first distinguishing steps between Anglo-Saxon justice and the ancient Roman justice followed by the rest of Europe, except, of course, England.

The judge did not represent the prosecution. He sat between prosecutor and defense, ideally impartial. At least that was how he was supposed to be. In other countries, the judge and the prosecution were often one with the burden of proof on the defense.

The Anglo-Saxon system had its flaws, but only in comparison to the ideal of what it should be. In relationship to the rest of the world, it was beauty in Bressio's eyes, and for a lawyer to function in this system with anything less than competence to Bressio was a sin. Which was why he liked to watch Dawson work even at a pretrial.

Dawson performed so casually that an uninformed observer would think he had just dropped in to say hello and gotten involved by mistake. He did not waste words, nor did he let anything slip by him.

The best comparison Bressio could think of was watching Joe DiMaggio play center field a quarter of a century earlier. No grandstand dramatics of diving catches, just consistent brilliant field work made ordinary in its appearance by his genius.

At something without publicity Dawson was his best. Bressio had never liked Dawson's use of the media because it took from what Dawson did best. To Bressio's occasional complaints Dawson would answer, "Pure, shmure, you ought to build a statue to the virgin of the law. I tell you, Al. That's where we differ. I think she's a great roll-in-the-hay whore and you think she's a stone goddess. And we both love her, so how do you explain it?"

Bressio signed in at the book downstairs, showed his permit to carry a weapon to the guard and took an elevator crowded with a group of elementary school students on tour.

The courtroom was the size of a medium supermarket, with fifteen wooden benches partially filled with people, leading to the high bench where the Honorable V. L. Gordon presided. It was a fairly full docket, and Bressio had noticed on the sheet at the door that the Fleish case was near the end. It did not list Dawson's name as representing. Bressio saw Dawson's white crown, three rows from the front. To the right in what would normally be a jury box, lawyers sat chatting.

There were scores of transactions going on in the courtroom, only one of which involved the Honorable V. L. Gordon sitting atop the head check-out line. Yet what was going on—the prosecutor, the lawyer, the client and the judge—was just as much the purity of the law as if the Supreme Court sat in majestic decorum.

"Al. Al Bressio," called a woman. It was Becky Hawkins, in a smart tan suit that screamed Bonwit Teller or Bloomingdale's or any of the good department stores that made women look so New York. This was the New York envied and feared outside of Manhattan by so many people, and the funny thing to someone like Bressio, who knew, was that this New York was made of the Becky Hawkins of the world.

The native New Yorkers lived in Queens or Brooklyn and the Bronx and felt just as envious of and hostile to Manhattan as might Des Moines, Iowa, or Troy, Ohio. New York's major league was no more New York than the New York Yankees. It was where the money was made.

Becky motioned to the empty shellacked wood space next to her. "We won't be up for a while," she whispered.

Was that Bobo's brand of perfume he smelled?

"You won't be up at all. This is a pretrial," said Bressio.

"Murray said I could watch. He's so sexy, isn't he?"

"He's all right," said Bressio. He felt Becky squeeze his arm.

"I'm so excited. You won't believe it, but I know this is my city. I belong here. This is where I always belonged. It's so alive."

"I believe you. Yeah."

"You think I belong, do you? Do you really?"

"You belong so much, Becky, you won't even be asking that question by this afternoon."

"That's the same suit you wore yesterday, Al. You shouldn't dress like that. I'm telling you this because I want you to be my very best friend. You've done so much bringing Murray and me together. I'll never forget you for this."

"Watch your ass, Becky. Bobo is no pushover."

"I know. Exciting, isn't it? Call me Bicky, it sounds better. Murray likes Becky, but I know Bicky is, well, distinctive."

"Bobo has got the money, Bicky."

"I know," she said and Bressio saw her young mind calculating.

The court clerk called up a case and Bressio watched Judge Gordon assign a lawyer who would be paid by the state. Everyone had a right to counsel. Unfortunately, Bressio recognized the lawyer and thought that one whale of a constitutional case might be made as to whether that man really was counsel. He would plead the defendant guilty and collect his fee. In this case it was a young black girl accused of embezzlement, the official charge, against Chase Manhattan Bank, N.A. She was probably caught taking home samples.

She would do better if she held up a liquor store and bought herself a real lawyer. In time served, Bressio calculated it was a good risk. She was going to do five years with that counsel. Sure as bank interest. With only a chance of getting caught with a holdup, she could do better with a good counsel on two offenses than she could with just the embezzlement and the public defender.

Then again, how would she know how to find a good lawyer? Too many, especially in Harlem or Bedford Stuyvesant, would delay trial until they had their fee, then go in and make the same plea she was getting for nothing. Nothing for nothing as opposed to nothing for something.

A very good question intrigued Bressio. In reality, could she be expected to be represented well? Probably no more than most Americans outside the very wealthy or the law fraternity.

Then again, could he or possibly even Dawson be assured they were getting the best doctors other than following the highest prices and hoping? What went on in the hospitals, Bressio suspected, might be far worse than what went on in the courts.

"What are you thinking?" asked Bicky, née Becky.

"Shhh," said Bressio.

"I can't tell anything that's going on up there. It's confusing."

"If anything happens, I'll tell you."

The court clerk made another announcement and Bressio leaned forward.

"Leland Fleish. Calvin P. Loring. Leland M. Fleish," called out the clerk. So Leland was L. Marvin's first name. Bressio suddenly noticed Fleish was sitting next to Dawson. He had his hair cut and was wearing a suit. That clipped blond head belonged to Fleish, Leland M. Dawson whispered something feverishly to Fleish and gave the back of his neck a little tap. Fleish nodded.

"That's us," said Bressio. "Over there is the U.S. Attorney, his name is Cartwright. He's got a bunch of papers in his hand: one of them probably is a bill of particulars concerning the evidence, another is probably the records of the defendants."

"You got the Arizona thing squared away so he won't introduce it, right?" said Becky.

"Dawson told you a lot, I see. Well, what will happen, probably at the trial, is the prosecutor will try to introduce it and Dawson will try to keep it out because it's not a conviction, a man being innocent until proven guilty. If Dawson were sleeping, Cartwright would try to get it established now so he could introduce it before a jury. But Dawson won't let him, and I'm pretty sure he knows that so he probably won't try. In a nutshell, don't look for Arizona here. We got it, as you said, squared away. Here comes your boyfriend, Becky."

Between guards came a gangling, nervous young man in a short-sleeved white shirt that hung like a flag over his scrawny shoulders. Bressio lowered his eyes. He knew what he had done to this young man. Well, he had done it and to hell with it. He noticed Becky. Her head was proudly erect and she was smiling. And he saw her give Loring one big fat wink. Loring's dejection became a light-hearted bounce. He returned the wink and the guards had to turn him toward the bench.

"That'll hold Cal for a month, that wink," said Becky. "He'll read reams of meanings into the slightest recognition."

Judge Gordon noted Dawson's substitution for another lawyer of his firm, noted the prosecution's presence and asked Loring if he had an attorney.

"Uh, no, sir, your honor," said Loring.

"That's so typical Calvin," said Becky.

"Are you going to live East Side or West Side, Becky?" asked Bressio.

"Bicky."

"Then we will appoint one," said Judge Gordon, who, as most men, looked dwarfed by the size of the bench over which he presided, and like many judges had black robes which made the disparity seem less glaring.

At this, the court clerk, sitting beneath and to the left of the judge, whispered something, and the judge called out the name of a lawyer who rose and went to Loring's side, scarcely noticing Loring, but looking for some recognition from Murray Blay Dawson.

Dawson ignored him. Fleish also looked straight ahead. Loring's lawyer was in his mid-fifties, and his hair was so heavily greased it glistened in the courtroom lights. He wore the kind of red and yellow jacket that gets left on racks for years. He was a "screwer," known for accepting clients' bodies as fees.

"Watch this," said Bressio. "I think you're going to see something."

"Murray's going to ask for a severance, I know that. It's sort of usual in these cases, isn't it? I mean, if you have someone tried for conspiracy without anyone present with whom he's supposed to be conspiring, then that's practically a won case, Murray says."

"Except that every lawyer worth two cents would attempt to ask for a severance," said Bressio. "You want to see it done right. Watch."

Dawson haggled slightly over the reading of Fleish's record of misdemeanors into the court record. Creating a public disturbance was one of them. Cartwright got it accepted, but only after a little hassle which he won easily.

"That was a feint," whispered Bressio.

Dawson finally agreed in a friendly tone with the judge and with Cartwright, dropping a hand into his pocket, and then as if he were being detained, he casually mentioned a little problem he'd like the judge to square away.

"Your honor, I'd like to sever our case if it's all right. My client doesn't even know this guy." Dawson's left hand went out in a casual flick to Loring. There was just the slightest note of indignation in Dawson's casualness, as though some legal mechanical mistake had been made, and the judge, being competent, would naturally straighten it out.

The U.S. Attorney was going through some papers, and just glanced up briefly, probably still riding on his little victory.

Bressio swallowed. "Shhhhhh," he whispered to Becky.

"Yes, of course," said Judge Gordon.

The clerk leaned back and whispered something over his shoulder. "I'm sorry," said Judge Gordon. "We can't sever. It's a conspiracy indicment."

After the trial date had been set, September 22, nearly a month away, Dawson returned up the aisle with Fleish who was shorn even of mustache, and looked incredibly vulnerable.

They talked outside the courtroom with Dawson getting occasional glances. Dawson said he wanted Bicky in on this discussion.

"Nice job. Almost," said Bressio.

"Yes, almost. A clerk makes a judge."

"Keep your boy out of Pren Street," said Bressio. "The place is loaded with smack. Loaded. Incredible."

"I thought you said they don't leave large amounts lying around."

"They have. In the millions."

"Maybe I can use it somehow. This means the FBNC is vulnerable."

"Don't touch it, Murray. There's going to be a blood bath. Guaranteed. Everyone is jumpy. Unless, of course, you want L. Marvin dead, which would not overly depress me."

"No. No. I wouldn't want that. You look as though you could use some sleep."

"I'm on the move."

"That bad?"

"That bad."

"How do you know?" said Becky.

"I saw it. I touched it. I felt it. Big."

"Maybe it's heavily cut with quinine. It could be cut with a number of things. Size doesn't always indicate quality."

"It's pure," said Bressio. "Uncut. Pure."

"Have you run a lab test?" asked Becky.

"My lab test is out in the street. I can count the bodies."

"Thanks for the warning, Al," said Dawson.

"You're talking about Marvin's loft?" asked Becky.

"No. The one beneath it," said Bressio angrily. "There's a bath-room floor full of it. Pardon the expression."

"Can I charge Cutler for Marvin's defense?" asked Dawson.

"Charge away," said Bressio. "But I'm first."

"What happened."

"He wasn't what I wanted him to be."

"So the goddess is a whore after all, huh, Al?"

"No. He just wasn't it, Murray."

"At what they do, they're good at."

"So was my father," said Bressio. He shook hands with Dawson, nodded politely to Becky, and ignored Fleish.

"Goodbye, Al," said Fleish. "Hey, Murray. I got a question. How come you didn't want me to say hello to Cal Loring?"

XIX

Bressio wanted to sleep badly. He felt the stickiness of his clothes, the dryness of his mouth and he wanted to take a nice cool drink and slip into his own bed. He told himself that it would be over soon, and that to stop, to let people get set on him, even have time to make a major decision on him, would be a foolish mistake. He would have all the rest he would need very shortly, and best of all he would wake up from it.

He checked in with Clarissa, who said they had a bill from Dr. Finney.

"Oh, that's right," said Bressio. "Pay it."

"I think we'll hold until the end of the month," said Clarissa. "We're a little flat."

"Okay, push the Cutler bill and add Finney's to it."

"You're okay, Al?"

"Clarissa, I never felt better. Just a little bit bored, that's all."

"Sure. That's all this is. Boring. I feel fine, too. You take care, now. Okay."

What a sweet person, thought Bressio. Was it possible he loved her or even, dare he think it, that she loved him? No. No. Impossible. He had seen the mirror that morning in the terminal.

"Impossible," said Bressio and realized the cabdriver was listening to him talk to himself. When had he gotten in the cab? He had just hailed one out of reflex. He had to get some sleep. He checked his watch.

"At twelve of three, two forty-eight, let me off at the corner of West End Avenue and Seventy-second Street. Drive up to Yonkers, then turn around. That should just about do it. Don't stop anywhere too long."

"I don't want no trouble, buddy."

Bressio put a ten-dollar bill in the money cup that was part of the wall that separated driver from passenger.

"I still don't want no trouble. I got two violations on the hack bureau. I don't need trouble."

Bressio put in two fifty-dollar bills.

"We won't have time to make it to Yonkers and back if you want to be at West End and Seventy-second at twelve of."

"Whatever," said Bressio and closed his eyes. He awoke four times when the driver stopped for traffic lights. By the time they circled back to West End Avenue Bressio had to be awakened, and this frightened him. Nobody who had not lived through something like this could realize the drain of energy.

"What about the fare? There's eighteen seventy-five on the meter."

Bressio gave the man two fives and a ten, and did not wait for change although he did not really want to give him a tip on top of the shmeer.

At ten of three he was at Dr. Finney's office and ringing the bell.

With flagrant red beard and flashing blue eyes, Dr. J. P. Finney wanted to know what Bressio was doing there without an appointment.

"Got to talk to you."

"How do you know I'm free?"

"It's ten of, you're always free at ten of."

"I have things to do between patients. This is awfully inconsiderate of you. You could have phoned, couldn't you?"

"I didn't want anyone to know I was going to be here."

"I don't know what it is, but I don't want any part of it."

"You got part of it, so c'mon, J.P., get off my ass."

"All right. Eight minutes, Al."

When Dr. Finney heard that Bressio wanted to discuss the Cutler case, he was furious. Bressio didn't have to come barging in. He could have made an appointment, and if the situation were so pressing for him, why did he have to deal with the Cutler case that minute?

"For one, I might as well get this thing cleared up because here and doing this is as good as anything else I can do, and for two I might as well just do it. So get off my back. What's your diagnosis?"

Bressio sat on the edge of the couch. Finney sat in a soft chair, his legs crossed.

"You know what it is, Al."

"She's not completely paranoid. A lot of that stuff she babbles about is true."

"So, what difference does that make? Mary Beth Cutler is incurable and you know that. There's nothing we or anyone can do for her."

"Yeah. I knew that after I spoke to her boyfriend when I saw him in jail. Five years she was on it."

"Amphetamines."

"And maybe some LSD."

"Well, unless the human body has changed drastically since we had that long talk at Fordham, I would say you didn't even have to send her to a therapist, unless of course she's that one in a thousand or two thousand or five thousand."

"Okay. Give me some fancy medical terms, put it on paper and mail it to my office."

"I don't do bullshit. Especially not when you send me one of those. Therapy is shooting craps enough without those kinds of odds. C'mon, Al, this is Johnny Finney you dumped that on."

It was at Fordham, in his doctoral thesis, that Finney had discovered addicts were never cured, they only withdrew. And having too small a sampling for that proposition, he had come to Bressio, who had gotten him in touch with someone who made his living writing doctoral papers. At that time Finney had laughed and called the dissertation "bullshit." It had given him a Ph.D. behind his name or a doctor before it.

"Okay," Finney said, knowing what the reference to "bullshit" meant. Now, however, he refused any drug-addicted patients because, as he had told Bressio a long time ago at school, you couldn't cure chemicals with talk. It was a standing rule of his. He hated failure.

"Today you don't bullshit. Well, okay. Still, I'm sorry," said Bressio softly. "I only found out after I spoke to her boyfriend. You can bill me for this."

"Of course I will," said Finney. "Well, I'm sorry. Your time's up."

Bressio had been walking ten minutes on Riverside Drive, glancing every now and then at the Hudson in the summer heat, when he saw he had again picked up a tail. He recognized neither of the men.

The tail stayed with him a few more blocks down Riverside Drive, and Bressio doubled back, cut up two blocks to Broadway and stopped at a Greek souvlaki place, where he ordered two of the pungent lamb and onion stuffed rolls. Now was no time to spend on a diet.

About 7:30 P.M. when he thought the last tail had dropped off, he hailed a cab to a middle-class neighborhood in Queens which had earned the reputation recently of being racist because it protested that a big low-income project would bring ghetto blacks to the neighborhood. Sgt. Philosophus Jones had lived there with his family peacefully for the last ten years, having moved there for the same reason as other residents—getting away from the crime. He could not join the protests as he told Bressio once " 'cause I still got to live with my people. But Jesus, Al, this wasn't racist when it started, but it's becoming that now. I'm gonna move out. I just may have to move out."

"Racism?"

"No. The damned project. My kids will be drawn right into all that shit. Needles in the arms. Pimps looking to sell my daughter's ass. Shakedowns on the way to school. No way, man."

Jones lived on the fourth floor of a neat red-brick apartment building. His daughter answered the door, a pretty little girl with a bright open grin, and two pink ribbons in her hair. "Hello. My name is Nancy Jones. What's yours?"

"Al Bressio, honey. Is your daddy home?"

"Who is it, Nancy?" came a woman's voice.

"It's someone for daddy."

"The department?"

"My mother wants to know if you're from the police department. My father is a policeman, a very good one, and sometimes he has visitors from the department, and he's sleeping now."

Bressio heard Mrs. Jones laugh from the kitchen at her daughter's explanation. She came out of the kitchen drying her hands on a towel, laughing at her daughter's openness. When she saw Bressio, the laughter died.

"Yes. Can I help you?" she asked coldly. She instinctively shielded her daughter's head with a hand, bringing little Nancy to the far side of her hip behind an immaculate white apron.

"I'm Al Bressio. I know your husband quite well, I'd like to speak to him."

"He's sleeping," said Mrs. Jones.

"I know. He would want you to wake him."

"Wait here," said Mrs. Jones. She disappeared into the apartment, pulling Nancy by the hand. Bressio heard muffled arguing from a far-off room. Finally Jones came to the door in his police trousers and an undershirt, rubbing sleep from his eyes.

"Phoss. I need a place for the night."

"I don't know, Al. I hear you're into the white powder now. I don't want anything to do with it in my home."

"I'm not in it. It's coming after me. I just need six hours. Six hours, Phoss. A hundred an hour?"

"What good's six hundred if this place becomes a shooting gallery?"

"It won't unless you spread the word I'm here."

Jones blinked himself awake. When his mind had time to focus, he shook his head emphatically. "Not in my house, Al. I'm sorry. Not in my living room. No way, man."

"Twelve hundred," said Bressio.

"That's a lot of money."

"It'll buy a nice trip to Bermuda and some nice school outfits."

"Al, truthfully, I would like to help you 'cause I would like to help you. Out in the street, okay. That's one thing. But back there is my living room, and my wife, and my daughter, and my son, and my kitchen, and my bed, and Al Bressio, you ain't coming in. Not with your connections or nothing. You want to come in, Alphonse, you gotta kill me right here at this threshold."

"What's this killing, Phoss? Here, let me pay you for yesterday." Bressio reached for some bills, but Jones waved him off.

"You use that to keep you alive. If it all works out, then you take care of me. I'm sorry, Alphonse. Truly. But don't come back here again."

Bressio watched the door close in his face. He needed sleep to be sharp. If he had to, he could stay awake for two days running, but the awareness dwindled to sub-nothing at that stage. Looking at the closed door, standing in the hallway, his hands at his sides, helpless, Bressio thought about Felli's offer.

With the family, he would have protection, with the family he could close his eyes and be rested and sharp and protected. Of course, when he was alert, he would be expected to perform certain duties, but even these would be made easier because the family liked to protect its talent. All he had to do was pick up a phone and say, "I'm yours." And then they would ask him to prove it.

It was a wise decision. All the odds pointed that way. Even the bookie knew. When he had called him the night before from Cutler's, he had found his credit turned off for the first time.

"So if I'm not alive, I couldn't collect if I won," Bressio had said.

"You'd be surprised who comes collecting for stiffs, Al. Sorry. No bet."

No bet. Bressio walked slowly down the hallway. Going to the family now would be a smart move. But he wasn't going to. No. He was a beautiful person. And God help anyone reaching into a pocket too quickly within the shooting range of that beautiful person. God help them.

XX

MEMORANDUM

At 6:38 A.M., agent Clyde Forrest, in charge of a maximum sensitivity operation, when inspecting area of highest sensitivity did discover upon personal observation that objects of that sensitivity were no longer on the premises. He reported said fact at 7:15 in a high state of anxiety, repeating quote—I should have sent the memos—unquote. He did not explain his comment.

cc: Special Investigation on Pren Street Operation.

XXI

"You're lying to me, Clarissa. I know there's an important message. Now, I can't stay on this phone too long. So what is it?"

"Al, I'm not going to tell you."

"You don't know about these damned things. You almost got me killed by withholding those other messages. Now do you want to get me killed for sure."

"It's Cutler. He got a phone call from Mary Beth last night. She's back with Marvin."

"She got out of the farm?"

"It's not a jail, Al."

"The hell it wasn't. Where is she now?"

"I don't know. Don't go looking for her Al. Just don't, please."

Bressio hung up and dialed Mitchell, Walker and Cutler. His eyes stung from lack of sleep. He could even feel and hear his heart beat. Morning was upon New York City, a gray, drizzly morning that made the world gray. Bressio watched the morning shoppers on Queens Boulevard bundled in rain slickers, covered by umbrellas, a people that got through the weather never enjoying it. You had to get out of the city to think of weather as more than a nuisance. He let the drizzle come in on him, for he did not wish to shut the door of the glass telephone booth. Sometimes they got stuck, and wouldn't he be a fine sight in a closed glass box. Glass shards were as good as bullets sometimes.

"Just a minute, please. Mr. Cutler said to put you right through to him."

Bressio listened to the clicks of the transfer of lines. He didn't

174

see any tails at the moment. Whether they had planned it or not, it was a good strategy to keep people on him. It was like a sword in his back. Yet in a way that strategy could backfire if he were a less reasonable man. He might be pushed to lashing out wildly at someone like Don Carmine . . . if he were not a reasonable man.

"Al, this is Jim Cutler. Mary Beth phoned me last night and said she was returning to Fleish. I thought you had assured me this wouldn't happen."

"Nothing of the sort. I said I would try."

"I got the impression she was going to Pren Street. That's a dangerous area now, correct?"

"Just how do you know that?" yelled Bressio. "How the fuck do you know that? What are you telling me she's in Pren Street for? What kind of shit is that?"

"I just said, Mr. Bressio, that I got the impression she was going to Pren Street. She mentioned the loft. In our agreement you were to provide her with protection, if I am correct. That is a dangerous place. If she is there, I would appreciate your getting her out of there. That is all I'm asking. I am a father and I am worried about my daughter. I was under the impression that your high fee covered a situation like this. Perhaps I am wrong. There really isn't too much I can do. Is there?"

"If I'm absolutely sure she's there, I'll get her out. If I'm 100 percent certain."

"That's all I can ask. And I am grateful."

"Yeah, well, I got the doctor's report on her yesterday."

"Yes?" Cutler's voice was anxious.

"She's, uh . . . she's coming along fine, Mr. Cutler."

"It's Jim, Al. I'm sorry for the harshness, but you understand the concern a father has for his daughter."

"Yeah. Okay."

From an open subway booth waiting for an F train into Manhattan, Bressio dialed Dawson's office. Dawson wasn't in. Bressio dialed his home. Bobo answered.

"He's right here, Al. We're together again, no thanks to you . . . It's your procurer, Murray."

Bressio heard the phone change hands.

"Hi, Al. What's up?"

"You seen Mary Beth?"

"No. Not for days."

"You know where L. Marvin is? He's not in that loft, is he? I mean, I fucking warned you and him about that loft."

"I don't know, Al. I don't know. He and Becky were talking about loft living last night. I loaned her my Rolls . . . Excuse me, I loaned the little farm tramp Bobo's personal car. Does that suit you, Bobo? . . . and she and Marvin drove off in it, and this morning the chauffeur found it parked in the garage, but without the keys. If you see Becky, would you get the damned keys from her? Bobo is the only person I know with a Rolls and only one set of keys. Will you shut up, Bobo? This is business."

"But you don't know for sure where she is or where Mary Beth is or where L. Marvin is, right? I mean you don't know that."

"Knowing the nature of the girl from Iowa, and knowing L. Marvin, I would say they took a look at the loft, and might still be there. Yes."

"That's not sure," said Bressio.

"You're not going there, are you?"

"Not if I can help it."

"You want company?"

"Thanks, Murray, but you'd only get in the way and get me killed probably."

"If you need me, Al, for anything, you know where to get me . . . Shut up, Bobo, you and your money can go piss up a rope. Just call if you need me, Al. I'll be here all day. Bobo and I are making up."

The Manhattan-bound train opened its doors, and Bressio dropped the phone and rushed into the maw of the car. He sat across from an old woman with a large brown paper bag of what appeared to be wool. She avoided looking at him. A transit patrolman seeing Bressio's pistol, flagrant in holster behind unbuttoned jacket, turned and walked out of the car.

In Manhattan, Bressio heard what he didn't want to hear. An unmarked car with two plainclothesmen signaled him over.

"You're Alphonse Bressio, aren't you?"

"Yeah."

"A Sergeant Philosophus Jones, twenty-seventh precinct, is trying to reach you." The plainclothesman checked his watch. "He's eating now. You can get him at that luncheonette on University Place near the Dardanelles Restaurant. Do you know the place?"

"Yeah," said Bressio. He was running out of small change, and with his last dime, he got the luncheonette's pay phone, and asked for Jones. He had the feeling that morning that he was living in telephone booths.

"Hey, Al. I got some information that may be of help. Big bad thing happened at Pren Street this morning, no one in the department knows what, the narcos are being super-hush about it."

"How many dead?"

"Don't think anyone's dead, but we're staying off that street as requested by their liaison this morning. I hear some people are being kept in their loft on the third floor and can't leave. Even the connected people don't know what's going on, but that street is an armed camp. Did you know that?"

"Yeah," said Bressio. "I know that. I'll take care of you if I'm breathing."

"That'll be nice, Al, but I didn't reach out for you for that. You know why I did what I had to do last night, don't you? You should know best of all."

"I do, Phossy. You've been better at it than I. I wish I knew how you did it so successfully."

"It's the small things, Alphonse. You don't even give 'em the small, meaningless things. You think about it there, fella. Good luck."

Maybe Mary Beth wasn't in the loft. Maybe other people were being held there? Maybe no one was being held there? All Phossy knew was what the precinct was talking about.

And maybe Mary Beth was there.

The rain was letting up, and Bressio felt his stubble of a beard, and his mouth tasted like wax when he entered a rent-a-car on Thirty-eighth Street.

"How long did you want the car for?"

"A half-hour. Make it a day," said Bressio, who told the clerk he did not care whether it was a coupe or a hardtop or an economy model. "A car. Just a car."

The clerk smiled with great effort and double-checked Bressio's credit card and driver's license.

Near Washington Park, Bressio parked the car, and waited for a car that might be a tail to pass from view down the block. He removed his .38 police special from its holster, checked the bullets that he knew were there, checked the hammer action again and put the gun back in the holster. The gun was in working order. God willing, he would not have to use it.

He picked up Pren Street as it came into Houston and at fifteen miles an hour drove slowly towards 285. For a street where the narcos had something big going, there seemed to be very few unmarked cars. There were only two parked cars on the street. The warehouse was closed, even though it was midweek. No one was on the street. In all the jarring, noise-grinding city of New York, this street was quiet as a cave. Bressio pulled up at the corner in front of 285. The metal door was closed. Bressio noticed a Venetian blind across the street move ever so slightly.

With great deliberation and very small movements he got out of the car. Standing by the door of the car with his hands clearly away from his shoulder holster and clearly empty, he looked up to the third floor loft. He saw a figure in the window, the very dusty window. Was it a woman? A man?

"Mary Beth," Bressio called out. "Mary Beth."

The figure did not move, and Bressio called out louder. "Mary Beth. Mary Beth."

Bressio saw the window nudge open, then flung open wide. His stomach jumped at its suddenness. He wanted to scream out for no sudden movements. For God's sake move slow. Who else was it but L. Marvin Fleish with his short haircut. He was wearing a T-shirt.

"Hi, Al," he yelled. "We're locked in here. Could you bring up something to eat?"

"Not so loud," said Bressio. "And don't make any fast moves. Nothing to rile anyone."

"Hey, baby. Don't hassle it," yelled L. Marvin. "If you're worried about all the creeps, I'll keep you covered." And with a booming yell lest anyone missed the threat, L. Marvin Fleish screamed, "I got you covered, Bressio. Go ahead." And to support this claim, out of the window came the Sea Scout training rifle.

The first nervous shot from across the street started the fusillade, and Bressio dropped to the pavement, his face in something smelly and sticky. The brat-brat of pistols and the bloom-blooms of shotguns and the pinging of bullets going into brick exploded down Pren Street. The weeks of quiet maneuvering, of back-alley killings, of frightened greedy people with guns all let loose on Pren Street. It only took one person thinking an artificial rifle was real.

Bessio felt a tug at his jacket, but he just stayed flat. That was how a bullet felt going through cloth.

"Al Bressio. Help me. Help me. Al, help me. They have guns. They have guns." It was Mary Beth's voice. There was firing inside the loft building also. Obviously some people had been planted there waiting, and they were exchanging shots with the narcos or with themselves.

Bressio was off the sidewalk into the building with his gun out and running up the steps, feeling a sharp sting in his ass and keeping on running. The hallway was floodlit now, and someone came fast at him falling backward into Bressio, who brushed him aside and down the stairs like a leaf. Past the damned second-floor loft, whose door was shut, and up a flight to the third-floor loft and into a rifle pointing down the stairs right at his face. Bressio's pistol was alive with two immediate and immaculate shots in the forehead, then chestbone. The rifleman convulsed and Bressio was at the top of the stairs on the third floor. The loft door was open. Fleish knelt with his hands covering his eyes. Before him was a body bubbling blood from the stomach. The body had sandy blond hair. Becky Hawkins.

"Who's in there? Who's in there?" yelled Bressio, getting close to a wall.

"It's me, Al. Your cousin Joey. Joey Bugellerio."

"Anyone else?"

"Just a friend. He's okay. You still heavy on that Cutler woman?"

"No. Never was," yelled Bressio.

"You were for the smack, right?"

"What do you think?"

"That's what I thought. We had a little accident in here."

"What do I care? What's the status of the smack?"

"I guess it's still downstairs. We heard the shooting and we came down from the roof. We caught some rifle shots and ducked in here. The broads got in our way."

"Who you working for?"

"Ourselves and some other guys. You want to join?"

"You join me."

"Who you with?"

"Myself."

"Okay."

"C'mon out," said Bressio.

"You come in."

Bressio heard the throat gurgle of a wounded person inside the loft.

With pistol in front of him he turned the corner exposing himself. Joey had a sawed-off shotgun pointed at Bressio's belly, his friend had a light pistol pointed at Bressio's chest. They stood in the middle of the loft. Mary Beth Cutler was curled in a fetal position by the bathroom door, surrounded by a small carpeting of blood. Bobbi sat by her mother, staring down at what was left of a face. Bressio knew what a shotgun could do to a face. L. Marvin trembled by the body of Becky Hawkins.

"She knew exactly where it was, Joey," said Bressio, nodding to Becky's body. Joey's pockmarked middle-aged face was flushing red. Bressio moved as if to put his pistol back in his holster. Seeing this, Joey relaxed and lowered his shotgun from Bressio's belly. As the barrel of Bressio's .38 touched his holster, Bressio moved towards his second cousin Joey as though to explain something.

"What you got to understand about this situation, Joey," said Bressio reaching out his left hand palm upward in an explanatory manner, "is that . . . "

His left hand gripped the barrel of the shotgun like a steel clamp, and the .38 police special suddenly came down, and Bressio's fine eye and reflexes put a loud hole in the chest of Joey's friend.

Joey tried to wrest the barrel free, but Bressio jerked it to his side, pulling Joey to his own massive belly and bringing a knee up into Joey's testicles, doubling him over and gaining control of the shotgun for himself.

With one hand he flipped up the shotgun, gaining the stock with his palm, and with his finger on the trigger stuck the wide double-barrel into Joey's ear and pulled the trigger.

Joey's head exploded as though turned on by three high-pressure nozzles of brain and blood and skull splinters. The loft floor was slippery with blood when Bressio went to Bobbi, and taking her by the hand, said, "Mommy's gone to sleep, honey. You come with me."

He brought her to a far wall, the stairs being too dangerous just then, and buried her head gently in his chest, keeping her clean dress away from the blood on his shirt. He felt a tearing pain there, but he knew he would live.

Fleish sobbed. "I didn't know. I didn't know. I didn't know."

The firing had stopped. Sirens were in the air all over the streets outside. Bressio heard lawmen in the process of arresting and searching and taking down information move up the stairs. He heard them come to the rifleman he had killed and heard that it was not one of theirs. He could probably beat this manslaughter charge and still carry his gun. If the guy wasn't law he had to be connected, probably with a record.

And Joey, Bressio knew, had done two stretches for armed robbery and assault with intent to kill. His "friend" undoubtedly carried a similar past.

"Forrest got it," said one of the men in the hallway.

"Where?"

"In the basement. He was with the supervisor when the hell broke loose. Ran into it."

Oh, no, thought Bressio. The kid hadn't made it either. All the grief of the senseless deaths came down upon him and he put his face to the little girl's shoulder and wept. He did not know why Forrest's death had unleashed this awesome sadness, why just one more life should do it, but it had. And there he was and he felt very frightened and very alone, and for some reason which he knew not either, he was without hope.

Several agents came into the room, remarking on the blood bath, and Bressio surrendered his gun. He felt a nudge at his shoulder and he looked up to find the U.S. Attorney Cartwright standing over him.

"Jim Cutler is here. Is that his daughter?" asked Cartwright.

"By the bathroom."

Cartwright went to the door and asked, "Do you want to look?"

"Yes. She was my only child."

Bressio caught Cutler's glance and saw the eyes move away from him. Cutler stood over his daughter's body for a few moments, bowed with a certain dignity. When he came back he toddled like a child to keep from slipping on the blood. Already one agent had taken a header.

"I guess I should have expected something like this," said Cutler bitterly. "Dealing with someone like you, Bressio. Thank you very much. Thank you so very much. Let me tell you, young man, you're through. I don't care what it takes, what I have to do, you're through in this city."

Bressio thought of spitting, but there was blood in his mouth. Surprisingly, U.S. Attorney Cartwright became engaged.

"You vile, goddamned hypocrite!" Cartwright bellowed. "You make any move against this man and I will be happy to indict your sanctimonious ass from here to Washington. Look at the floor. Is this enough spit for you? Did your FBNC put enough spit into the casual fight against drugs? Yes, you, Cutler, and your Washington friends with your bright ideas. Every time someone wanted to back off on this thing, they had you people screaming how casual they looked in their fight against drugs. Show me the winner here. Out in that street as of this morning is enough smack to turn on the East Coast for a year. Congratulations, Mr. Cutler, and thank you on behalf of the city's junkies for your firm's pro bono work in narcotics."

"You talk as though you have a lifetime appointment," said Cutler menacingly.

"Long enough to make life miserable for you."

"You can't indict me for the mistakes of the FBNC. I was only on the President's advisory panel on narcotics. We only helped shape policy."

"Screw all that," said Bressio heavily. "This is your granddaughter, Cutler." Bobbi refused to lift her head.

"That's Fleish's child, if I'm correct."

"The papers have been filed. She's an orphan and she's your granddaughter and she's entitled to whatever that entitles her to."

"Well, you take care of it, if you can without getting her killed. Get her into some kind of home. I'll take care of the bill. Keep my name out of it. There have been too many people into my pocket already. Including you, Mr. Bressio. I've had a very trying day. Seventy-five dollars an hour. What gall. What incredible gall."

Alphonse Joseph Bressio began to laugh and despite the wound he could not stop laughing even when the doctors told him he had to. Finally, it was decided he should have a sedative, and he agreed, but noted that it did not seem to have any effect. He went to sleep pointing this out.

XXII

The heroin failed to surface on the streets of the cities, thus justifying the FBNC's request for secrecy from the press. As it was explained by the public relations officer: "If we keep a lid on this thing, we still have a chance for a major breakthrough against organized narcotics rings."

So the press knew about it, the police knew about it, the major drug dealers knew about it and even some Senators and Congressmen knew about it, but no one was talking publicly. It did not get the heroin returned, but for a while did save the new FBNC a major scandal as its special investigative body gathered more evidence to prove that agent Clyde Forrest had been responsible for perhaps the biggest gaff in narcotics history.

Naturally the agency instituted new procedures so that "one bad apple" would never again be allowed to hold such a sensitive post.

One newspaperman did report the rumors of this gaff to his city desk, but was told his newspaper did not wish to take the responsibility if their story should send the people who had the heroin under cover.

"But the pushers know about it. If I know about it, the pushers certainly do," complained the reporter.

"When a cop tells me that, I'll run the story." And everyone waited for someone else to take the responsibility for making the news public. An underground newspaper made an inept attempt, with almost all the facts wrong, which didn't really bother their writers since they were trying to prove that the U.S. government wanted heroin to reach the streets to "dull the consciousness of the revolution." It was the concept that counted, not the facts.

The shootout at Pren Street was attributed to the growing gang wars in the city, and a former business writer transferred to the crime beat explained the violence as a result of too rapid expansion of the gangs without enough capital. This article received very favorable comment from the business community, many of its members feeling that this writer had produced the first intelligent and coherent analysis of organized crime. He also offered a solution: Take away crime's markets through massive funding of urban housing, the theory being that slums bred the markets for organized crime, and why not dry up their consumer markets at the source, especially since crime was having trouble anyway. Naturally the builders, like Arnold Farnsworth of Alpen Realty, saw this as an excellent solution.

Al Bressio quickly recovered from his physical wounds, which were called minor, and was allowed to keep his weapons permit when the grand jury failed to indict him for manslaughter. It was considered self-defense since ballistics while sorting out which fatal bullet came from which gun, found that all of Bressio's slugs came from people with records. The coroner, when removing and tagging the bullets from Bressio's body, remarked, "Hell of a shot on that .38 police special. Like he put these things in with calipers."

One of the things that helped Bressio before the grand jury was the government's knowledge that Murray Blay Dawson was raring to bring the whole Pren Street situation "to public light." The U.S. Attorney submitted the evidence against Bressio to the grand jury as though he were counsel for the defense.

William James Cutler thought the bill submitted by Bressio's firm was "incredibly excessive, something akin to extortion." Clarissa Duffy handled the situation with one phone call to Murray Blay Dawson.

"I'd like to get this thing settled by the time Al comes out of the hospital."

"A pleasure," said Dawson, who promptly instituted a half-dozen suits from breach of contract to conspiracy to defraud, the latter really being the province of the District Attorney, but very serviceable for "hellos."

Dawson had three young lawyers badgering Mitchell, Walker

and Cutler in both their Washington and New York City offices, attempting to get depositions.

Hedding "Puff" Mitchell kept telling Jim Cutler, "These suits are groundless. Not a feather's weight of case in any of them." But the prestigious firm found itself totally consumed in fielding these "absurd little cases," while it took Dawson less than a half-hour each day to think up a new one.

"The bastard is ruining us, Jim," said Mitchell and was backed up by Walker from Washington. The three partners met one afternoon in the Washington offices of their firm, with Walker saying one word to open the meeting.

"Settle."

"It's like robbery," protested Cutler.

"So?" said Walker. "We've been robbed before. If someone came in here with a gun, would you try to wrestle it out of his hand just so you wouldn't be robbed?"

"I have looked into the face of guns recently. Of guns, I know," said Cutler indignantly.

"Dammit, fellas," said Mitchell. "Let me take on this Dawson and see just how good he is in the courtroom."

"We can all pay one-third of Bressio's bill," said Walker.

"It's the principle of the thing," said Cutler. "It wasn't your daughter who was killed. It wasn't you who was terrorized by gunmen, it wasn't you who had to walk through a room slippery with blood. I am willing to settle with Bressio, but dammit, I want peace with honor."

"Let me at Dawson," said Mitchell, and Walker blinked and Cutler sighed with the resignation of the defeated.

"Do you doubt that I couldn't make a good showing against that publicity whore of a kike Dwarshkopf?" said Mitchell angrily. "You all know he doesn't have a damn thing to come in with. It'll be like a slingshot against a heavy bomber. I'll bomb him back to the Stone Age."

"What was his latest figure this morning?" said Cutler.

"As of this morning," said Walker. "It was a hundred and ten thousand dollars. That included punitive damages."

"Punitive damages for what?" demanded Mitchell. "Give me five minutes with him in front of a judge, and I'll show you punitive damages. I'll get that hotshot disbarred is what I'll punitive damages him."

Cutler and Walker thought a moment about Mitchell and Dawson in front of a judge and Cutler spoke first.

"Offer him ten thousand dollars. I hate to pay it, but I'm weary of this thing."

"I won't pay, gentlemen," said Mitchell.

Walker ignored the comment and reached for the telephone, telling his secretary to get Dawson on the line.

"The ingratitude of the man," said Cutler. "The ingratitude. I offered him a place in this firm, in Mitchell, Walker and Cutler. With his background, I offered him a chance to be someone in this world."

"You weren't serious about that Bressio in Mitchell, Walker and Cutler, were you, Jim?" asked Mitchell. The thought of it outraged him.

"I was serious about the offer. I wasn't exactly serious about taking him in."

"Oh," said Mitchell, satisfied with the explanation.

At the little game of who speaks to whose secretary first, Walker lost. He was on the line waiting for Dawson.

"Hello, this is William Walker, Mr. Dawson, of Mitchell, Walker and Cutler. We've been playing with your little suits now for a week or so, and we wondered what it would cost us to save postage and carfare back and forth on these things . . . I see. Well, I was thinking of something more in the neighborhood of ten, maybe twelve thousand dollars . . . I don't like to haggle either, Mr. Dawson, that's why I'm phoning you personally. Give us a realistic figure to deal with . . . I see . . . Well, look, this fellow Bressio only put in a week at the most . . . I see. Twenty-five thousand. That's awesomely reasonable. I might remind you, Mr. Dawson, that some of my partners want to go into court with you . . . Well, we have nothing to lose either, we are lawyers, you know . . . You have twenty-five thousand dollars to lose, is what you have to lose . . . I couldn't get my people to agree on fifty. I'm just a partner, not God."

Walker put his hand over the receiver.

"Thirty-three five," he whispered.

"Yes. Yes," said Cutler. "But that has to include taking care of Fleish's daughter, putting her in a home or something."

"Thirty-three five," said Walker. "There's the matter of the child that must be taken care of . . . Correct. We don't wish to read in the papers about the granddaughter of William James Cutler . . . We understand. There was nothing anyone could do about the daughter. Her name had to be in the paper—she was dead, after all . . . Correct. Fine, Mr. Dawson. I'd like to add I have a great admiration for you . . . Yes, I'd love to. Sometime when I'm in New York City, that would be absolutely fine . . . Yes, I knew Bobo briefly. Exquisite, charming, delightful woman . . . Yes, yes, of course . . . Well, we are considering transferring some business. We could work out your firm's retainer very easily . . . Yes. Yes. Of course, well, it has been obvious through this last week that we should have retained counsel for criminal matters. Frankly, we would have gone to fifty . . . I am not full of shit, Murray . . . Heh-heh. You'll never know . . . Well, let's make it next Thursday for lunch . . . Certainly. I'd love to meet Helmer and Burns. Next Thursday for lunch it is then. Give my regards to Bobo. 'Bye."

Walker hung up. "Thirty-three five," he said.

"I know," said Cutler.

"I still think we should have fought," said Mitchell, lighting his pipe with decisive motions.

"For thirty-three five?" asked Walker incredulously.

"Were you serious about retaining Dawson, Hemler and Burns?" asked Cutler.

"Absolutely," said Walker. "I like the way that man operates. He can add dimension to our resources."

When Bressio returned from the hospital, Clarissa presented him with a welcome-home check from Mitchell, Walker and Cutler, for services rendered.

"C'mon, Al. Don't be so gloomy."

"What do I do with the kid?"

"Put her in a home, Al. I've had her ever since Pren Street and I think a home will be a good place for her. There are loads of Catholic orphanages."

"I thought you said the Catholic Church was a reactionary oppressive force? You said it did a lot of damage to you."

"For me, yes. For Bobbi Cutler—I mean Fleish, no. It would do her good. Get some order into her life, an order that she never had. Do you know she eats with her hands? I can't get her to use a fork."

"No," said Bressio. "No orphanage. I don't know what I'll do, but no orphanage. I'm going out. Leave me alone."

"Are you okay, Al?" said Clarissa. She placed a gentle hand on his arm, and he moved away.

"Don't touch me," he said "Just leave me alone."

"Is it because of what I said about Bobbi, Al?"

"Just lay off me," said Bressio and left his office and went to the Cedar Tavern and despite doctor's orders got somewhat drunk, and went home and locked the doors behind him. The phone rang promptly on the television introduction of Dick Schaap. It was a Dawson call though.

"What is it, Murray?"

"Get over here right away, Al. I'm scared and I need you. I don't know what to do. We just got the trunk of our Rolls open."

XXIII

Dawson poked his head out of the basement's garage entrance. "C'mon in, Al. I kept the servants out."

"Anybody else know? Bobo?"

"She's inside here."

Bressio had to suck in his stomach to move between wall and Rolls. It always amazed him about this garage that it never smelled of oil. The massive Rolls trunk was open. Bobo stood by a taillight drumming her fingers on a fender.

"Thanks, Al. Thank you very much for all that you've done for us," snapped Bobo. "We needed this. This makes the season complete. I have had to spend three weeks in New York this summer and now this. Oh, thank you so very much, Al Bressio. This here is carrying the Mafia a little too far, just a little too far. Don't you think?"

Bressio saw the plastic bags stacked, wedged and pushed into a mass that filled the trunk. He shook his head while calculating.

"What do you think, Al?" said Dawson.

"I think I'd better think," said Bressio.

"Why bother to think? Aren't you going to set up a connection here?"

"Bobo, shhh. Please," said Dawson.

"Murray, this is a nasty, nasty thing. I thought we were through with it. Well, it was not inconsistent with Becky's character to do something like this."

"How could she do it?" asked Dawson.

"She carried it in her paws," said Bobo. "Can I leave now."

"No," said Dawson.

"Stay here just a few minutes," said Bressio. "Yeah. Okay. The loft above. You cut through a little hole for a look, then a larger hole for crawling. You bring up the stuff one bag at a time, hand it up through the hole. All right."

Bressio went around the car and got in the rear seat. He began pulling out the back seat cushion. It was loose.

"All right. They take down the stuff, slow, maybe four hours leaving the car in the street, maybe making a few trips with the car, but never unloading."

"Wouldn't they hear in the basement?"

"Maybe," said Bressio. "I don't know. What I heard in the hospital was they found that bathroom had been cut into from four sides, the hallway cut being three weeks old, so you figure it out."

"You mean someone else was working on it, too."

"Undoubtedly. I was just trying to figure out how Becky Hawkins might have done it. I didn't hear anything about this car, though. I would have heard if it had been parked outside. They would have been through this car within five minutes of the stash being missing. She must have had the car parked several blocks away. Maybe she had Mary Beth and L. Marvin help her. Each carrying five bags apiece per trip. I don't know. I don't know. But I knew one thing for sure—someone was going to figure out a way. Maybe she had help from one of the narcos downstairs. She knew how to peddle her ass good."

"Shut up, Bobo," said Dawson.

"I didn't say anything," said Bobo.

"All right. We've got to get rid of it," said Bressio.

"There's death in that trunk. Let's make sure it doesn't kill again. Let's flush it bag by bag down the toilet," said Dawson.

"And then Bobo tells just one friend and you have vicious company that can't believe someone would flush millions of dollars down the toilet. They'd keep sticking lighted cigarettes into you until you told them where."

"But if I tell them nothing but that it's gone?"

"You'll be very burned."

"But certainly there's some amount of reason. I know, contrary to popular belief, the Mafia is a profit-making organization. Take away the profit and you're safe."

"But they've got to know it, Murray," said Bressio, talking loudly with his hands. "They've got to know it, and they're never going to know it just because you tell them."

Dawson was quiet, mulling. Bobo took this lull to bring up something that bothered her. "What makes you all so sure I'd talk? I've kept lots of secrets very well," she said.

"Name one," said Dawson absently, looking at the trunk of plastic bags of pure heroin, probing avenues, twisting around corners, weighing possibilities. "Name one."

"You liking to stick it in my ear and hair," said Bobo.

"Thanks," said Dawson.

Bressio said they could not phone the police or narcos because Dawson had too many enemies there who might like to forget the phone call and stage a raid . . . with the U.S. Attorney General helping to get everyone involved, afterwards a nice promotion.

"That settles it," Dawson said. "A man likes to be sure he has done one good thing with his life. Often we cannot separate self-interest from charity. But if I had to die for something, for one thing, then I am sure this thing would be it. That is a trunkload of human tragedy. And with my life I will destroy it. I have never been so sure of anything before, as sure as I am sure of what I do now. It's my gift of gratitude for being alive."

"That's beautiful, darling," said Bobo.

"Have you been drinking, Murray?" asked Bressio.

"It's not the alcohol talking, Al. At first I saw it as a tragedy visited upon me, but now I perceive its true nature. It is an opportunity few men have. I shall not let it pass, for it may never come again. Bobo, help me with these bags."

Before either of them could reach into the trunk, Bressio closed it forcefully. Dawson's pinky caught briefly and he yanked it away, hopping and wincing and blowing on it.

"You motherfucker!" screamed Dawson. "Ooow! You mother-fucker!"

"We are going to very publicly and very finally get rid of this stuff and we are going to deliver it with someone of unimpeachable stature with us, so in case we are stopped he can verify what we are doing. Case closed. Is that the phone over there, Bobo?"

"Yes. But I like Murray's idea better. I've never done a great humanitarian act—and with millions of dollars worth of something, too."

"That's because you're bored, Bobo," said Bressio. "You want to be a humanitarian with your life, fine. Not with mine. I hate dying with a passion. I hate the thought of it, even the possibility of it. It's my thing. You people will just have to indulge this little whimsy of mine. Think of it as a neurosis."

"And I thought you were a tough man, Al Bressio," said Bobo.

Bressio phoned the Cutler residence in Old Lyme. Mr. Cutler could not be disturbed, Bressio was told. Then Bressio would just have to make up his own words for the reporters, he said. There was a pause and then William James Cutler was on the phone. What was this nonsense about newspapers? Hadn't Bressio been paid?

"You'd better come into the city, Cutler, or your fat name is going to be in the *Daily News*."

"Have you no decency, Mr. Bressio?"

"No way," said Bressio and gave Cutler Dawson's address. This seemed to relieve him somewhat, knowing that it was not a dangerous neighborhood.

While waiting for Cutler, Dawson asked Bressio why he thought this trunkload would be any safer than it was in Pren Street or the other heroin in police headquarters.

"Because they've already made the mistake. Maybe they won't do it again. That's how people learn."

"But you don't know, do you?"

"No, I don't," said Bressio.

"Then you're taking a chance with the lives of thousands of people, aren't you?"

"That's right."

"I would have thought better of you, Al. I would want to think better of you." Dawson sucked on his pinky.

"You know what wax is used for, Murray?"

"Candles."

"And what else?"

"There's a lost-wax method in making metal tools."

"Anything else?"

"Engraving, I imagine. Make your point, already."

"I already have," said Bressio and they waited in silence for

Cutler. Shortly before 1:00 A.M., Bobo noted that the rustling noise
they heard outside was probably Cutler.

"They're waiting for you down here, sir?" Bressio heard one of
the servants say.

"Bored to death," muttered Bobo.

Dawson gentled the hand with the injured pinky.

Cutler looked somewhat haggard despite the neat business suit.
Bressio motioned him in and for the door to be shut behind him.

"We found the stash," said Bressio when the door had been
closed for a good minute.

"So?" said Cutler.

"It's in that car."

"So?"

"You're going to drive with us to headquarters, so in case any
policeman stops us, you can verify our destination and purpose."

"You're assuming an awful lot, Mr. Bressio."

"I'll take my chances."

"And if I refuse to go?"

"You're going."

"Where is this thing that has become so famous? I would like
to see it."

"It's just smack. A lot of it," said Bressio.

"I've never seen the substance, and I would like to see what it
looks like. That's the least you can do since you are in the process
of kidnapping me to be its escort."

Bressio opened his mouth. The words did not come right away
but when they did they were weak with shock and wonder. "You
mean you were on the President's advisory panel and you never
saw heroin?"

"We set policy," said Cutler haughtily.

"For an entire country," said Bressio incredulously.

"Well, I did see a sample they bring around to schools and
things. Part of the national educational program for high schools."

"Open the trunk, Murray," said Bressio.

With his good hand, Dawson opened the trunk.

Cutler sidled along the car to get a view. "So that's it? Doesn't
look like much. Just plastic bags. How do you know it's not
Bromo-Seltzer in there?"

On the way to the station, with Bobo driving, Cutler allowed

Dawson to know that what happened this evening certainly wouldn't advance his case for a retainer from Mitchell, Walker and Cutler. But Dawson hardly paid attention. He was explaining to Bressio in the back seat that it was not so unusual for a high government official to have a profound unawareness of what he was doing, nor was it limited to any particular government, democratic, fascist, communist or down-on-the-farm commune. When Germany had decided to invade Russia, the chief of the German general staff went out and got a world atlas fifteen years old. They didn't have a map of the place on hand. Field Marshal Haig of Britain, responsible for more English deaths than the Black Plague, visited the battlefield only once during World War I to exclaim, "My God, I didn't know it was like this."

Dawson nudged Bressio. "They're no different from most of the lawyers we know, Al. Same thing. People."

"I was thinking," said Cutler from the front seat, "if someone with Bressio's contacts were to market that material back there, how much do you think he could get in very liquid cash, twenty million, thirty million, how much? Just a supposition."

Dawson scarcely blinked and Bressio's gun was out of its holster and pointed to the back of Cutler's head.

"This much," said Bressio. "Turn around."

When Cutler looked behind him he saw and heard the pistol cock. "Just a supposition," said Cutler.

"Sure," said Bressio. "You're William James Cutler, whose single life is vindication enough for an entire university, a former Under Secretary of State, one of our leading Washington attorneys, a member of the President's advisory panel on narcotics. Sure it was just a supposition."

Bressio kept the gun out of its holster all the way to headquarters.

XXIV

Clarissa expressed a certain satisfaction that Bressio had destroyed her note calling him "beautiful." Bobbi, she said, was driving her up a wall. Dawson, she said, had probably wanted to destroy the heroin for some devious publicity move and settled for the big exposure in turning in the heroin. She was sure that as bad as Cutler was, it was his noble motivations that prompted the turning in of the stash.

"All right, all right," said Bressio. "What's wrong?"

"Nothing's wrong," said Clarissa. "I'm your secretary, not your wife. You can't dump that kid on me. You have no right. Get her out of my house by week's end. God, to think I'd ever call you beautiful—the pressure must have been incredible. You threw the note in several places, you say?"

Since there were times when Bressio assiduously avoided aggravation, he left the office as he had been leaving the office for the last several weeks when the subject of Bobbi came up. Each time Clarissa would angrily point out that she was not his wife, did he see a wedding ring on her hand? did he ever sign for a wedding license? did he ever say he did? Well, then, he should get the little monster out of her house, and yes, she felt a little bit guilty that Bobbi's mother was dead, but she had her own life to live also. It wasn't as if she were tied down by some marriage contract.

"I do not know what is troubling her," Bressio told Bill, the bartender at the Cedar Tavern.

"Sounds like she may love you. Sounds like she may want to marry you from what you tell me. A woman sends you a note saying you're beautiful, she must love you, Al. No offense, but you're not a physically attractive person."

"No kidding," said Bressio. "No. She doesn't have those feelings for me. The kid is getting on her nerves. I should get that kid out of her place, she's right."

"Maybe she's asking you to put a ring on her finger and then she'll keep the kid."

"I went to a couple of Catholic orphanages the other day, and a couple of boarding-school-type things."

"Yeah."

"I think the kid would have been better off dead than with the nuns."

"So what are you going to do, Al?"

"Fleish is coming up for trial tomorrow."

"What are you going to do?"

"Dawson's going to plead him guilty just to keep him off the streets. There's no contract out on him, but some guys who got hurt by that Pren Street thing may break him up fatally if they see him."

"What are you going to do about the kid, Al?"

"I come here for some peace and quiet and all I get from you is what I get from Clarissa."

"I don't want to marry you, Al."

"Neither does she," said Bressio. "All I hear is about the kid. The kid. The kid. What is it with that kid.?"

Thus Bressio left the Cedar Tavern into the afternoon sun that was becoming not at all unpleasant for September. I'll get rid of the kid, he told himself, and I'll put an end to all this aggravation.

After all, he didn't bring her into the world. L. Marvin Fleish did. He didn't charge unarmored into the vessels of pleasure, why should he have to wipe up the spillings? He didn't even know the kid. The only time he ever touched her was at the blood bath on Pren Street. She never even spoke to him. What was she? She was a legal package. Since she was a legal package, he knew what to do.

Harriet Whitmore Fleish. With Mary Beth Cutler dead and the papers only in the works at the time, Harriet Whitmore Fleish was the legal mother. There was a legal obligation Harriet and L. Marvin Fleish had to the child. Since L. Marvin was back in jail,

Bressio having revoked bail money at Dawson's request to keep L. Marvin off the streets, Bressio couldn't very well deposit the kid with him. Besides, he was destined to do a bit, probably Danbury.

Harriet Whitmore Fleish was best known in the West Side for her fight to bus West End Avenue children to Harlem schools. In this district that traditionally voted liberal to left, she was shocked, said she was shocked for television over the lack of support she encountered.

Privately, according to Clarissa, who had heard it from L. Marvin—an unreliable hearsay chain if ever there was one—Harriet Whitmore Fleish confided that she did not expect support, but just wanted to "rub their noses in it." The "they" being West Side liberals.

From what Bressio knew she was one of those who believed that only a massive armed revolution throughout the world, in every capital, in every village, would bring peace to mankind. She was fond of quoting Ho Chi Minh, who, as Bressio understood it, thought peace was so much nicer after a very bloody war. Ho Chi Minh died in bed, as did Lyndon Johnson. Thus it would ever be, thought Bressio as he rode up to the seventh floor in the elevator on West Eighty-fourth Street.

Harriet Whitmore Fleish's lust for integration did not deter her from using a police lock, reinforced by several bolt locks, backed up by a massive German shepherd that—she kept telling Clarissa—did not bark specifically at black men. This little did Bressio know about Harriet Whitmore Fleish. What he did know and what made him massively uneasy was that he was trying to foist a child on a human being who apparently married L. Marvin Fleish of her own free will.

He rang the buzzer and heard the locks click down when he yelled who he was upon being asked. The door opened on the tow-headed moppet in a New York Mets T-shirt, untied sneakers, and relatively clean blue shorts.

"My name is Al Bressio. What's yours?"

"Robert Peter Fleish."

"I'd like to speak to your mother."

"She's fucking."

"That's not a nice thing to say, Robert."

"There's nothing wrong with fucking."

"That's not a nice word."

"It's legitimate," said the boy in the Met's shirt.

"Who is it?" came a woman's voice from inside the apartment.

"A reactionary, Ma."

"I'll be with him in a minute. Tell him to come in."

"C'mon in, mister."

Bressio followed the boy into the living room, where he discovered at least that the boy did not lie. A woman who by the rolls of her stretched stomach appeared to be in her early forties had a bearded youth clasped between her legs. They occupied a sofa.

"Just a minute, I'm coming soon," said the woman.

"You're Harriet Whitmore Fleish?" asked Bressio, examining very closely the base of a lampshade.

"Yes. Does this bother you? I should be more thoughtful. Sometimes people aren't as liberated as I would hope them to be."

"It bothers me."

"Robby, take this gentleman into the kitchen."

"Can I have a Kool-Aid Pop?"

"No. You've had enough carbohydrates for today. And it's not even supper time."

"Brown rice is a carbohydrate," protested Robby.

"Brown rice is good for you. It's not a . . . Just a minute—oh, that feels good . . . Where are you going?"

"My name's Al Bressio. I may be back."

"Marvin and Clarissa have talked so much about you. It's a pleasure to meet you. You almost got sucked into that capitalist conspiracy on Pren Street, didn't you? Where are you going? You just got here."

Bressio was slightly tipsy when he arrived at Clarissa's apartment that night in Rego Park. He wanted to speak to the kid, he said.

"She's watching TV," said Clarissa.

"I want to talk to her."

"Have you been drinking heavy, Al?"

"A little."

"Talk to her tomorrow."

"Now," said Bressio.

"This isn't your apartment. You don't pay the rent. The lease isn't in your name. You can't come in here if I don't want you to."

Bressio brushed her aside and found Bobbi in the living room. Bobbi was eating an apple and watching *Maude*. Clarissa waited by the door to the living room, her arms folded, her foot tapping out impatience.

"Hello, Bobbi," said Bressio. "I want to talk to you."

Bobbi did not take her eyes off the television screen. Bressio turned off the set. Bobbi still refused to look at him.

"This is probably too important a decision for you to make, Bobbi, but I think you're going to have to make it anyhow. You can't stay here any longer, and there are two places you can go. You can go to a home with a bunch of other kids your age, or you can live with a woman who has at least one son about five years older than you. Which would you like?"

Bobbi bit into the apple, taking a too big bite for her mouth.

"Where would you like to go, kid?" asked Bressio. "If you don't make up your mind, I'll have to do it for you."

"She's just a kid, Al, what the hell do you think you're asking her?" snapped Clarissa.

"She might as well make a choice. She's got to live with it."

"It's you who doesn't want to make the choice, Al. You're the one."

"Do you talk, Bobbi?" asked Bressio.

The little girl shook her head. Clarissa had put her hair up in curlers. They bobbed when she shook her head.

"Who do you want to go with?" asked Bressio, and as the little girl turned to him to bury her head in his massive stomach he was awesomely sorry he had asked that question.

"I want to go with you," said Bobbi, and she began to cry and Bressio was beginning to cry, and as if he wasn't in bad enough shape, Bobbi Cutler Fleish explained she wanted to go with him because he was a nice man.

"He's a very nice man, honey," said Clarissa. "He's a beautiful man. He's our man." And she went to Bressio and Bobbi and made it a threesome by enfolding them with her arms.

"Rot in hell, L. Marvin," screamed out Alphonse Joseph Bressio whose arms were so occupied he couldn't even get to his gun to put a bullet in his own head, even if he wanted to, which he fleetingly considered with a multitude of other current nonopportunities. "Damn you, L. Marvin."

And he heard Clarissa confide to Bobbi that he always made a lot of terrible noises, but really he was just one big teddy bear. "You'll find a lot of people think he's dangerous, but he's just a big roly-poly pushover. See. Push here."

With great will, Bressio resisted the strong desire to run into a wall, and finally the women let him go when he promised to go outside and bring back a pizza. Both of them were laughing when he left the apartment.

At the pizza parlor, two big toughs in black motorcycle jackets and black boots, with chains dangling from their wide black belts, wanted their slices immediately before the counterman made Bressio's pizza to go. There was a minor discussion over this matter, when one Alphonse Joseph Bressio did suffer an assault by said young man, who in front of witnesses did lay hand to arm of one Alphonse Joseph Bressio. In defense of his person, Bressio beat the pair groggy.

This did not go unnoticed by the landlord, who was passing by for an evening stroll. He commented that Bressio had helped bring a certain peaceful order to the neighborhood, which had been suffering lately from a rowdy element.

"I am glad that I could be of service, Mr. Felli," said Bressio.

The two walked down Queens Boulevard together with Bressio steadying the pizza carton to keep the oil from his clothes.

There was a matter that Alphonse might be concerned with, said Felli. It concerned the tragedy of Joseph Bugellerio and his poor mother, who was now left with only one son to support her. There was no one, and this should be well understood, who blamed Alphonse for the accident at Pren Street. Yet here was this poor widow who had lost three of her four sons, and Don Carmine was being strapped by his charity. She did not need much of a contribution from other sources for her maintenance. Just a little thing. Twenty-five dollars a week. A little thing.

"Yes, a small thing," said Bressio. "The small things." Bressio noticed that the pizza carton was beginning to sag, so he quickly agreed to make that small contribution, saying he felt better about the tragedy now that he knew his mother's second cousin was being taken care of.

"I must run now. With all pardons," he said. "Please give my respects to Don Carmine."

About the Author

RICHARD SAPIR is a graduate of the Columbia University School
of General Studies and has won awards for newspaper stories. He
is co-author of the *Destroyer* paperback series and has been an
editor on two newspapers, a reporter on four, and has worked in
public relations. This is his first hardcover book. He lives now in
Pittsfield, Massachusetts.